BRIGHT BEFORE SUNRISE

ALSO BY TIFFANY SCHMIDT

Send Me a Sign

BRIGHT BEFORE SUNRISE

Tiffany Schmidt

WALKER BOOKS
AN IMPRINT OF BLOOMSBURY

First published in the United States of America in February 2014
by Walker Books for Young Readers, an imprint of Bloomsbury Publishing, Inc.
www.bloomsbury.com

For information about permission to reproduce selections from this book, write to
Permissions, Walker BFYR, 1385 Broadway, New York, New York 10018
Bloomsbury books may be purchased for business or promotional use. For information on bulk
purchases please contact Macmillan Corporate and Premium Sales Department at
specialmarkets@macmillan.com

Library of Congress Cataloging-in-Publication Data
Schmidt, Tiffany.
Bright before sunrise / by Tiffany Schmidt.
pages   cm
Summary: Jonah and Brighton are about to have the most awkwardly awful night of their
lives. For Jonah, every aspect of his new life reminds him of what he has had to give up. All he
wants is to be left alone. Brighton is popular, pretty, and always there to help anyone, but has no
idea of what she wants for herself.
ISBN 978-0-8027-3500-3 (hardcover) • ISBN 978-0-8027-3501-0 (e-book)
[1. Self-acceptance—Fiction.   2. Emotional problems—Fiction.   3. Love—Fiction.
4. High schools—Fiction.   5. Schools—Fiction.]   I. Title.
PZ7.S3563Br 2014   [Fic]—dc23   2013025425

Book design by Nicole Gastonguay
Typeset by Westchester Book Composition
Printed and bound in the U.S.A. by Thomson-Shore Inc., Dexter, Michigan
2 4 6 8 10 9 7 5 3 1

For the Schmidtlets

You brighten each of my days . . .
even the ones you choose to start before sunrise

ONE NIGHT CAN CHANGE HOW YOU SEE THE WORLD.
One night can change how you see yourself.

BRIGHT BEFORE SUNRISE

1

JONAH

☀ 12:57 P.M. ☽

TIME MOVES SLOWER ON FRIDAY AFTERNOONS

"You dropped something."

I totally miss that the girl is talking to me. She's sat next to me in English for five months and other than her falsely sweet "Welcome to Cross Pointe" on my first day, the only interactions we've had are her *indulge-me* smiles when she leans across my desk to talk to the girl who sits on the other side of me. One is Jordan and the other is Juliana—I'm not sure who's who. Both have long, light brown hair and toothpaste-commercial smiles.

She clears her throat and taps my desk with her pencil. Then points to the pink baby sock at my feet. It must have fallen out of my sleeve or the leg of my shorts. Even though all of Sophia's laundry is washed separately in her organic, hypoallergenic, dye-and-fragrance-free, all-natural, probably-promises-extra-IQ-points detergent, it seems to get everywhere. Especially her socks. She's just found her feet, and her favorite pastime is freeing them.

It drives my stepfather, Paul, into panics about her

catching cold. Even when it's eighty degrees out. What can I say; the baby is cute *and* crafty.

I reach down and grab the sock—that little monkey must have managed to kick it into my pocket or stick it down my shirt while I was holding her this morning.

"Thanks," I say to Jordan/Juliana.

"Is it your daughter's? It's so cute." She's smiling, but there's something off about the question. Besides the fact that it's none of her business, she looks too eager, almost hungry for my answer. "You're from Hamilton, right?"

"What's that mean?" I ask, crushing the sock in my hand. I already know the answer. I'm the new kid from *Hamilton*. And because I didn't grow up in Cross Pointe, with nannies and beach homes, I must be a teenage father.

At least she has enough decency to blush when she stammers something about, "Well, it's just—I've heard that in Hamilton . . ."

"It's my sister's." I hate myself for answering. For caring even a little what my Cross Pointe classmates think of me.

"Oh." She looks me up and down again, like I'm a new person now that I'm not someone's baby's daddy. "But it *is* true about Hamilton, right? Did a lot of your old classmates have kids? I heard they even have a program where you can bring your babies to class. I can't even imagine a *baby* in a classroom."

She draws out "imagine" into three syllables: im-ma-gine. And ends her statement with this absurd giggle.

I bite my tongue so hard.

She leans over and takes the sock from my hand. I could've held on to it, but I'm too shocked by her complete disregard for my personal space. "This is so little! I can't believe you have a sister who's a *baby*."

I wonder what part of my body language or expression makes her think I want to continue this conversation. Does she think I've been waiting all semester for her to wake up and notice me? Or maybe she's just bored because the other half of Jordan/Juliana is absent.

"I just can't get over it—that's *so* much younger than you. Talk about an *oops*—I bet your parents were shocked." She's turning her whole body in her seat, leaning toward me; like she's starving and will feed off whatever information I'll share about myself. "Whole sister, or half?"

"When I left for school this morning she was in one piece. I hope no one's halved her by the time I get home," I say, taking the sock back and shoving it into my pocket. Then I turn around and continue filling out the I-don't-feel-like-teaching-on-Friday busywork sheet on the themes in the fussy Gothic novel we're reading.

I hear her exhale in a huff. I'm sure she's rolling her eyes and getting ready to make some insulting comment about me to someone nearby, but I don't care.

I am not providing fuel for their gossip. I am not playing any of their Cross Pointe games.

I'm surviving.

Counting down the school days until graduation. Eleven. Then I'm out of here.

2

Brighton

☀ 1:16 P.M. ☽

23 HOURS, 44 MINUTES LEFT

"Brighton! Why weren't you at lunch?"

I freeze at the familiar voice. I'd been hoping—just this once, just today—I could make it from my locker to class without being seen, but Jordan latches on to my arm as I walk by the door of Mrs. Watson's room.

"I had to do something for yearbook." The "something" had been to take a moment just to breathe. The yearbook room had been a convenient place to hide out and do it.

"Why didn't you tell anyone?" She *tsk*s like I'm being silly and gives my arm a playful shake. "Everyone was looking for you."

Which is why I hid.

I thought I'd be fine. Until the moment this morning when we were getting ready to broadcast announcements and I glanced at the first story I was supposed to read and almost burst into tears. I don't know what I would've done if Amelia hadn't noticed and stepped in with a quick lie: "Oh, Brighton, your mascara is smudged! Go, I'll take your spot—"

so I could run off to the bathroom, pull myself together, and lecture myself on being ridiculous. So the captain of the baseball team is named Ethan—same name as my dad. This isn't news to me. It certainly isn't a valid reason to cry like an idiot during a live broadcast.

Since then, I'd done a fairly decent imitation of *fine* during my morning classes, but skipping lunch had been necessary.

"Sorry." I pluck off my headband, smooth my dark brown hair, then put the band back, using the motions as an excuse to extract my arm from her grip. "What did I miss? Do you need something?"

"Not really." Jordan shrugs, leans toward me with a conspiratorial smile. "But since you weren't there, you didn't hear how Natalie wants to have her graduation party the same day as mine! And we both want the yacht club; so one of us will have to use the clubroom instead of the ballroom. I'm sure Natalie is going to have a fit if it's her—which isn't fair, why should I have to be the one to settle? Regardless, you'll come to *my* party, right?"

I stare at her for a moment; she's serious. "Why don't you two just throw your parties together? You'll be inviting all the same people, and that way no one has to choose."

She squeezes my arm again. "B, you're brilliant! This is why you need to be at lunch! I'll go find Natalie and tell her it was your idea."

She dashes down the hall, and I fight the urge to lean against the lockers and shut my eyes. Not just because I hadn't slept well last night. Or any of the nights this week. Or because seniors do not need party planning advice from juniors—especially not advice that's so obvious they should've thought of it themselves instead of creating drama or asking people to pick sides.

Except now I'm just being rude. I'm sure they're already combining their guest lists and moving on to debating invitations, colors, and food—

"Oh, I almost forgot to tell you—" Jordan is back, standing in front of me and trying so hard to fight a grin. I force myself to look engaged and interested in whatever the new gossip is. "Since you weren't at lunch today, you also missed my big announcement: I got off the Brown waiting list! I'm in!"

"That's amazing! I'm so proud of you. Congrats!" My last word gets buried in her shoulder as I pull her into a hug. For a few moments I can shake off my exhaustion and be happy for her. "Oh my gosh! How could you possibly not tell me that *first thing*? You've got to be so excited."

"Next time come to lunch and you'll be in the know!" She fake-pouts at me. "Seriously, I only have two weeks of school left—get underlings to do your yearbook tasks; I don't want you missing any more lunches."

"I promise." And I can do that. It's only today. Today and tomorrow. If I can just survive the next thirty-six hours, I'll be able to breathe again. But just thinking about them deflates me, drains all the enthusiasm from my voice. "Brown! Wow. I hope Rhode Island is ready for you."

She doesn't even notice, just laughs and says, "Of course they're not! Okay, gotta get to class, but I'm sure I'll see you tonight. Later, gator."

I call another weak "Congrats" after her and head toward my own class.

"Hey, Brighton!"

"Hi, B."

"What's up, Brighton?"

The hall seems so crowded. All the people passing by, throwing smiles and greetings at me—each one feels like a minor assault of friendliness. Each one makes me more aware of how many sets of eyes are watching—and how big an audience I'll have if I let myself fall to pieces.

I twist the ring on my finger. I expected it to provide some comfort today, but mostly it just feels heavy, foreign—a constant reminder of what's happening tomorrow.

I need to shake this off.

Dad had two favorite sayings: *Everything looks better when you're wearing a smile* and *Eighty percent of any achievement is making the decision to achieve.*

So I'll pull on a smile and be okay. If I can't quite achieve *okay,* at least I'm 80 percent closer to it.

I can fake the rest.

3

JONAH

THAT TIME OF DAY WHEN MY LOCKER FIGHTS BACK

I want to kick it open. Leave a big, ugly dent in the front of the metal door. Ruin the perfection of the bank of shiny green lockers. It would earn me a trip to the principal, who would be shocked and horrified at vandalism in her precious school. But maybe then I could get my books without wrestling the lock every damn time.

"Need some help?"

I shouldn't be surprised she came over. I ignore her. Hope she'll go away. Not likely, but a guy can dream. She was just talking to Jordan/Juliana from English—who probably told her that I'm the father of an illegitimate child. Or, if Jordan/Juliana *had* believed me, they were gossiping about how weird it is I'm seventeen years older than Sophia.

Up until the sock thing, the only people who'd acknowledged me today were teachers and the freshman who said "excuse me" when he bumped into me during lunch. Which is fine. More than fine, it's my preferred way to pass a day in Cross Pointe. And with fifty-seven minutes standing between me and dismissal, all I want is for my crappy locker to open so I can get my Spanish book.

"Sometimes they stick." It's the same voice, and it's closer this time.

"Did I ask your opinion, Waterford?"

Most students in this school couldn't pick me out of a lineup, but Brighton Waterford can. Which is why she's standing in front of me with an expectant smile. And why I have a sudden urge to skip Spanish class, just so I can avoid having to get my book or interact with Cross Pointe Barbie.

"Here, Jonah, let me."

She reaches for the lock. I'm still jamming the release lever up, but even though the combination is in, it refuses to give.

"I can do it," I say through my teeth, but she nudges me out of her way, then hands me her books. I watch her wiggle the lever side to side.

The green door pops open. Of course it does. She's Brighton Waterford. Even the lockers adore her.

"There's a piece of paper in the mechanism."

"I know. The idiot who had it before me kept it propped open."

She slides a thin finger into the space and pries out the paper wad, presents it to me like a gift. It's a math test from two years ago.

"Lots of people do that. It's not like you need a lock in Cross Pointe."

I scoff, then realize she's serious. She's not just spouting Cross Pointe dogma like the Homeowners' Association or Welcoming Committee. Of course not. No need for locks and no teenage pregnancy. The town's like a freaking modern Stepford, except robots have more personality than most of the trophy wives here.

"Sure," I say as I grab my Spanish book.

"Jonah, no one *here* is going to steal."

Was that *here* a dig at my old school? The teens in Cross Pointe may have more zeroes in their bank accounts and less on the odometers of their shiny cars than they do at Hamilton High, but it doesn't make them better people.

This is the one bit of the school I can claim as mine.

I want it locked.

I slam the locker door.

"You're welcome," she chirps, tugging her books out of my hand.

I ball up the math test and toss it in the trash can across the hall. It's a dismissal and she gets it, nodding once and flashing me a smile full of perfectly straight, perfectly white teeth.

"Real quick, may I ask you a question?" Apparently she's not really looking for permission because she rushes on, "I was wondering, are you busy Sunday?"

Any other guy in this school would be falling over himself right about now—I've watched them do it for the past five months. I could understand their attraction to her glossy perfection: long, dark hair and the type of milky skin that begs to be touched—if she wasn't . . . *Brighton*.

"I can't."

"But I haven't even told you the details yet." She laughs like I'm trying to be funny instead of just trying to cut the conversation short. "You know the book drive we've been having at school?"

I shake my head.

"Really?" She reaches out and taps a fluorescent pink flyer hanging on the wall beside my locker. "Well, we've been collecting books to send to needy elementary schools. This Sunday we're sorting and boxing them up."

She pauses. Looks down at her hands. A flash of gold band, flash of green stone—she's twisting a ring around her finger. It's huge. And probably real. She looks back up at me.

"So, I was thinking . . ." She moves the ring from one finger to the next. "I'd really like it if . . . Will you come?"

"I can't," I say again. We've had this conversation before— she's tried to recruit me to count pennies for Build a School in Some Other Country, to seal envelopes for Let's Write Letters to Senators So They Can Ignore Us, and wrap presents for Care Packages to Last Year's Seniors, Because Former Students Can't Pass Finals without Cookies and Fancy Post-its.

In fact, that's probably how she sees me, as yet another charity case: Integrate the New Student.

"I could pick you up."

She's sliding the ring off again. Clenching it in her fist, then trying it on her other hand.

"You're going to drop that." I don't know why I care. If she wants to lose a ring worth more than my car, that's her choice.

"What?"

I point to her hand.

"Oh." She slides the ring back on her finger. "If I give you a ride, will you come? Is your address in the school directory?"

"What, you're worried my crappy car will ghettoize the library parking lot?"

"No." Her fingers fly back to the ring. Spinning. "That's not—"

"I'm not interested."

"Oh." Her face flashes to *damn!* for an instant before she plasters on a yearbook-photo smile and straightens her headband. It's the first crack I've seen in her I've-got-it-all-together image, and I kinda feel bad—but then she barrels on and my sympathy is gone. The girl looks like a dream, but she's got the determination of a pit bull. I'm sick of being her prey. "Well, if Sundays are bad for you, is there another day you're free? I'd really like to—"

"No, not another time. When are you going to get that I want you to leave me alone?" I almost add "please," but catch myself.

Her face freezes in a shocked expression. A blush starts at her collarbones and spreads to her hairline.

I swallow my guilt. This is a *good* reaction. Maybe she's finally listening to me. Hopefully it's finally sinking in.

"I . . ." She shakes her head slightly. "I'm—"

"Brighton! I love that top. So cute!"

And she's back to normal. Smiling. Done with me and turning toward her fan club: a preppy blond girl walking by with another preppy blond girl. She's absorbed back into the flow of the hallway, surrounded by people who want those smiles and live and die by her advice.

I pull out my phone so I can text the girl whose smiles I want: Carly.

R we still on 4 tonite? Can't wait.

4

Brighton

23 HOURS, 41 MINUTES LEFT

"Leave me alone" is way worse than "No." It's more of an "I can't stand you" than an "I'm not interested." The raw annoyance in his brown eyes and deep voice add intensity to his rejection. I feel it from the curl of my toes to the fire in my cheeks. It hurts—as much as the places my new sandals have rubbed my feet raw, or the pulse point behind my ear that's pinched by my headband. But I can't let it show on my face.

I won't.

Sarah's interruption is a welcome distraction. I could hug her and Miranda for buying me a moment to pull myself together.

"Thanks. Your shirt is too. Both of yours. Really cute."

They chime, "See you later," and keep walking.

My gaze snags on the hallway clock, and I bite my lip. The clock is not my friend today. It keeps moving forward, carving minutes out of the day and cruelly pushing me toward tomorrow.

And I'm not ready.

Each click of the second hand feels like a catch in my breath, each bell that announces another class is over heaps more pounds of pressure on my shoulders.

There's only a fragile strip of time between me and Mom.

I don't know if I can do it.

Eighty percent of any achievement is making the decision to achieve.

I take a deep breath and spin back around. Because I should say something, right? Apologize, or let Jonah know that I got his message. Something.

The space in front of his locker is empty. Craning my neck and standing on tiptoe, I catch sight of the top of his head, his disheveled light brown hair passing the entrance to the courtyard. He's too far away for me to catch up and I doubt he'd appreciate me chasing him. What would I even say?

"Brighton!"

"Hey! Brighton!"

The two voices each call out again. Louder. From opposite ends of the hall. I feel like I'm being tugged in both directions, like I should fracture myself into pieces. Whoever I pick, I'm letting the other person down.

"B!"

Amelia's nearly at my elbow. Maggie's farther away, but louder, and much less patient. She's waving her hand to get my attention. I smile in Amelia's direction and call "Hi" toward Maggie.

Amelia reaches me first. "Is it the weekend yet?"

"Not quite." I want to lean my head on her shoulder and

confess—if not the harder stuff, at least I could tell her how I just made a fool of myself with Jonah.

She does a little dance. "I'm so impatient! And you should see Peter! He said the cutest thing—"

"Hey, Brighton! Hi, Amelia." Maggie skids to a stop on my other side. "Sorry to butt in, but this is *important!*"

Amelia responds with an unenthusiastic, "Hey."

I focus on the word "important" and rally some enthusiasm. "What's up?"

Maggie waves her phone in my face. "I just got the proofs for my senior pictures! I've been looking for you all day, Brighton. Why weren't you at lunch? So tell me, which one do you like?"

Important? We must have different definitions of the word. But then again, on any other day I would see this as important too. It's not *her* fault.

"Let me see."

"I've just got to pull up the link." Maggie's fingers fly over the screen of her phone, then she pauses. "Oh, since you're here, you can help too, Amelia. My mom likes the one where I'm leaning against the tree—is she crazy or what? My nose looks deformed, and I practically have a double chin."

She holds her phone toward us: scrolling through photos with the words "Emerick Studios" watermarked across them. I try to concentrate on the screen, on pictures of her cute round face and brown hair, but she gestures as she speaks; the freckles on her photographed nose blur with the motion.

"You're so prepared. I can't believe you've taken senior photos already—I can't believe we're almost seniors." I tip my head to match the angle she's holding the screen.

"I wanted time in case I needed retakes. And I didn't want to—"

"Here, give me that." Amelia snatches the phone and holds it steady between us. A moment's scrutiny later, she taps a picture. "Not the tree. This one." She hands it to me.

"That one? Really? How can you like that one? It's awful. My ears look totally crooked. Don't they, Brighton?"

She steps in front of Amelia to look over my shoulder. Amelia scowls and feigns claws behind Maggie's back. I fight a smile and sidestep to make room for her. "I think your ears look fine. Amelia's got a great eye for this sort of stuff. I'd go with her pick."

"But which do *you* like?" she insists, pushing my hand away when I try to return her phone. "I've got a favorite, and I'm trying to figure out if it's really the best one, or if I'm fooling myself into thinking it's good."

No pressure there. I wish Maggie had given me a hint; not only which pictures she doesn't like, but some clue about which one she does. I *like* the tree picture. I *like* the one Amelia chose. I scroll through them again, but they're starting to blend into indistinguishable smiles and poses.

"Really, any of these would work." I force the phone into her hand.

Maggie frowns. "So you think I should get retakes? Yeah, you're probably right."

"What? No, that's not what I mean!" I don't know how to speak more carefully than I already am, yet I still managed to say the wrong thing. "They *all* look good. You're really photogenic."

"But none of them have that standout, wow factor? And

my senior photo should, since it's going to be hanging on my parents' wall forever." Maggie sighs. "Okay, retakes it is." She gives Amelia a look; I get a hug. "Thank *you* for being honest with me. You're so right. I can get a better photo than these."

There's no way to contradict that without insulting her, but my stomach sinks as she types a response into her phone.

The bell rings. Maggie doesn't stop typing. I clear my throat and Amelia laughs. "B, you know Ms. Porter's not going to care if we're late."

Maggie finally pockets her phone and starts walking. "So, what are you doing this weekend?"

What are you doing this weekend? It's a normal question. One I've answered every Friday since I reached the age of plan making. Today it glues my tongue to the roof of my mouth. I fidget with my ring, turning the emerald side in and squeezing my hand shut so it hits my palm. I don't want to think about this weekend.

"—anniversary with Peter," finishes Amelia. I should remember what her plans are. And which month anniversary it is. We spent last weekend picking out cologne for him. I can't remember which one she bought. I should know this. Why can't I remember? Six months? Eight?

Maggie nudges me with an elbow. "What about you? Do you want to come to the movies with us? We're seeing *Shriek 3.*"

"Oh, I can't." I really hope she lets it go. Doesn't pressure me or ask a lot of questions. "Thanks, though."

"Come on! You should totally come."

"I've already seen it."

"So, what are you doing?" Maggie demands. "Are you going to Jeremy's party?"

"I . . ." I stare at the groove Jonah's locker left across the polish on my index finger. The tip of my thumbnail fits in it perfectly, and I scrape at the edge, making a scratch into a chip. "This weekend?"

We're too far from the classroom door for me to avoid answering.

"Um, I'm . . ." I swallow.

My face doesn't give anything away, but Amelia knows me well enough that she doesn't need a signal. "Who's going to the movies? It's freakin' scary. I'm surprised Peter and Brighton can still feel their fingers—I gripped their hands tight enough to cut off circulation."

"I've heard it's the scariest so far. I know I'm going to be terrified!" Maggie starts listing parts of the movie trailer, interrupting herself to name the group of people she's going with.

Amelia bumps her shoulder against mine and gives me a small smile. It's nice to know I don't have to return it, because she knows what I'm thinking, but I force my lips upward and bump her shoulder back. If she could, she'd gladly share some of my dread about tomorrow. She'd pass me tissues and rub my back if I let her see me cry.

I can't, though. I never could cry in front of other people. Not even when it first happened. Grief always feels too personal to be made public.

Five years tomorrow.

Five years. And it's still so raw.

Ms. Porter starts class as soon as we slip into our seats. While my fingers dutifully copy her notes off the board and

I nod as if I'm fascinated by her insights on Thomas Hardy, my other hand is clenched into a fist in my lap.

I take a deep breath and uncurl my fingers, straighten my ring, smooth out my capris. It's two weeks till the end of school and the last period on a Friday, so no one's paying much attention. Ms. Porter even breaks off her lecture early and tells us to start reading the next few chapters aloud. I try to focus—turning pages when I notice the others doing so and staring at the book like the words make sense, but my mind is miles from *Tess* and her misfortunes.

Evy's coming home from Glenn Mary University tonight. The relatives descend tomorrow.

"Brighton, next page."

I blink at my book, blood rushing to my cheeks. Someone coughs. Someone shifts in a chair.

"I'm sorry, I lost my place. What page?" I squeak.

"Three seventeen." There's a week's worth of exasperation in the number, and I cringe under the weight of it.

I stumble over a word, one I know. Then, like an avalanche gathering snow, my mistakes double and triple—collecting and muting me so my last paragraph is read at a whisper.

I finish to silence and stares. Even Ms. Porter has lowered her book to study me.

Amelia clears her throat. "Can I go next?" Without waiting for an answer, she starts reading.

Slowly all the eyes turn back to their books, the blood drains from my cheeks, and the clock ticks its way to dismissal.

Five years.

5

JONAH

☼ 1:24 P.M. ☽

HOW DO YOU SAY "FIFTY MINUTES OF TORTURE" IN SPANISH?

Group work. Like we're eight.

As soon as Señora Miller gets to the word "partner" in the English repetition of her directions—"*estudiantes*, I'm going to let you work with partners—" eyes go wide, darting around the room looking for others whose eyes are darting too. Then faces flush with relief. I wonder if they miss the rest of her directions: "—on this assignment. It's a review for the final. Come get one worksheet per group. Pass it in at the end of the period."

I watch their reactions but look away whenever anyone glances in my direction. I don't want a partner, and if I make eye contact some idiot might feel obligated to ask me out of pity. The threesome on my right is looking at me and having a whispered conference. Before they can decide they'll do me a favor and subdivide to include me, I grab a worksheet off the stack on Miller's desk and return to my seat.

Writing "Jonah Prentiss" large enough to fill the whole

name line, I scan the worksheet. It won't be hard. Despite the boasts that "Cross Pointe is a top-tier school—our grads go to such prestigious colleges"—it's no harder than Hamilton. The difference is the teachers here are younger, dress in labels, drive nicer cars, and spend more time coddling my classmates. I glance at the threesome, relieved to see they've gotten to work. The other pairs are scattered around the classroom, gossiping and occasionally jotting down answers.

Thirty-four filled-in blanks later, I stand to hand in the worksheet. I've checked my phone under my desk after nearly every question; it's only five minutes to the bell and Carly still hasn't responded to my text. Which could mean I've done who-knows-what to annoy her, or her phone battery's dead, or—

"Señor Prentiss, *uno momento por favor*?"

I pause halfway to my desk and turn back toward the teacher.

"This looks *muy bueno,* but you forgot your partner's name. You don't want to steal all the glory, do you?" She's smiling an overly cheerful teacher smile, expecting a chuckle and an "oops."

I meet her eyes. "I did it by myself."

Her smile dims a bit. "By yourself?"

"*Si,* Señora."

"You know our school emphasizes the importance of collaborative work."

I think: *Our* school? Not so much.

I say: "I know."

She leans forward. "In the real world, people don't work in isolation."

I resist the urge to point out a dozen jobs where people DO, in fact, work pretty much alone: artists, plumbers, postal workers, forest rangers . . .

Señora Miller isn't ready to let this go. She's counting the students in the class. "There are *dieciocho estudiantes* in here. Even."

The threesome is shooting dagger glances at me, daring me to rat them out for being exclusionary. About half the class watches with passive curiosity.

There's a copy of the Cross Pointe High Educational Philosophy hanging in every classroom. I've spent way too many hours using it as a hypocrisy checklist for my class-mates' actions; I have the damn thing memorized, which is an advantage right now. "I thought I'd find it *more personally meaningful* if I worked by myself."

Miller tilts her head as she considers this. "Fair enough. All right, *estudiantes*, hand in those worksheets and have a great weekend. I'll see you all on *Lunes*."

There's the usual *adioses*, "have a good weekend"s, and *graciases* during the scramble for the classroom door.

A girl with pearls and a ponytail touches my arm as I exit the room. I look from her hand to her face and raise my eye-brows. She removes her fingers and smiles tentatively. "You could've paired with us, you know. Maybe next time?"

I just stare at her.

The girl's smile fades to a scowl. "Or maybe not."

I stay silent, just like my phone. She takes the hint and leaves.

Why hasn't Carly answered me? I can't think of any-thing I've done to earn her silent treatment—*again*. I push my way through the hallway congested with people making plans and wasting time. I pull out my phone's battery and reinsert it, hoping it's a glitch in the programming or it needs to be reset. It's old, so either of these is possible. The two minutes it takes to reload are painful.

I have a new text message. I curb the urge to fist pump and click on it. Carly.

How soon can U get here?

I do a victory slam of my palm against my locker—the door pops open. So much for Brighton's fix. But who cares? I exhale as I shut the door. It's more than forty-eight hours till I'll have to open it again or walk the halls of a school that'll never feel like mine.

I make my way to my ten-year-old blue Accord, climb in, and wait impatiently in a line of tricked-out Benzes and BMWs for my turn to make the left down Main Street and drive the two miles to Mom and Paul's subdivision.

ASAP I text Carly, and fight the urge to blare my horn at the Escalade in front of me where a blonde is holding up traffic to lean out her window and kiss a guy in a CPHS baseball shirt.

"As soon as possible" is not soon enough.

6
Brighton

22 HOURS, 45 MINUTES LEFT

Amelia pulls me to the side of the hall as soon as class is over. "Let's go get mochas and talk. I know you're stressing."

"Can't. Friday—manicures with Mom." My answer is quick, my mind immediately shuttering off tempting thoughts of sinking into a cozy chair at Bean Haven and having an honest conversation with Amelia. "Thanks, though."

"I think she'd understand if you wanted to skip this week."

"I really can't. I can't mess with her routine right now. She's . . ." I flutter my hand and try to think of the right word, "fragile."

"And you're not? B, you—"

"Brighton! There you are!" Silvia's a sophomore, but I work with her on yearbook and dance committees. She moves a million miles an hour—both on and off the soccer field— and speaks everything with exclamation points. Her energy is contagious . . . normally. "Did you get my texts? I need help on my lab report!"

Amelia frowns. "We're kinda in the middle of something."

"Oh, sorry! I know, it's Friday afternoon—finally! You probably want to leave. It's not due till Monday. Want me to e-mail what I have and we can meet up tomorrow?"

"Can't you ask someone else?" Amelia suggests. I know the hand she's put on my arm is supposed to be supportive, but it feels like yet another weight, another demand, another expectation.

"Mr. Leland told me to ask Brighton. But I guess if you don't want to . . ." I hope the statement ends with "I'll ask someone else" or "I'll figure it out," but Silvia just shrugs and sighs.

"She doesn't."

"Amelia!" I exclaim.

Silvia takes a step backward, but I protest, "It's all right. Really, it's okay. Show me now." I squeeze Amelia's arm and give her an apologetic look. "Have fun tonight with Peter."

"Call me later." It's a command, and I nod before I follow Silvia toward the computer lab.

"Brighton!" Jake Murphy calls down the hall. "What time should I be at the library on Sunday?"

I don't want to yell, so I hold up eight fingers.

"Eight a.m.? You're killing me," he bellows.

"I try," I say, shooting finger guns in his direction.

This earns me one of his booming laughs and a "For *you*, my coffee and I will be there. Large. Coffee."

Ellie Cooper stops me next, and it's hard to maintain a smile. Just this once I'd like to get from point A to point B without having twenty conversations. Invisibility sounds like the most desirable of superpowers—I'll have to ask Peter which radioactive creature needs to bite me.

"B, I'm going to be a little late on Sunday. Tennis lesson."

"That's okay. We'll probably be at the library until noonish."

"Great! I'll be there by ten. At the latest. Who's coming?"

The list is at the bottom of my bag—and if I pull it out, she'll want to talk about everyone on it. So I wink. "Wait and see."

"You're the worst. Ugh, okay, I guess I'll be patient. Oh, almost forgot, Mr. Donnelly wants to see you before you leave."

"He does?" Mr. Donnelly is the Key Club advisor. I'm sure it's nothing, just some last-minute reminders about the book project, but it's yet another thing between me and my car. I pull on a smile. "Thanks, Ellie. See you Sunday."

Three interruptions later, we finally reach the empty computer lab. Silvia inserts a thumb drive and pulls up her lab report. My chest tightens when I look at the screen. She's normally a good student, but her equations are a mess. This isn't going to be simple or fast. I look at the clock and pull out chairs.

"Silvie, this is kind of . . ."

"A disaster?" she suggests. Laughs. Then drops her head into her hands. "Ugh, I know! I was just so distracted!"

"Well, it shouldn't take us too long. Let's get started." I scroll down the pages looking for something to compliment. I know from yearbook that Silvia needs to hear something positive before a negative. "Your conclusion is solid; we just need to swap around some of the chemical names and results in the procedure so they match."

"Yeah, I copied most of that from Izzie. I just *couldn't* pay attention today!"

"Then we'll need to change the wording, or Mr. Leland will notice." I take the mouse and start this process.

She sighs. "Sorry! You're probably totally impatient to get out of here. But, honestly, *this* is not my fault. Anyone would have flaked in my situation." She looks at me and raises her eyebrows, waiting for me to ask.

I swallow my sigh and let go of the mouse. "Everything okay?"

"Adrian! Forrester!" She says this like it's an answer, but I'm not sure how it matches my question. When I shrug, she continues. "Do you know him? Super tall? Super blond? Super *hot*? Both our lab partners were absent, so Mr. Leland paired us up for this . . ."

She stops talking and stares dreamily at the computer screen.

"And?" I prompt.

"Oh! And nothing." She frowns. "But, *gah*, he's too adorable! He's wearing this yellow polo today, with a blue stripe that is the *exact* same color as his eyes. How am I supposed to pay attention when he's wearing that? And he was telling Max at the next table about his new car—he just got his license. I'd die to be his copilot!"

I don't have time to be relationship therapist *and* chem-tutor, so I offer the obvious solution and hope we can move on. "So, why don't you ask him out?"

Silvia laughs and plays with the mouse. "Yeah, right! We're not all *you*. I could never. When it comes to Adrian, I'm just . . . *hopeless*!"

I'm not going to bite this time. I'm not going to play

Who's More Popular or list the reasons any guy would be lucky to date her. I know she expects this, and it would only take a blink to conjure up the words.

But I can't. I just can't.

"Well, then, let's focus on something less hopeless, like getting you an A on this lab."

It's kinder than what I'm thinking—*it must be nice to have your biggest problem be a hot lab partner*—but my tone is sharper than I intend.

Silvia's face crumples. "Sorry. I shouldn't have bothered you. You can go. I'll—I'll stop being so stupid and figure it out."

My stomach clenches. Hurting her feels like punching myself in the gut. "Oh, Silvie, *I'm* sorry. That came out wrong." I give her a one-armed hug and say what I should have said the first time. "Any guy would be lucky to have someone as adorable, funny, and wonderful as you. Your snickerdoodles alone would make most guys drool—combine those with how pretty you are, and how nice? If Adrian hasn't noticed, then *he's* the one who's stupid."

"Yeah. Sure. Thanks." But there aren't exclamation points on these sentences. She turns her face toward the screen. "I'll get started so you can get out of here."

I'm trying not to watch the clock, and not to guess how long everything will take. I'm impatient—I don't want to keep repeating myself for Silvia or go make small talk with Mr. Donnelly—and knowing that makes me feel worse. I *adore* Silvie. I *like* tutoring. I *love* organizing service projects.

At least, I usually do. I should probably apologize again, make sure she's okay, but she's finally focusing on the computer screen and it's taking all my energy not to clench my hands into fists, so I don't interrupt.

"Great!" I tell her. "You're getting it."

My job is purely moral support, company, and prompts to keep going. A talking doll could do this job—probably better than I could, since a doll wouldn't have snapped at Silvia. A doll wouldn't make Silvia feel like she had to apologize for every question or thank me for every answer.

It takes me until she hits print to convince her that *I don't mind*, that *she's not stupid*, and *really, I'm not annoyed with you. How could anyone be annoyed with you?*

Silvia thanks me *again,* and hugs me. "I mean it, B. You're the best! I'm so glad I don't have to worry about this over the weekend."

"Anytime." I hug her back. "But I should get going if I'm going to catch Mr. Donnelly before he leaves."

As I walk down the hall I catch sight of a tall guy wearing a yellow polo with a blue stripe standing at a locker. I'm only two doors from Mr. Donnelly's room, but I'm still suffocating on computer lab guilt, so I pause and smile at him.

"Hi! Adrian, right?"

He looks startled, then grins. "Yeah. Hey, Brighton. I didn't know you knew me—I guess from that animal-shelter thing earlier in the year?"

"Of course!" I agree. "Anyway, could you do me a quick favor? Please?"

"For you? Yeah. Sure! What's up?" He pops the tab on a can of Red Bull and takes a sip.

"Do you know Silvia Lombardo?"

"Tall, bouncy girl with brown hair? She's in my chem

class." His locker is still open, and it's a mess of energy drinks, papers, Sharpies, and a trio of Cross Pointe High hooded sweatshirts.

"Great! I forgot to tell her what time Key Club is meeting Sunday, and I'm already late for a meeting with Mr. Donnelly. Would it be a huge inconvenience if I ask you to run back to the computer lab and tell her it's at eight a.m.?"

"Is that the library thing? I'm going to that."

"Fabulous!" His name is so not on the list in my bag, but I'll take all the recruits I can get—plus, Silvia will be thrilled. "And did I hear you just got your license?"

"Yeah. Yesterday." He blinks and stands a little taller, leans toward me. "I can finally use the parking space my parents reserved for me. Crazy, right? Them paying for a space I only get to use a dozen times before summer break—not that I'm complaining."

I'm supposed to giggle or roll my eyes at his parents' excess, but really I want to yank the Red Bull from his hand and chug it. Hope that there's enough caffeine in the can to get me from now until whenever I can collapse on my bed.

I giggle.

"You know—" He shifts his weight and puts a hand on my arm. "I'm old for a sophomore. My parents kept me back in kindergarten, so I'm practically a junior. If you want to see my car—"

If Silvia walked by right now, she'd be crushed. I'm not flirting. I don't have a quarter of the energy required to flirt. I have less than zero interest in flirting with Adrian, but he thinks I am. Instead of helping Silvie, I'm making things worse. I pull my arm away from his hand.

"You know what would be awesome?" I don't pause for

his answer. "If you could carpool on Sunday. Since you can drive and most sophomores can't—and there's not much parking there. Maybe you could drive . . . *Silvia*?"

"Silvia?" He steps back, message received. "Yeah, I could totally do that. I'll go find her for you."

"Thanks," I say, turning down the hall. "You're the best, Adrian! See you Sunday."

Mr. Donnelly's shuffling through stacks of student work, moving piles back and forth on his desk and looking through his bag. He's so absorbed in this process, he doesn't acknowledge my knock or notice when I cross the classroom to stand on the other side of his desk. I shift my weight a few times, check the clock on the wall above the projection screen, and finally fake a ridiculous-sounding cough.

He looks up and adjusts his glasses. "Oh, Brighton! Sorry, I didn't hear you. I can't seem to find the list of volunteers for Sunday."

"I have it. Remember? You gave it to me yesterday."

"Did I? Well, I've got a few more names for you to add. Where did I put that note?"

My heart picks up a beat, and for a moment it's easy to ignore that the clock is ticking away my downtime while Mr. Donnelly rejects a variety of illegible notes on scraps of paper. Could Jonah have changed his mind? If so, I can just apologize in person at the event.

"Here it is: Mallory Freeman and Jake Murphy. How many volunteers does that put you at?"

I swallow and bite the inside of my lip. Not Jonah.

I need to sit. Now. Like disappointment has a weight to it. A weight heavy enough to make my knees refuse to hold me up. I lower myself onto a table and steal an extra moment by pulling the sign-up sheet out of my bag and adding their names. Adrian's too.

It's not just Jonah I'm upset about. It's my dad. Everything seems to be leading back to Dad right now.

I take a deep breath and count the names on the sheet. "Twenty-two. That's plenty, even if a few of them are no-shows."

Mr. Donnelly nods and pulls a coffee-stained catalog out of a drawer. It figures he knows exactly where *that* is, and he even has a sticky note marking the page. He flips it open, and I'm faced with a glossy photograph of the plaque I picked out back in October: green marble mounted on dark cherry wood. The words engraved in gold. A row of people holding hands across the bottom that look like the chains of paper dolls I used to cut out and decorate in elementary school.

It's perfect—an exact duplicate of the plaque already hanging in the lobby outside the main office, the one inscribed with my father's name—but that doesn't matter anymore. Ninety-nine point whatever percent isn't good enough.

"Brighton, the deadline for club purchases is next Thursday."

I nod and tighten my fingers. The date is circled on my calendar at home.

I look at the wording I'd deliberated over this fall—it's printed on the sticky note, just waiting for an order that won't be placed:

Cross Pointe Key Club
100% Participation Award

2013–2014
Club President: Brighton Waterford
Club Advisor: Mr. Donnelly
Making the world better, one day at a time.

"I've got a lot riding on this. Principal Jencks and I made a bet, you know."

"You did?" I ask.

"If you pull this off, I win—and my schedule next year will have a coveted end-of-the-day prep period. If we don't get a hundred percent student participation, I lose. And then I'm in charge of coordinating the halftime bake sales at all the football games. Please don't make me lose. I can't cook."

"I'm trying." I want to tell him I don't need the added pressure. That I'll make all the cookies, cupcakes, sugary whatevers he needs next fall, but I can't do this.

"I know you are." His face softens into affection; he's never made it a secret that I'm one of his favorite students. It's a blessing that often feels as heavy as a burden—especially now, when I want to make him happy but can't. "You remind me so much of your dad—and if Ethan were still alive, he'd be so proud of you for doing this."

I'm used to people comparing us, and I know Mr. Donnelly went to school with Dad, so it shouldn't surprise me, but I'm unprepared, caught off-guard, and a soft "I hope so" escapes my lips.

"Of course he would. I'm sure I've already told you all this: how he was a couple grades above me, but he knew everyone, and everyone wanted to be his friend. He was such a leader—like you—I think if he'd wanted us to dye our hair green instead of raising money for starving Ethiopians or Mexican earthquake survivors, we would've done it. You couldn't listen to him and not get caught up in his enthusiasm. There's so much of him in you. *You* are his legacy."

I suck my bottom lip and refuse to let myself blink. If I don't shut my lids, then my eyes are just glistening. It's not the same as crying. I hadn't realized how badly I needed to hear that. Or how much it would hurt.

It's not that I don't want to answer, thank him. It's that I can't.

After several weighty seconds, Mr. Donnelly nudges a box of tissues in my direction and clears his throat. "So, have you had any luck with our little situation?"

I twist a tissue in my fingers while I take some steadying breaths. I doubt Jonah Prentiss would appreciate being referred to as a "little situation"—or maybe he wouldn't care, just like he didn't care about harbor seals, drinking water in Africa, litter along the highway, or any of the other causes I've invited him to help out with.

"He's busy on Sunday. Sorry."

Mr. Donnelly sighs and slides the catalog another inch or two closer to me. "It's always hard when new students move into town; they don't understand the Cross Pointe philosophy of giving back to the community. If Brighton Waterford can't convince him to participate, that says it all. Some people are takers, and there's nothing you can do about it."

For a moment I'm relieved. There is nothing I can do. Jonah is just a taker. There are no magic words I can use to persuade him to volunteer. The whole situation has gotten overhyped and out of hand.

Mr. Donnelly continues, "You know, maybe if I talked to him . . . It's not too late: we could get him to commit to tutoring someone during finals or we could stretch the rules a little and get him to sign up for a summer service project after he graduates. Maybe if I tell him how much it means to you. We could even talk to him togeth—"

I shake my head so emphatically that Mr. Donnelly stops midword.

"No. Really. You don't need to."

The last thing that would work is Mr. Donnelly cornering Jonah and telling him to do it *for me.*

If I could just figure Jonah out: who he is, what he likes, why he refuses to play by the same social rules as everyone else.

"We've worked so hard on this all year—I'd just hate to see all that effort go unacknowledged if you fail."

I flinch at the words "you fail."

He smiles reassuringly. "And I'd really hate to have to figure out how to turn on my oven."

"I'll try, but . . ."

I look down at the catalog again. Mr. Donnelly spins the picture so it's facing me.

"Don't give up hope just yet. There are still a few days until that ordering deadline." He taps the photo. "I have faith in you. I still think we'll be ordering this, and the Waterford volunteerism legacy will continue. Your dad wouldn't give up, and you won't either."

I stammer a thank-you and leave the room. I *want* to give up.

But I can't.

My father's the only one who's ever done this: gotten the

whole school to volunteer. And Mr. Donnelly's right: Dad never would've given up on 100 percent; he never would've given up on Jonah.

I spin the ring on my finger—I have no idea how I'll change Jonah's mind, but I won't disappoint Mr. Donnelly. I won't fail my dad.

The hallways are nearly deserted, and I'm grateful. I'm itchy in my skin, fidgety in ways I haven't been since I was little and Mom lectured me about standing still. I need to keep moving, keep making progress toward home. Take a few minutes in my room, maybe even climb into bed and pull the covers over my head.

But Amelia's Land Rover is still in the parking space next to my car: the Audi Roadster my sister, Evy, picked for her sixteenth birthday four years ago. I hate how conspicuous it is—like a bright red jelly bean. I open my door and climb in, lowering my window when Amelia opens her passenger door to talk. Peter's behind the wheel. He calls his greeting across her and turns down the radio.

"You didn't have to wait for me," I say, but I'm touched that she did. She shrugs this off and asks, "What time is the memorial tomorrow?"

"One." It's that squeaky voice from English class.

Twenty-one hours and fifty-six minutes from now. Not enough time to prepare.

"Want me to come over before?"

I wish I could get out of the car and hug her, but I can't without crying. If Amelia sees a single tear, she'll never let me leave. And my mom needs me. "Thanks, but that's okay— I'll see you at the church."

She ducks under the shoulder strap of her seat belt to lay her head on Peter's shoulder. "If you change your mind, call me. And call me later."

"Sure. Have fun tonight."

But her attention's on Peter now.

I watch them for a minute before I raise my window and put the car in reverse. It only takes six minutes to drive home; I still might have fifteenish minutes to decompress if Mom's running at all late.

After eight minutes of impatient stop signs and pausing to let joggers, dog walkers, and baby strollers cross at every corner, I pull into the driveway and hit my garage door remote. Mom is waiting at the top of the stairs. She's still in a gray pencil skirt and white-collared blouse, but she looks rumpled. Her sleeves are rolled up, and wisps of dark hair have escaped from her bobby pins. So much for fifteen minutes. Or even five.

I want to turn around and retreat to my car, to make up an excuse and go get the mail—anything to create just a minute of me time. Instead I notice her nervous energy, the way she's half reaching for me, as if she's going to pull me up the last step and into the kitchen. I take a deep breath, close the space for a quick hug, and manage a calm voice: "You're home early."

She laces her fingers together and looks down at the toes of her pumps. "I took a half day. It was too hard to focus. I keep thinking about tomorrow. I need everything to be perfect for your father."

I look beyond her shoes to the mess she's already created in the foyer: her coat slung over the banister, a coffee mug on the antique bureau, her purse on one stair, her briefcase on another, and her keys—for some reason—on the floor.

"How about we stay home? I'll make tea and you can change out of your work clothes."

Mom looks up. Almost-formed tears cling to her eyelashes as she blinks with surprise. "But it's Friday, we've got manicures. And look at that chip on your nail."

"I can just touch it up. We could reschedule. What if we go on Monday?"

"We always go on Friday. We've got appointments."

I open my mouth to protest, but a smudge of mascara under her left eye stops me. She's been crying. "Okay."

Mom nods. "Go on, put away your bag, then we'll leave."

I obey, climbing the stairs to my bedroom, hanging my bag on its hook on the back of my door, swapping my wallet and phone into a purse, and grabbing that instead. I allow myself one forlorn glance at my bed, flipping over the pillowcase so I can't see the mascara tear stains from last night. Then I head downstairs to where Mom is waiting, keys in hand.

7

JONAH

☼ 2:29 P.M. ☽

HALF-PAST GUILT

Mom meets me at the door wearing my baby sister in a sling around her neck. She's also wearing a burp cloth, a splatter of baby spit-up, and a frazzled expression. She looks like a walking advertisement for birth control, but she claims to love her new life as a stay-at-home mom.

"Jonah, buddy—" she begins, reaching up to unwind the sling and smiling hopefully.

I step to the side before she can get it off. "Hey, Mom. I've got to get going, I'm meeting Carly."

"Could you change your plans? Have Carly come here instead?"

"No way in hell—"

She cuts me off with a disapproving frown and mouths the word "language" while covering Sophia's ears.

I look around for Paul, because Mom's still rational most of the time. I don't see him. "She can't even talk yet."

"But she can listen. Is that the example you want to be setting?" She's smiling though, so at least she recognizes she's being insane.

"Damn, I guess I'm a crappy big brother then. You wouldn't want a screwup with such foul language around Sophia."

She laughs. "I'm glad to see the swear jar was effective. We'll have to charge this one a dollar instead of a quarter."

"That one" will be able to afford a dollar a swear. I'm sure Paul will pay her allowance in gold coins if she asks.

"Oh, please, Jonah. Our babysitter canceled, and Paul and I have dinner reservations. You'd really be helping us out."

She must be desperate if she'd ask me. Paul always hovers when I'm holding Sophia—like he needs to be ready to swoop in and rescue his precious daughter in case I decide to shake or drop her. And Carly—well, if I see Sophia as a reason to use birth control, Carly views her as an argument for abstinence.

I try to look sorry. "Maybe if I'd known earlier, but we've got plans."

Mom sighs and runs a hand through her hair, smearing some of the spit-up from her shoulder. If this lifestyle wasn't a prison of her own making, and if I wasn't trapped in it too, maybe I'd be sympathetic.

But my life is waiting in Hamilton.

"It's okay. Have fun. Tell Carly we say hi."

I turn to go up the stairs just as Sophia wakes and starts to wail. Mom begins to bounce her and coo, "Shhh, baby girl. Please, please shhh. For me?"

Dammit, she sounds so pathetic. And exhausted. I sigh and make a 180, holding out my arms. "I can wait a little while. Go take a shower or a break or something." I even tolerate the hug she gives me along with my sister.

"Twenty minutes tops, I promise! You are my best son ever," she calls from halfway up the stairs.

I switch Sophia to my other arm and put down my backpack. Then bob and weave around the living room, catching my reflection in Paul's sixty-inch flat screen—I look like a poorly controlled marionette. Sophia's noises go from a screech to a whimper. I add a singsong, "Your mom is nuts. Totally freakin' nuts," and my sister has the good sense to smile up at me. Then she yawns, shuts her eyes, and goes back to sleep.

It's so easy to make this baby happy—I'm jealous. The warm weight of her against my chest and the little sighs she gives as she nestles closer and grasps a tiny fistful of my shirt almost distract me from how long Mom's been upstairs.

I whisper to her, "Make a mental note of this for later: your mom is the slowest showerer ever. She uses up all the hot water and takes at least twice as long as she says she will."

The mom who comes back downstairs is the one my sister will recognize, but she no longer looks like the parent I grew up with. My mother used to come home from her job as an office manager at an insurance company and change into sweats or jeans with holes. My mom was nineteen when I was born—*I* was the oops Juliana/Jordan mentioned in English, not Sophia.

Her mom is someone I don't know. A woman who wakes up early to do her makeup before going to Zumba and spends an hour cleaning *before* the cleaning woman comes. She finds staying home "fulfilling," can spend a whole week trying out different recipes for zucchini bread, and laughs it off whenever I comment that she looks exhausted.

"There's nothing like a shower to fix things. I feel so much better, you don't even know." Gone are the spit-up, the ponytail, and the gym clothes. She's in her Cross Pointe costume, some extremely matching outfit with precision hairstyling and makeup application. Mom pats my head, and even that's different now. Her gel-tipped nails are another Cross Pointe addition. I hate the way they feel when she touches my shoulder or scratches my back. Really hate the clacking sound they make when she drums them on the marble counters while lecturing me about moving on and accepting my new life.

Her new life.

I'm staring at her—she gives me a funny look and I try to relax my posture so she doesn't decide now's a good time to try out another parenting-book technique for "opening communication pathways" or some other crap.

Mom picks up a glass of sparkling water from the coffee table and takes a sip. "Oh, good, you got her back to sleep. You can put her in her swing if you want."

I shrug and lean against the back of the couch. "She's fine. I don't want to wake her."

"So, what did you learn in school today?" she asks with a wink, knowing I hate this clichéd question. At least it's not "What's a goal you've set for this weekend?" or "How would you describe your current emotional outlook?" or "Can you tell me one thing you did today to make the world better?" or any of the other obnoxious conversation starters she's gotten from her library of What-do-I-do-with-my-teen? books.

I roll my eyes as she reaches out and touches my hair—ruffling it and then smoothing it back into place.

"You need a haircut."

"Yeah, I know." I used to keep it short so it didn't get in my way on the diamond, but now that I'm not playing, I can't be bothered.

"I miss seeing you, bud. You're always running off to Hamilton or you're locked in your room."

I open my mouth to say "then you shouldn't have moved," but what comes out is, "Miss you too."

"Do your Sox play this weekend? Now that we get every channel known to man, I'm sure we get all their games. Want to order Chinese and watch? I'll get Paul to take the baby to the park so it's just you and me. It'll be like old times."

I want to give in—except it won't be like old times. Dad won't be there to spill popcorn whenever a batter strikes out, and Mom will pay more attention to whether or not I'm using a coaster than to the lineup.

I should say no, but her eyes are pleading. "Maybe."

"Good." She smiles. "Sophia looks so comfortable with you."

"She's pretty cute," I admit.

"Am I making you late?" Mom asks.

"I've got a few minutes." I don't remember the last time Mom and I had a conversation that didn't include her telling me everything I'm doing wrong. I can be a few minutes late to see Carly if it means prolonging this. I give Sophia a gentle squeeze; maybe I'll put her in the swing after all. Then I'll talk Mom into making her famous nachos while we catch up.

"If you've got some time, you don't mind if I just duck out for my manicure, do you?"

"What?" I freeze halfway to the swing and spin around to face her.

"I won't be long. Paul should be home any second. He's running late because one of his clients needed a last-minute appointment before a race tomorrow."

She says this with such expectation. All my nostalgia and goodwill vanish. None of it was real.

"What the hell? Are you kidding me?" This time I'm not swearing for her amusement, but she pretends not to notice.

"Come on, Jonah. I'll give you gas money." She reaches inside her purse and pulls out her wallet, looking at the bills instead of me. "Forty dollars for twenty minutes? Sound good?"

The way she holds out the cash is like she's daring me to protest. And I could use the money. Back in Hamilton, I had a job, but Mom and Paul made me quit when we moved so I could "focus on school work and making friends." Now, if I need money, I'm supposed to "ask Paul." I don't even like asking him to pass the salt; I'm not going to beg for handouts.

I take the cash.

"Will you make me nachos?" The question is a fragment of the conversation I thought we might have, and it slips out in a sulky voice.

She's already putting her wallet away, leaning down to kiss Sophia on the forehead. "Right now? I'm on my way out."

"What about for the game?"

"The game?" Either she's distracted by locating her keys on their hook, or she's already forgotten.

"The Sox game?" I prompt.

She pauses. "Right. Sorry. I really want to do that, Jonah. We'll find a time and, yes, I will make you a huge plate of nachos." She reaches for my hair *again*. I shift out of her reach. "Did I already tell you to say hi to Carly for us?"

I nod. She tosses a hasty "thank you" in my direction and shuts the door to the garage behind her.

Carly's first impatient text arrives ten minutes later. **Where R U?**

Haven't left yet. Soon. It'd better be soon. Paul better be home soon like Mom promised.

My phone beeps again and I hope for a teasing pout-faced picture or a tempting: **If u were here right now . . .**

For the first couple of months after the move my phone never stopped beeping. She flooded it with **I MISS U** messages and updates about everything/everyone. But lately they haven't been as frequent or friendly.

I click on her text:

I hope U don't think Im waiting all nite.

I call. Voice mail. I don't bother leaving a message. When Carly gets like this, face-to-face is the only way to reason with her. And I should be leaving soon, definitely before four. Plenty of time to have dinner and some us time before Jeff's party.

I pace with Sophia in my arms. My sister's like me that way: she craves constant motion. Paul, the king of not-fidgeting, says it's a baby thing and she'll outgrow it. I hope he's wrong; it's the only part of me I see in her. She's got Paul's blue eyes, while I have Mom's brown. Her hair is dark like his—I was a white-blond and looked bald until I was two. Other than hair and eyes, she's a mini-Mom in ears and nose and mouth. When I look in the mirror all I see are my dad's features, and it reminds me all over again that he hates me now.

We pace and I bounce her, humming hybrid versions of rock anthems and the ABC song.

Twenty minutes pass. Then thirty. Forty. How long does it take to paint nails? Where the hell is Paul?

The garage leads into the kitchen via a half flight of stairs. Normally I'm startled by the alarm's obnoxious *beep-beep* each time a door or window is opened, but I'm humming a particularly enthusiastic version of "Rubber Ducky" and trying Carly's phone again, so I don't hear Paul until he's a few feet away.

"I would appreciate if you could show enough restraint to not text while holding my daughter. If what you're doing is so important it cannot wait, then put her down somewhere safe until you can give her proper attention."

His criticism hits at the same time as Carly's voice-mail message. I hit the cancel button on my phone and wish I could mute him as well. He holds out his arms and crooks his fingers impatiently until I pass him the baby.

"You're welcome," I say, responding to a "thank you" that won't ever come.

Paul doesn't disappoint. He ignores me and starts examining Sophia—checking her hands and pulling out the back of her leggings to see if her diaper is clean. "Daddy's home. It's all right now."

I get way too much satisfaction from the fact that in *his* arms, Sophia wakes and cries.

"Nice job. I just got her to sleep. And I think it's pretty ballsy for *you* to accuse me of not keeping her safe or paying enough attention."

He ignores this too, but I know I've hit him in his most vulnerable spot. His face turns a mottled red. It starts at his collar and spreads up to his ears. I remember this from back in the days when he was my physical therapist and one of the employees in his practice would arrive late or when a client would be a no-show. Back then it intimidated me—now, it's my goal to inspire these angry flushes as often as possible.

Mission accomplished.

I head to my room for a quick shirt change, deodorant reapplication, and to check the contents of my wallet.

A quick text to Carly: **Leaving now.**

I take the downstairs at a run, earning a fly-by frown from Paul as I dash through the kitchen where he's now singing and feeding Sophia a bottle.

"Does your mom know where you'll be and do you need—"

I slam the door, leaving the second half of Paul's question in the kitchen. Thirty seconds later I'm in my car—driving away from Mom, Paul, Sophia, and their game of Happy Family—sending **On my way** texts to Carly.

I'm speeding—not pushing it, I can't afford another ticket—but I'm sixty-two miles per hour in the fifty-fives. At least I am until I hit rush-hour traffic—something I could've avoided if I hadn't let Mom guilt me into waiting. The thirty-minute drive turns into forty-five, and I'm cursing every car on the road, counting down the miles until Carly's skin is on mine, and I can taste her, taste the first beer of tonight's party—and feel just a little bit like myself again.

It's only Friday night to Monday morning that I exist anymore. Only once I've crossed the boundaries of Cross Pointe and come home to Hamilton.

8
Brighton
☼ 3:28 P.M. ☽

21 HOURS, 32 MINUTES LEFT

I roll the bottle of It's Raining Luck between my palms and let my eyes drift over the other colors lined up on the neat racks. I tune out the chatter and background noise in the spa and breathe in the dizzying scent of Friday afternoons: aromatherapy oils mixed with nail polish and acetone.

"Really, Brighton, I don't know why you even stop and look. We both know you're going to get Pointe-Shoe Pink like every other week." Mom takes the bottle from my hand and laughs as she replaces it on the wall rack. "Green glitter? Who would wear that? Take off your ring, Mina's waiting."

I stick my ring in the front pocket of my purse and take the chair next to my mother's, across the counter from Mina. She has my polish ready, a pale wash of pink half a shade darker than my bare nails.

"Evy's flight lands at five thirty. We'll go pick her up from here," Mom announces while settling herself into her chair and paying Mina and Pearl so she won't have to handle money with wet nails. "Your sister is going to be the death of me."

"Why? What'd she do this time?" Freshman year she'd organized a naked race around campus on the last day of finals.

"She was almost mugged last night," Mom answers as she dips her fingers into the bowls of warm water and beach stones Pearl has set before her.

"What happened? Is she okay?" I ask shrilly. Mom gives me a don't-cause-a-scene look.

"She's fine. Honestly, Brighton, what kind of mother do you think I am? Would I be here if she wasn't?" She gives me a look of pure exasperation.

"Sorry."

"Now, this is Evy's version of the story, so you know it's exaggerated, but according to her, she turned to them, told them they'd picked the wrong girl. She told them she was a black belt—which we both know is not true, unless she spent her spring semester in a karate studio, and even then, she would've told us about it *in detail*. And she screamed at the two would-be muggers until they backed down. Then she got in her car, locked the doors, called the cops, and *followed them* until the cops arrived." Mom removes one hand from a bowl and rubs her temples—leaving watery streaks in her foundation that roll toward the collar of her crisp white shirt, but don't drip; like they know stains aren't tolerated in Mom's world. "Your sister has far too much 'fight' and not an ounce of 'flight' or common sense."

"What am I?" I ask. "Fight or flight?"

Mom smiles indulgently at me. "Baby, you'd manage to make friends with them. But, barring that, flight. You hate conflict."

"And Evy loves it."

"Evy's more like me. You're just like your father."

"How so?" I lean forward, sloshing water over the edge of my bowl and causing Mina to tut and tug on the hand she's jabbing with cuticle scissors.

I need this—concrete answers to this comparison everyone keeps making. I want to know more than we had the same eyes, or we both ran Key Club. I need to know *real* things. I feel like I'm forgetting everything that matters.

Mom's face softens to sadness and I backtrack, "You don't have to talk about that, sorry."

She nods a little and stares down at the wet hand that's creating a damp circle on the fabric of her skirt.

I bite my tongue and want to curl my fingers into fists and trap all my questions there. *Don't you miss him? And the way things used to be?* Stupid questions, because I know she does.

But I wish family dinners hadn't died with him. I wish I still started my mornings by sitting beside him at the breakfast bar in the kitchen while we ate cereal and he drank coffee. His mantra had been: "Your goal each day should be to make the world better by being in it," and before I'd leave for school he'd kiss my forehead and say: "You've already 'Brighton'd' my day, now go get the rest of 'em." Each night we'd go around the table and share one thing we'd done to make the world a better place. Evy was sometimes snarky, Mom often complained about it, but I always took it seriously and mentally screened my whole day for the story that would make him proudest.

I still lie in bed each night and whisper my answer to the ceiling.

If I say this to Mom, she'll sigh. One of those long breaths that are drenched in her desolation and whisper, *Why would you tell me this when you know it's only going to upset me?*

I need to change the subject, but my thoughts are stuck and it hurts to breathe.

"He was the perfect therapist . . . ," Mom says softly, and I don't dare look at her for fear she'll stop talking. "He made each of his clients feel like the most important person in the world, yet he left all their sob stories in the office—shook it off and came home. You're the same, baby. You make every-one feel better about themselves, but not much touches you."

Could he *really* compartmentalize like that? Or had he been haunted by his clients' problems, like how I can't forget the way my thoughtless words hurt Silvie earlier? There's a difference between not caring and not *showing* that you care.

"Teflon girl," I mutter, switching hands for Mina.

"What?"

"That's Amelia's new thing—she says nothing sticks to me. Of course, *everything* sticks to her." My best friend with her *causes du jour* and debate club presidency wears her heart on her sleeve. Actually, she wears her heart like a billboard.

Mom laughs. "I like that. So, what are your plans tonight?" This is usually her first question once we are settled in our chairs. I guess we're back on script.

"After we get Evy?"

"Sure. Or I can drop you home on my way to the airport."

I pick my words carefully. Is there a non-insulting way to say I didn't make plans because I'm waiting for her to break down?

"I figured the three of us would do dinner and then I'd wait and see."

"I can't do dinner—I'm meeting Aunt Joan. Maybe Evy? But no. I'm pretty sure she mentioned plans with Brooke." Mom's inspecting the cuticles Pearl just trimmed, her voice matter-of-fact.

"Oh, but . . ." I swallow the rest of the sentence.

"Do you want me to cancel?"

"No, you don't have to." I pull my hand out of my bowl and set it dripping in my lap. Mina clucks her disapproval but continues to shape my other hand with her file. "It'll be good for me. Relaxing." My mind is cycling through surprise to extreme relief. I need to hold it together now for Mom, summon enough energy to be excited to see Evy—but then . . . then I can climb under the covers and hide until tomorrow.

"You could call that boy you went out with last week. What was his name? Joshua?"

"Jeremy," I supply. "Maybe. We'll see."

In the six years we've been coming to this salon, I've become accustomed to treating it like the kitchen table. Mom used to say, "It's not like they understand us anyhow," which makes me uncomfortable in an is-that-racist-or-just-stupid? way. But Mina doesn't offer her opinions, and Pearl never says anything but "thank you," "sit," and "other hand." They communicate with us in gestures and nods, gossiping among themselves in Korean, though I know they're both fluent in English. They take their cues from Mom, and she insists that our "girl time" include confessions and no interruptions.

Not that I ever have much to confess. It'd been way more scandalous when Evy sat between us, but she'd quit coming when she was fifteen—choosing to color her nails with Sharpies, highlighters, and Wite-Out and refusing to play Gossip Quest on Mom's terms.

"Excuse me." The woman at the table to my left leans over. "You're Andrea Waterford, right? We met a few weeks ago at Emma Murphy's jewelry party. You made that fabulous spinach dip. I have *got* to get that recipe. This must be your lovely daughter; and did I hear you say you've got no plans tonight?"

She's breaking Mom's cardinal rule of manicures—do not eavesdrop or join our conversation—but I can't be rude; even though Mom's brief nod and the tone of her "Oh, hello. Lovely to see you again" treads the line between cordial and dismissive.

I force a smile and a cheerful "A night of downtime every now and then can't hurt."

"I'm Brenda Shea. You're Brighton, right? Your junior prom queen photo in the *Gazette* was beautiful. You are much prettier than the senior queen."

I blush and make an embarrassed noise of acknowledgment. Compliments like that are so awkward. Mom's too annoyed to save me, sighing loudly as she watches a soap opera on the television mounted behind Pearl's head.

"My son goes to school with you."

I've never heard of anyone with the last name Shea, which immediately makes me feel guilty. Cross Pointe isn't big. Mrs. Shea seems to know all about me, and I can't even identify her son. "I don't think I know him. Sorry."

"That's okay, he's quiet. Anyhow, if you don't have plans tonight, would you be free to babysit?"

I jerk out of Mina's grasp and am rewarded with a Pointe-Shoe Pink stripe that stretches from my thumb across the tops of my fingers. "He needs a babysitter? I'm not really comfortable—"

"No." Mrs. Shea laughs. "He's going off to college next year—I hope he doesn't need a babysitter! He's on a date. I'm talking about my daughter, Sophia. She's five months."

"Oh." I apologize to Mina and turn to give my Mom a relieved look. She's ignoring me, tapping her foot impatiently against the leg of the table.

"Normally I would never ask, but our babysitter canceled last minute and my son refuses to change his plans with Carly. We moved here not that long ago, so I don't have a backup sitter yet. I thought if you weren't doing anything . . . but if you can't, I completely understand."

I don't know Carly either. Who are these people?

"Um . . ." I give her a once-over. She's pretty much a typical Cross Pointe mother: Tory Burch bag at her feet, hair highlighted and sculpted, cardigan set coordinated with her sandals.

Then it hits me. New to Cross Pointe? And there's a similarity in their dark brown eyes and the shape of their mouths—although her polite smiles are so different from his leave-me-alone scowl. "Wait, is your son Jonah *Prentiss*?"

"Yes!" Mrs. Shea beams and leans forward. "You know Jonah? Oh, that makes me happy. He's really struggled with this move. He used to be so social, but since we've gotten here, he's seemed withdrawn. I'm relieved to know he has friends, even if they're not always over at the house the way they were in our old town. In fact, with the baby, it's probably good I don't have to worry about kicking out noisy teens at one a.m."

This is the type of thing she shouldn't be telling me. I'd crawl under this table and cry if my mother told a stranger such personal details. And I have no idea how to respond—it's hardly like I'm going to correct her, not when she's this excited about the idea of his "friends." So I smile. "He seems nice."

"That's so sweet of you to say. And here you are with no plans—would you even consider it? Sophia is an angel. I promise she'll be easy. I bet my husband will even have her asleep before we leave. And we won't be late. What do you think?"

"Mom?" I wonder if she'll object to my going to a stranger's home—But, no, if you're in the jewelry/candles/scrapbooking party circuit, then you're trustworthy.

"It's up to you—but I want a home number and address."

"Of course!" says Mrs. Shea.

Both of them are waiting for my answer. Me, in Jonah's house—I'd wished for a way to figure him out and this is backstage access. Almost *too much* access—I just want to know a little more about him. I don't need to see where he sleeps and eats his morning cereal.

But if I want to meet the deadline for ordering the plaque, if I don't want to let down Mr. Donnelly, if I ever want Jonah to give me more than a moment's attention, then this could be the opportunity I've been waiting for.

"Will Jonah be home?"

"No, sorry. As soon as school ends on Friday he's off like a shot. I barely see that boy all weekend." She looks disappointed. I'm melting with relief.

All that's left for me to do is agree—and despite my desire to spend the night hibernating, I nod.

"Great!" She carefully claps her hands, now tipped with dark red nails. "Why don't I bring you straight to our house

from here. That way I can go over all the emergency numbers and instructions with you."

"Sure, I guess." I wish I had even half a spine and the
ability to say that word that starts with an *N* and ends in
an *O*. It's a word Jonah clearly has no problem saying . . .
maybe after tonight I'll understand why.

9

JONAH

☼ 5:03 P.M. ☽

CARLY TIME

Normally Carly is waiting out front when I pull up, eager to kiss me, burrow beneath my chin, then kiss me again. It's an impatient-Carly thing, but also a practical one; if I enter her house, it's at least an hour before we finish talking to all her family members and get back out the door.

Tonight she's not sitting on the steps, but that's no big deal. I love her family. I'd even asked my parents if I could move in with them and finish my senior year at Hamilton High. Mom had said, "Don't you understand the opportunities I'll be able to give you now that I'm married to Paul?" Dad had been speaker-phoned into the conversation. When Mom mentioned "Paul," he'd hung up.

But tonight, if we end up watching a Brazilian soccer game with Carly's parents, sister, and brother before going to Jeff's party, I'm okay with that. One of the best things about her is that she'd probably be okay with that too.

Seven-year-old Marcos answers the door. "Hey, Jonah."

"How's it going, little dude?" I brace myself for an

ambush—for him to jump on me and demand a piggyback ride or whip out his Nerf guns and begin a foam-bullet assault. When he just stands there eyeing the toes of his scuffed blue sneakers, I ask, "Do we have time for a quick catch? My glove is in the car. Or want to play a round of *MLB Showdown*?"

"Can't." Marcos's sigh is so exaggerated I have to fight a smile. "I'm supposed to go watch TV. Carly's in a bad mood—she said I'm not allowed to play with you. It's not fair."

I put my hands on my knees and stoop to make eye contact. "Level with me. On a scale of one to ten, how cranky is she?"

Marcos sucks on his pointer finger while he thinks about this. "Eleven. She's been yelling at Ana all night and she slammed her door—twice."

"Hmmm. How about I come over tomorrow and we play catch? I haven't seen Carly all week—I was cranky today too."

Marcos nods and sticks out a hand to shake on the deal, then disappears downstairs to his playroom. I take another step into the kitchen and look around—the house is abnormally quiet for a Friday night.

I'm disappointed Mr. Santos isn't around. We typically talk baseball until Carly's tugging on his sleeve and whining, "Papai, we need to go." Or until his wife intercedes. But the only one here is Carly's grandmother, Avó. She's sitting at the kitchen table reading a magazine devoted to her soap operas. It must be a high-drama article, because she doesn't get up to hug me and fuss. She raises her eyebrows over the glossy cover and then turns a page. I lean down and peck her cheek and scan the headlines.

"Do we want Dr. Drake to come back from the dead? Or is it better for Cordelia if he stays gone?"

"She's better off without him; he's a cheating scoundrel." Avó lowers the magazine and adds a string of rapid-fire Portuguese that reminds me, yet again, what I'm being taught in school is not at all helpful in the real world. At least not in *my* real world. It's probably useful for my classmates who spend their spring breaks on Ibiza. And those who pat themselves on the back for being *so* cosmopolitan when they use their textbook Spanish to give condescending instructions to their Hispanic housekeepers. Cross Pointe High offers six languages—I could study Latin, which isn't even spoken anywhere but stuffy universities—but I can't learn the language my girlfriend's family uses when they're pissed off.

Avó turns another page before looking up and adding, "Carla's in her room."

I walk to the bottom of the stairs. "Hello?"

No response. Normally Carly's little sister, Ana, is my shadow—fluctuating between a curious kid who peppers me with questions and an awkward preteen who's trying to figure out how to flirt. It drives Carly crazy—which could be why they were fighting. Though they're always in these huge fights—followed by dramatic apologies and what seems like instant forgiveness. Having spent my first seventeen years as an only child, I can't imagine Sophia and I will ever have that type of volcanic relationship.

"Carly?" It's a well-established rule that I'm not allowed

on the second floor, but it's uncomfortable to stand here and bellow, so I go up a few steps and try again. "Carly? Are you almost ready?"

Her door opens. She dyed her hair a few weeks ago, and I'm still not used to it being cinnamon colored. She's wearing jean shorts and a black T-shirt that slides off one shoulder so I can see a hot-pink strap underneath. It's either a tank top or a new bra—I'm hoping for the second.

"Hey. You ready to go?"

She nods and calls back over her shoulder, "Papai, I'm leaving. I won't be late."

It's her mother who meets us at the door, giving her daughter a long look and a hug. I get a quick nod as she holds the door open.

Either Carly has been in a brutal mood or something's up.

"Where do you want to eat?" I reach for her hand, but she's holding her cell phone.

"I already ate," she says. "Why are you so late?"

It's barely five. I'm tempted to make a joke about her catching the early-bird dinner with Avó, but she huffs out a breath, so I answer her question. "I got stuck on Sophia duty."

She rolls her eyes.

I pull her into a hug beside the hood of my car. "I missed you this week."

She puts a hand on my chest and leans back to look me in the face. "Can we skip Jeff's party? Let's go to the state park and talk."

She means the always-empty parking lot that borders the state park. We must be fine. I kiss her greedily and don't argue. Carly pulls away to climb into the car. It's a shorter kiss than her usual greeting—especially since we haven't seen each other in five days, but like me, she's got to be impatient to get to the park. I pull out of her driveway and try not to speed for the ten-minute drive.

Talk? Yeah, sure.

I want Carly's hair between my fingers. I want her voice in my ear. I want to erase the doubts she's planted in my head lately and forget everything but how she feels.

She bites her lip as I park the car—glances at me out of the corner of her eye with a look that makes me want to stop and thank the inventors of zippers. I know what comes next: she'll climb over the console into the backseat, squealing "Jo-nah!" when I tickle her on her way by.

But she doesn't. Instead she fiddles with her seat belt.

I lean across the console to kiss her, but she leans away to apply another coat of her inescapable cherry lip gloss. Then she pauses, the cap in one hand, tube in the other. Both hands fall to her lap. She sucks on the left side of her bottom lip and pulls a knee up to create a barrier between us.

"Okay, Carly, what's going on?"

She brings the gloss back up to her mouth, touching up the spot she'd been sucking and rolling her lips together. "Where were you *really* tonight before my house?"

"Watching Sophia. Waiting for Paul to come home and tell me what a failure I am. Why?"

She pulls a folded piece of blue paper from her pocket and flips it over twice, before shoving it back and saying, "I don't want to go to Jeff Diggins's party. I want you to take me to one in Cross Pointe."

"There are no Cross Pointe parties." At least, not that I know about. None that I'm invited to.

She juts out her chin. "Really? They don't party in Cross Pointe? What do they do all weekend—listen to Mozart? Eat caviar? Count their money? What?"

"Carly, why do we have to do this again? I thought we were done with this."

"Because I want to see who you're with when you're not here."

"I've told you, I'm not with anyone." I'm being careful to keep my voice level, but the pauses between my words are a dead giveaway that I'm annoyed she's brought this up again.

"Are you ashamed of me or something?" she asks. Her chin's not out anymore. She's lowered it and is barely looking at me through her eyelashes.

"You're kidding, right?" I schedule my life around when she's free for phone calls. I've driven an hour round-trip just to watch one of Marco's soccer games with her, or study next to her at her parents' kitchen table with our ankles and fingers linked beneath it. "I'm sorry this week was crazy and I couldn't get over here—" But I don't know why I'm apologizing. *She* was the one who was busy, not me. She's the one who turned me down every time I offered to drive up.

"If you're not ashamed of me, then why won't you ever take me to things at CPH? You've lived there since January; why haven't I met anyone yet?" She narrows her eyes. "Why couldn't we go to *your* prom?"

There are so many answers to that last question: because I didn't want to spend a night in a rented tux surrounded by snobs who probably own theirs, because then you'd see what a loser I am, because I already emptied my bank account to rent a limo for Hamilton's prom after you hinted—"I hear all

Cross Pointe girls get them; what do you think it's like to ride in one?"

Carly can't seem to grasp that just because Paul has a bottomless checkbook doesn't mean I do. I have no clue how I'm going to pay for the post-graduation dinner she wants at La Fin, Cross Pointe's most expensive restaurant.

But I won't tell her any of these things. I can't. Carly's always asking for funny anecdotes about Cross Pointe excess so she can mock their superficiality. The last thing I want is for her to make a poor-little-rich-boy joke about me—or turn my new life into a punchline.

There's nothing I can say, so I don't say anything. A pattern that's becoming too common with us lately. When she gets sick of waiting, she snaps, "What are you hiding?"

"I don't know what you're talking about."

She looks away and says quietly, "You think I don't know what's going on, but I do."

I touch her face, trace the line of her cheekbone, and slide my hand to the back of her neck. "Carly, nothing is going on. Nothing's going on in Cross Pointe tonight, and nothing's going on with me."

She grasps my hand and places it back in my lap.

I know I'm only going to antagonize her—bring out the famous Carly temper—but I can't help it. "I don't believe I drove all the way over here so you can play prove-you-love-me games."

"Games?" Her eyes snap wide open. "*I'm* not the one playing games! Screw you, Jonah."

Except, apparently, I'm not getting screwed tonight. I turn away and glare out the window.

Carly speaks first: "I think we should break up."

"What?" I sit up so fast I hit my head on the roof of the car. "Why? Because I won't take you to Cross Pointe? All right, let's go. When we get there we can buy eight-dollar coffees at Bean Haven or try and have a civil conversation with Paul and my mom—it'll probably be a fascinating discussion about something important like if the landscaper is cutting the lawn too short or their endless debate about whether Paul has enough support to run for a spot on the country club's board of directors. Sounds like fun, doesn't it?"

She shakes her hair out of her face and meets my eyes. A lock sticks in her gloppy lip gloss and she frowns as she extracts it and smoothes it behind her ears. She's wearing large gold hoops, not the ruby studs I saved up to buy for her birthday.

"You've changed."

"I haven't," I lie.

"Yes! Yes, you have. You've become another Cross Pointe snob and you treat me like I'm not good enough for you anymore."

"That's crap."

"Oh, really? Convince me you're my old Jonah. Tell me one thing that happened at school today—to *you*, not one of your classmates. Tell me one fact about your life."

I look away. What good will come from me whining about how I eat lunch in the library because there's no place for me at the cafeteria's round tables? How it's almost physically painful listening to the baseball players who sit near me in bio talk about organizing a father-son summer league? How my math teacher still calls me "Noah"? Or what about how the Empress of Cross Pointe graced me with a lesson on operating my locker?

"Please?" she says, leaning forward and putting a hand on my knee. "Just talk to me, Jonah. *Please.*"

I flip my hands palm up in a half shrug. I can either tell her I'm a loser, or I can lose *her.* "I figured out how to lock my locker."

"You mean unlock," she says with an eye roll, pulling away from me.

"No, *lock.*" I shift in my seat, trying to find a comfortable position where I can face her without the steering wheel impaled in my ribs. "See, in Cross Pointe the lockers—"

She waves a hand, cutting me off. "Don't talk down to me."

"What?"

"*In Cross Pointe,*" she mimics with an affected accent. "Please, Jonah, explain to me how lockers work, because since I'm not from Cross Pointe, I'm clearly not smart enough to know."

"Forget it." I'm shaking my head and we're both sighing. Frustrated exhales that are the only sound in the car.

"So that's it? That's all you can come up with about your day?" It's an accusation, but I'm not sure what I'm being accused of. And when I try to think of something to share, something that would make today stand out from every other day of invisibility and over-polite refusals to acknowledge my existence, I can't.

"Let's talk about something else. It was just a normal day—nothing happened."

"Just because I don't go to your fancy high school and I'm not headed to an Ivy League college doesn't make me stupid—" I try to interrupt, but she's on a roll. "And just because I can't make out with you in the back of the Jag I got for my sixteenth birthday and seduce you with the perfect boobs I got for my seventeenth—or is it the other way around, Jonah? How do Cross Pointe snobs order their lives: cars or plastic surgery first?"

I laugh. I can't help it. "Plastic surgery. Then the cars."

"Oh, so this is a *joke* to you? I guess you'd know. So tell me: Exactly how many sets of Cross Pointe boobs have you seen?"

The nail of her pointer finger is inches from my face. I push it away and snap back, "You think I'm cheating? Are you crazy?"

"We both know you are. At least be man enough to admit it."

"That's such crap. I can't believe—"

"Don't even try to deny it. I found *this* in your backseat last week." She pulls the bright blue paper back out of her pocket and holds it like a murder weapon.

I have no clue what's on it or why it's made Carly psycho. I take it from her hand and hope it contains the logo from *Punk'd*. The creases are deep and smooth, like it's been unfolded repeatedly.

She crosses her arms and watches my face expectantly. I look down—it's a single sheet of paper. A flyer from Cross Pointe, like the hundreds of others that are hung on the school walls at neat intervals.

"So?" I'm baffled. So confused that I'm not even angry anymore.

"Are you kidding me?"

"Did you want to help put together care packages for last year's seniors? I don't know what the problem is. Yes, it's a stupid project—but who cares if some idiots wanted to mail snacks and instant coffee to a group of spoiled college freshmen?"

Carly's face is red, her lips pressed together so tight they disappear. "Who. Is. She?" She snatches the flyer from my hands and it tears in the corner. I'm left holding a jagged scrap of blue paper. Carly points to some handwriting at the bottom of the page: ten digits and a name.

Brighton.

10

Brighton

☼ 6:07 P.M. ☽

18 HOURS, 53 MINUTES LEFT

The Sheas gave me a tour and left three different ways to contact them. Sophia's already asleep and they promised to be home by ten, so the only real directions for the next four hours are: "Check the baby monitor and call if you need us. No, actually, if she wakes up at all, call us."

It seems straightforward, and she hasn't woken so I haven't called. But this hasn't stopped Mr. Shea from checking in three times already.

I reassure him, for the third time, "Everything is quiet here."

"And the monitor is definitely working?" he asks.

"It is." I hold it up to the phone and turn up the volume so he can hear the steady raindrop sounds of Sophia's white-noise machine.

"Okay." He exhales. "So, you're all set?"

"Go enjoy your dinner," I tell him. "Everything here is fine."

"Great. Great, great. Thanks so much, Brighton. We'll see you in a few hours."

I hang up and pace from the kitchen to the living room, through the dining room and one of those never-really-used rooms with new "antique" furniture and a grandfather clock that bongs about seven minutes early. It almost looks like every other house in Cross Pointe, but there's a hint of not-quite-there-yet—it's apparent in the price tag still dangling from a throw pillow, and the dining room chairs, which look like they've never been sat on. Everything is slightly too matchy-matchy and too new. But the Sheas are still new, still trying too hard.

Not that everyone else in Cross Pointe doesn't try; we just don't let our efforts show.

I circle back to the kitchen. They have one of those floor plans where the rooms all connect with multiple entrances; it all flows around the staircase to the second floor where Sophia sleeps in the only room with an open door. Behind one of the other seven is all the information I'd ever need to know about Jonah.

The Sheas said I don't even need to go upstairs—as long as she's quiet, I should just let her sleep. I click the video button on the monitor—not awake.

On my second lap of the first floor, I check for photos of Jonah. Picking up frame after frame and trying to replace them in the exact same positions. The house is a baby shrine. There are an absurd number of photos of Sophia in every state of dress and pose—I particularly enjoy the one of her half-buried in a basket of laundry hanging above the washing machine in the mud room—but the only photo I find of Jonah is in the back corner of a bookshelf. It's of him in a middle-school baseball uniform.

I fail at my attempts to translate the tanned, dirty-blond boy with a wide, metallic grin to the taller, darker-haired ghost who sulks in Cross Pointe's halls. I can't stop the comparisons. What happened to make him stop smiling so wide his eyes wrinkle in the corners? How come his broad shoulders are always creeping up and forward instead of squared and confident like his thirteen-year-old self?

I carry the picture frame to the kitchen without even realizing it. I lean against the marble countertop and tilt the photo so it's fully illuminated by the track lighting—he was thin, didn't quite fill out his red-and-white uniform. But even then you could see hints of the muscles he would develop. I can't stop studying his grin—it's confident, carefree. So open and sincere that I'm jealous of the boy he'd been.

If Jonah had attended middle school with the rest of us, he would've been prime crush material. If he'd stop scowling long enough to acknowledge anyone at CP High, he'd still be.

I flip the frame facedown on the countertop and check the baby monitor again—sleeping. Though I'm still curious, I make myself walk away from the photo and into the living room.

It isn't even curiosity, really, just restless energy. I thought tonight would be different. I thought it would be nightmarish, like the night before Dad's funeral—tidal waves of Evy's tears. Mom's grief, which demands and judges and suffocates and needs an audience. And me—helpless and guilty because I couldn't cry, couldn't stop their tears, and couldn't fix anything.

I spent today preparing for *that*, and in the end I wasn't

needed. I could be at Jeremy's party with everyone, making Amelia ridiculously happy by giving him a chance. I could be catching up with Evy. I could be home right now, sleeping. Or watching mindless TV and eating popcorn. So how did I end up in some stranger's house watching Sophia sleep on the video screen of her baby monitor?

I didn't have to agree to babysit. Really, it's just a plaque—Mr. Donnelly won't be too disappointed if we wait until next year to order it. I don't need it as filler for my college apps. Dad would hate that I'm stressing over this. I need to let it go.

And who cares why Jonah doesn't want to volunteer?

Or why there's no trace of him in this house besides a photo that's four years old? Not even a hat or a sweatshirt or a backpack on the first floor. Nothing of his written between the playdates and Zumba classes on the calendar on the fridge. No magazines with his name in the rack by the couch.

I've scoured the whole first floor, and there's nothing here to teach me anything more about him. But it's not like I'm going to go snoop in his room. That would be ridiculous.

I turn up the volume on the baby monitor until it's slightly staticky and I can hear the soft splashes of the rainfall setting on her white-noise machine. Instead of soothing me, the rhythm makes me feel useless. I need a distraction, a purpose, an outlet.

There are four remotes aligned with military precision on the coffee table. These are framed by a neat stack of parenting magazines and a pink basket of teething rings, bibs, pacifiers, and burp cloths. I pick up the remote on the left and study it. Pick up the next one and compare them. I press the power button on the third one and the stereo blares to life with, "My teddy loves me. He's got a big red bow—" I jab at the button again and hold my breath. The music dies instantly and the sound isn't replaced by crying. Returning the remotes to the coffee table, I double-check the baby monitor. Sophia's still sleeping and I still have nothing to do.

I cross to the bookshelves. Since I don't want to read *What to Expect When You're Expecting* or during the *First Year* or any portion of a child's life, I hope there's something tolerable and diaper free in their library.

On the top shelf is a book I recognize too well. It's stuck between a battered copy of the *Mayo Clinic Guide to a Healthy Pregnancy* and a hardcover bio-thriller. I pull it out and sit on the floor with it cradled in my lap, tracing the cover lettering like I did when I was seven and Mom would bring me to visit Dad at his office. This cover is different—a newer edition. What new criteria have they added to *Teens in Flux: Adolescent Psychology* by Ethan Waterford, Ph.D. And who is Roberta Schell?

Why does the cover advertise that she's written a brand-new introduction to my father's book? I flip the pages— turning past highlighted passages and pencil notes in the margins—wondering how a book like this would assess *me*. What would Dad think about how I've turned out?

If Dad were still here, would he be able to explain how to make *Teflon* work in my favor? How to let that barrier down occasionally and who to let in?

If Dad were still here, everything would be different. Tomorrow we'd be making pancakes and going golfing. Maybe I'd even finally figure out how to play. I used to tag along just so I could ride in the cart, hand him clubs, and have four hours of his attention. If Dad were still here, tomorrow I wouldn't be putting on black and dueling with my grief.

I don't want to go to the memorial tomorrow. I'm not ready to say good-bye again. I want to shut the door on those feelings—the ones that might consume me if I ever allow myself to acknowledge them—and run away. I thumb through the index of Dad's book, knowing there's probably a section on "repressed emotions"—and that's the closest I'll be able to get to *him* helping me deal with his death.

I shut the book's cover. I should have told Mom "no" when she asked for my help with planning. Instead, I chose caterers and florists; picked out hors d'oeuvres and flowers. Called all our relatives to invite them, which meant listening to all of their reminiscing and tears. And I made sure we were stocked up on tissues, because every time I had to ask Mom a question, she would cry and I'd feel guilty for not being able to answer it myself.

There's a quiet sneeze over the monitor—it isn't followed by any other sounds, but I click on the video. Sophia's in the same position as the last fifty times I checked.

I wish I had something to do—anything. Anything but sitting here thinking about Dad . . . or Jonah.

Which is just pathetic, because I'm sure I haven't crossed his mind once since he walked away and left me standing at his locker.

11

JONAH

☼ 6:20 P.M. ☽

TIME TO BEG

On the drive back to Carly's house I plead with her to listen to me, but she's stubborn. She's always been stubborn. It's a cute personality quirk when she's arguing about which movie we should watch, or which MLB pitcher is best, or with her father about extending her curfew, or with my mother about making me move to Hamilton for the second half of senior year. Tonight it's not cute—it's damn infuriating.

There's no convincing Carly the flyer is nothing more than a piece of paper—one Brighton had shoved in my hand a few weeks back as part of her never-ending campaign to save my soul through volunteer work, and that I, in turn, had tossed on my backseat.

No, Carly had found it, googled Brighton, and decided she was the kind of girl I'd go for and the reason behind my so-called change.

"She's even got dark hair—I *know* that's your type and why you were so weird about me dyeing mine."

"I wasn't weird about it; I was surprised." I reach out to

touch her hair, but she leans away. "And Brighton's definitely not my type. There's not a girl in Cross Pointe who is *less* my type."

"How many girls did you have to go through before you figured that out?"

"I'm not a cheater," I say through gritted teeth. After two years together, how could she even *think* that?

"Funny, that's just what Daniel Diggins said."

"That's really helpful, Carly. Bringing up your ex is *exactly* what we need right now. Too bad you didn't warn me I'd be driving around all your baggage tonight. I would've asked Mom to borrow the SUV." She hates when I get sarcastic, but I can't stop myself. I'm almost shaking with furious helplessness. "You dated Digg *three years* ago. You're really going to blame me for his screwups?"

"Jonah . . ." Her eyes are on her hands as they pick at the crumbs collected in the seams of the seat. "I don't want to end it like this. Let's stop fighting. It's just . . . over."

I know how to argue back when she's pissed off; I don't know how to handle her sadness. I've never been able to handle her sadness. Not the time she accidentally ran over a squirrel and cried for hours. Not when she got a rejection letter from her top choice for college. Not when I had to look her in the eyes and tell her I was leaving Hamilton High. And none of the times lately when she's seemed depressed and distant—like she's still a zip code away even when I'm sitting right next to her.

And not now, when she's blaming me for something I've never even considered and all I want to do is yell that I'm innocent and that she's acting insane.

"How can I convince you I'm not lying?"

"You can't."

I turn the car off, and we stare out the windshield at her driveway. We're so quiet the crickets start chirping again and lightning bugs flash right outside my window.

She's curled in on herself, like those caterpillars we used to catch and poke when we were ten. She's been in my life forever. First as the girl who wanted to be part of the neighborhood boys' group. Then, because of her stubborn refusal to be excluded, as the girl who *was* part of the boys' group. Finally, in what seemed like an overnight transformation, she turned into the girl who could no longer be part of the boys' group because I couldn't stop seeing how very *girl* she was. That was the summer before freshman year, but it wasn't until May of tenth grade that she broke things off with Jeff's sleaze of an older brother and agreed to date me.

Now what? Will she just not be part of my life anymore? The thought pushes all the air from my lungs, replacing my anger with chilling fear.

"But I love you. Why would you do this to us?"

Carly gives me a look: lowered eyebrows, mouth pressed in an angry slash, nostrils flared. "*I* didn't do it." She reaches for the door handle.

"Wait," I ask, and she does—even though I don't say anything else. I've apologized. I've begged. I haven't cheated. I don't know what else I can offer her.

Losing her will be losing her family too. It's the second family I've lost this year—and it sucks just as much. I've known Marcos since before he was born. He was the first baby I'd held, my eleven-year-old's bravado melting into

"Am I doing this right?" as soon as Carly placed him in the bend of my elbow.

I want to beg her again to reconsider. Instead I say, "Will you apologize to Marcos for me? I told him we'd play catch tomorrow."

She nods but doesn't say anything. Her angry face has disappeared. She's breathing in quick, short breaths and blinking a lot—trying not to cry.

There's a flicker of brightness when she opens the car door. A slam. A silhouette in my headlights. An absence.

How long has she been planning this? Have I missed some big warning signs? I know our relationship isn't perfect, but *damn*! How can she believe ten numbers on a piece of paper and not believe me?

I scramble for my iPod, scrolling past the playlists of "Carly music" and choosing a band that growls more than sings. Turning it up until the floor vibrates with bass and the words distort into monster sounds, I put the car in reverse and leave her driveway so quickly my tires squeal. Like pulling off a Band-Aid, I need to get out of here as fast as possible—maybe then it won't hurt so much.

I want to hit Jeff's party. To drown myself in noise and beer and people I know. But do I know them anymore? What has Carly told them? If my own girlfriend assumed I was cheating, can I really expect any of them to believe me?

Did the guys know what Carly had planned? Jeff's hooking up with her friend, Maya—he should've given me a heads-up. He's been my friend since grade school—but now Carly knows more about him than I do. His house, this town, it had been my domain, then ours. Now is it just *hers*? I clench my jaw and point my car back toward the suburban hell that others refer to as Cross Pointe.

It's thirty minutes from Hamilton to Mom and Paul's house. By the time I reach the highway the speakers aren't the only things shaking in the car; I'm trembling with rage. *How dare she?*

And how dare my *mom!* Moms aren't supposed to change. They're not supposed to be one person for seventeen years and then sit you down one day and tell you they're divorcing your father. Oh, and they're pregnant with your physical therapist's baby and they're getting married. That was all bad enough, but how dare she make me move for the second half of senior year? And expect me to be okay with walking away from *my life* and think that a bigger house or expensive things with remote controls made up for leaving behind everything that made me happy?

I'm just supposed to accept it all—and swallow the fact that my father's definition of divorce involves walking away from me too.

Playgroups and pediatricians and everything Sophia— these are Mom's priorities now. Me, her leftover kid, the doggy bag of her first marriage, I'm supposed to adapt. *It's only one semester and then you're off to college. You're never home anyway. Hamilton isn't that far. We'll buy you a car . . .*

And now Carly's gone.

I stare at the highway barriers blurring outside my automotive bribe. I could jerk the steering wheel just a little to the left, turn my Accord into a scrap-metal smear. But I don't really want that; I want *others* to hurt. I've been hurt enough.

If mercy exists in Cross Pointe, Paul will be out with his

bowling team and Mom will be home watching TLC. She'll let me escape upstairs without an inquisition about how my date went and why I'm home so early.

But I don't expect mercy—I expect them to be brooding because they missed their dinner reservation. Mom will be nursing some imagined slight by one of the neighborhood ladies: not being invited to join a walking group or insufficient praise of her flower beds. Paul will be brainstorming ways to solve her drama. And when I walk in, all that fix-it energy will be focused on me. *Why don't you still play baseball? Have you joined any clubs? I heard about this great charity project the high school is doing—that pretty Waterford girl is running it—why don't you sign up? Do you know the average CP teen spends three hours a week volunteering? When was the last time you spent three minutes thinking of anyone but yourself? How about we all go to the art fair on the town commons tomorrow? Mrs. Glenn's son, Patrick, will be there—you boys could do something afterward.*

Why can't the town leave me alone? Why can't Paul and Mom leave me alone? Why can't Brighton? Haven't they all taken enough from me—my address, the second half of my senior year, my identity—did they really need my girlfriend too?

I just want to make it to graduation. Fourteen days, that's it. A few more months beyond that and I'm gone. I'll be in a dorm on the other side of the state. I don't think anyone has ever looked forward to going away to college as much as I am.

When I reach the exit for Cross Pointe, I accelerate. I blow by the exit for Green Lake too. I'd keep driving all night, except in East Lake the highway becomes something with traffic lights, and my rage and red lights aren't a good mix. Since the forty dollars from Mom is the only cash in my wallet, I need to park before I impatiently rear-end the SUV in front of me. I end up sitting in a diner with a forced-retro decor, picking at a half-decent burger and plate of salty fries.

It's fine. I can direct my anger at the pink stars on the tabletop and the obnoxious jukebox music while the grease congeals on my plate. At least I can until a teen mob comes in and crams themselves into the booths on either side of mine. They aim conversations over my head and annoyed glances in my direction.

This makes *three* towns where I'm unwanted. I signal for my waitress.

The teens overflow into my booth before I'm out the door.

In the car, I call Carly. An hour later the breakup doesn't make any more sense, doesn't make me any less angry. It's probably a good thing I get her voice mail. And that I hang up instead of leaving a message I'll regret.

A horn honks, then a car flies past me. I glance at my odometer—I'm driving ten miles under the speed limit. When I reach my exit I can't think of a good excuse not to take it. I can't think of anywhere else to go.

The looming cul de sac makes my muscles tense. I hate this town: a "planned community" constructed at the inter-sections of Hamilton, West Lawn, Green Lake, and Summer-set. Everything about Cross Pointe is artificial and obnoxious.

Mom and Paul still love exclaiming that they're "so lucky to have found a house here! No one ever moves from Cross

Pointe!" as if that justifies the insane cost of one of the super-sized matching colonials laid out in straight lines with sidewalks that are too perfect to meander and meet at right angles under streetlamps with hanging flower baskets.

Hate. This. Town.

I take the left into our neighborhood too fast, and my overcorrection tears a tire stripe through the lawn. I hope I took out some of the sprinkler heads on Paul's automatic watering system.

I try to psych myself up to turn into the driveway. Maybe after this song. Or maybe after the next one. I drop my chin and take a deep breath. My head fills with chemical cherries, the smell so strong I half believe I'll find Carly beside me. But when I turn, the seat is still empty and her lip-gloss residue is smeared on the collar of my shirt.

12

Brighton

☼ 7:53 P.M. ☽

17 HOURS, 7 MINUTES LEFT

The grandfather clock is chiming 7:53 p.m. when I finally give in to my urge to climb the stairs. The monitor is telling the truth: Sophia's fast asleep, lying on her back with her arms and legs spread out in starfish formation. Her pacifier has fallen out of her mouth but her lips still twitch in a sucking motion.

Her nursery is decorated in pink and white—matching polka-dot crib sheet, dust ruffle, rug, curtains, and overstuffed glider. Board books fill a carved white bookshelf, and I'm sure the dresser is full of sweet, ruffled outfits.

In this room, the pictures are of her parents. They're everywhere—it's like the Sheas are afraid their daughter will forget what they look like overnight. Jonah's in one. A small frame decorated with pink grosgrain ribbon on the bottom shelf of the bookcase. It's a candid shot of him holding Sophia. He's half-turned from the camera, but in profile it looks like he might be smiling down at the baby gripping his finger.

I flip on a lamp to see it better, and Sophia stirs. She lets out one quick whimper and her face creases for an instant before I click off the lamp and back out of the room with hasty steps.

Next to Sophia's nursery is a bathroom. I don't realize I've made up my mind to peek into Jonah's room until I've shut the door again and am reaching for the next knob. This room is a home gym: yoga mats, treadmill, and free weights set up facing a flat-screen TV and a bookshelf full of fitness DVDs.

I don't hesitate to try a third door; at this point there's no pretending I'm doing anything but snooping.

Guest room. Decorated with stiff, expensive-looking fabric in green-and-navy stripes.

Fourth knob—master suite. I shut that door fast; it's weird to see where Mrs. and Mr. Shea sleep. If there is underwear or anything on the floor, I don't want to see it or I'll never be able to face them when they come home from dinner.

Door five—linen closet.

Door six—home office.

The seventh door opens to reveal another guest room with furniture identical to the first. This one is decorated in the same striped fabric, but the green stripes are burgundy instead. I start to shut it until I realize I'm out of doors. There are no more rooms to inspect.

A second glance over this room and I notice a history textbook on the nightstand. One dresser drawer is open a crack, and I can see the green T-shirt Jonah wore to school today.

This isn't right. I don't know what I expected his room

to look like—some sort of mash-up of the teen-boy clichés from TV: car, band, or bikini-model posters; big stereo; video games; dirty dishes; clothing all over the floor. In fact, it's probably statistically more likely that I'd see underwear on *this* floor than in the Sheas' master bedroom. My eyes shoot to the ceiling and then creep back to the hardwood that doesn't contain so much as a stray sock.

This is how Jonah lives? How am I supposed to learn anything about him in a bedroom that's as generic as a hotel room? I take another step through the door and do a slow 360-degree rotation. There's a backpack leaning against the closet door. TV cables and power cords snake from the wall up through the back of an armoire in the corner. There's a similar set up with laptop cords on the desk, but the actual surface doesn't hold so much as a pen. Except for the history book, the bedside table is empty. The bureau looks blank too—except, no, it isn't. There's a frame on its back corner.

With a glance back at the silent hallway, I cross the room and pick it up. It's heavy, made of some dark wood, and holds two pictures.

In the top photo Jonah's dressed for baseball, though it's not a copy of the middle school one from downstairs; this is a Hamilton High uniform. There's a man next to him with his arm around Jonah's shoulders. I pull the picture closer. It's hard to really study it in the dark room, but the man's got to be his father. The resemblance is uncanny, from their sandy hair to their tans to the smiles they're both aiming at the camera.

The second picture is from a prom. Jonah looks good in a tuxedo—that's my first thought. But then again, who doesn't look good in a tuxedo? I look beyond him to the rest of the photo. It must be Hamilton's, because ours didn't take place in a gym, and the country club wasn't decorated with Mylar balloons and paper streamers.

Jonah looks alive, animated. And the girl beside him must be why. His girlfriend? She's wearing a short pink dress, tight enough to showcase her gorgeous curves. She's looking up at him with laughter written all over her face. His arm is tight around her, pulling her up against his side, and she's got a hand on his chest.

So playing baseball and this girl, that's what makes Jonah happy.

It's hopeless.

What a waste of the night.

I want to go home.

13

JONAH

☼ 8:05 P.M. ☽

YES, MOM, I'M HOME EARLY

It's quiet as I cut through the laundry room and into the kitchen. I expect Mom and Paul to be sulking over a glass of wine or consoling themselves with some fancy takeout, but the only thing on the counter is my eighth-grade baseball photo.

Maybe they want the frame for another picture of Sophia.

I lean into the family room to tell them I'm home. If Mom's paying attention, she'll read my expression and wish me a good night. If she isn't, if she gives me crap about my attitude to Paul earlier, then the gloves are coming off. I'll make it clear that no matter how much she forces Paul and me to watch sports together or discuss current events, we aren't going to bond. We are never going to be the magical blended family she reads about in her parenting magazines.

And Paul, I'll tell him all the things I've kept in, starting with: I don't care what you read on the *Modern Father* blog, real men *don't* wear pink polo shirts to match their daughter's onesie or carry diaper bags with butterflies. Once, I heard him pull into the garage with some baby bopper music playing—and Sophia wasn't even in the car. I mean, hooray, he loves his daughter, but get a grip. And I am *not* your son.

The family room is empty. It looks exactly like when I left, except one of Mom's postdivorce self-help books is on the floor. Or, at second glance, it's one of her teen-help books. The type she highlights the hell out of and then quotes like she's reading fortune cookies. "Jonah, I understand that you're *experiencing a time of intense feelings and urges*, but I want you to remember: *Quick decisions have lasting consequences*." Or, "*Change is a choice*, bud, and I feel like you're *choosing not to change*." I'm still fuming about the sticky notes she's started leaving on my bathroom mirror: "Your goal each day should be to make the world better by being in it," and "Adapting to change is an important life skill," or "80% of any achievement is making the decision to achieve."

The book on the floor plus the photo on the counter aren't good signs—she and Paul must be planning some new Jonah intervention.

Dammit, that's the last thing I need right now.

I lean against the wall, suddenly too exhausted to have this confrontation. I want my bedroom, door shut, music on. Video games under my thumb till I've blown up everything that can be destroyed.

I start up the stairs. Since they're not anywhere down here, that means they're in their bedroom and I'm not going to knock and let them know I'm home. Once they shut that door, I like to pretend they don't exist. I'll do just about anything to avoid thinking about what goes on behind it or how my sister came to be.

My door's open.

Is it too much to ask that she give me that much privacy? It's a room that barely feels like mine to begin with—designed by her interior decorator without my input so that my belongings have to fit into the cracks and closets.

The lights are off, and Mom's back is to the door. She's standing in front of the dresser. It makes me sad for a time when if she wanted to know something about me she'd just ask—and trust my answer, not go snooping through my stuff.

"I'm not on drugs." This seems like the most logical explanation: she read something in one of those books about the signs of addiction and is up here looking for evidence.

She jumps and drops whatever she's holding—I step through the door and turn on the light.

14

Brighton

16 HOURS, 53 MINUTES LEFT

I scramble to pick up the picture frame, horrified by the splintering sound it made when it hit the floor.

"What the hell!" Jonah yells. "Are you stalking me?"

His anger makes me drop it again. This time there's no question: it's broken. Triangular splinters of glass rain down from the mangled wood when I pick it up a second time.

I swallow. My whole body has gone hot, and my shirt is sticking to my back. "I'm so sorry."

"For stalking me or destroying that frame?"

"I . . ." One corner is split, and I push at the two pieces of wood. They resist and I press even harder—I'm not sure why, since it's useless without the glass and the wood is cracked. It just seems important, like if I can fix this . . .

"You know what, I don't care. I don't want to hear it. Just get the hell out of my room." Jonah grabs the frame from my hand. He starts to retrieve the prom photo, then swears under his breath and drops the whole thing in a trash can under his desk.

"I'll clean it up. And replace it." I want to run for the door, but my feet won't move and my mind won't come up with any explanation that will make this situation better.

"Do I need to call the cops?" he demands. "Get out of my house!"

"What?" He thinks I broke in? I grab the baby monitor off his dresser and hold it up as proof. "No, you've got it all wrong! I'm watching Sophia."

He gestures around his room. "In here? Really?"

I duck my head. "Can we go downstairs and talk about this?"

"No. No, let's stay. Let's go through the rest of my drawers." He reaches around me and starts yanking them open, dumping a handful of T-shirts on the floor. "Would you like to know if I'm boxers or briefs?"

"I didn't— That drawer was already open."

"Sure. And I bet you didn't put my baseball picture on the kitchen counter."

"No, I did that." I clench my hands into fists.

"Was I not clear in school today? Leave me the hell alone." Jonah sinks onto the edge of his bed and kicks at the shirts on the floor. "Just go home. I'll have my mom drop off a check tomorrow."

"I can't. She drove me here." I wish I had my car so I could put distance between me and my humiliation. I wish I could go back in time to the salon and say no, or back further and not approach his locker today.

He looks at me like I planned it this way. Like I want to be here any more than he wants me here. I can't stand him looking at me like that. I slink out of the room and chew the inside of my lip as I head back downstairs, cursing myself with each footstep.

Thankfully he stays put, but through the baby monitor I can hear him talking on his cell phone: "Mom, I'm back. The babysitter's still here. When will you—?"

I consider texting Amelia and confessing everything, but I can't. It's too embarrassing. She'll tease me and tell Peter. The idea of anyone knowing makes my stomach turn. Jonah won't tell, will he?

I grab onto the back of a kitchen chair and take a few deep breaths.

No. He wouldn't have anyone to tell.

I hear his footsteps coming down the stairs and start babbling before he's even fully in the kitchen: "I'm really not stalking you. I didn't know it was your sister at first. I met your mom at the nail salon and she introduced herself as Mrs. *Shea*."

Without looking at or acknowledging me, he goes straight to the cabinet next to the fridge and takes out a glass. The collar of his shirt is folded crookedly in the back and I want to go smooth it. I can't stop staring at the crease or the inch of skin between his collar and where the ends of his hair curl just slightly. Messily.

"Listen, we got off on the wrong foot and you clearly don't want to be playing host, so you don't have to entertain me until your parents get back," I say.

"Wasn't planning on it, but glad to know I have your permission." He opens the refrigerator and studies the contents. "My mom's on her way."

"Thanks." This is it, my last chance to persuade him to

volunteer. I suck in a breath and squeeze my fingernails into my palms. "I'm not sure what I did *before* today to make you so unfriendly, but tonight I gave you every reason to be mad and I'm sorry."

Jonah pulls milk and chocolate syrup from the top shelf. He puts these on the counter next to his glass before facing me.

"Can we start over?" I hold out my hand. My nails shine in the kitchen's track lighting. "Hi, I'm Brighton."

He turns his back to me and fills his glass with milk, squirts in far too much Hershey's syrup, and leaves his stirring spoon in a chocolate puddle on the counter.

My hand is still extended, and he doesn't show any signs of taking it. After swallowing a big gulp, he says, "Class president, yearbook editor, swim team, head of the CPHS Spirit and Key clubs. And Little Miss Popular, junior class."

"Dive team."

"Dive team. So glad you clarified." He pushes off the counter and turns to leave, but I can't let the conversation end like this.

"Wait! Hang on a second." I'm surprised when he does, but he's still looking at me like I'm contagious or confusing. "The only things I know about you are: you moved from Hamilton, you used to play baseball. And your mom says you have a girlfriend named Carly."

His face changes and the knuckles holding the glass turn white. For a second, he almost looks sad. It's just a flicker before he reverts to his mocking grin. "But you're not stalking me."

I should back down, but I'm angry too. The emotion sits unfamiliar in my mouth, making my teeth feel pointed and my tongue taste coppery. "What's your problem? I've done nothing but try and make you feel welcome at Cross Pointe."

"You're right. I should probably be thanking The Great Brighton Waterford for taking time from her busy social life to follow around a nobody like me." He bows low in my direction, his face a mask of contempt. "Don't trouble yourself anymore."

There's something hot and wicked curling in my stomach, forcing its way up my throat and through my lips in a sharp voice I don't even recognize. "You act like I'm the world's biggest snob. But you're wrong."

He raises his eyebrows and snorts.

"I'm not some stereotype. I'm not a bully or backstabber, or any other label you'd like to slap on me."

"If you say so."

"I'm not! What have I *ever* done to you? And why are you acting like being popular automatically makes me evil? Isn't the definition of "popular" someone people *want* to be around?"

"Maybe some people, but I'm not interested in your pity or stalking or whatever it is. Go find some other lost cause— I'm sure there are a dozen guys who'd be thrilled you even know they're alive. Go mess up one of *their* lives and stay out of mine." He drains his glass and places it on the counter, then turns and heads up the stairs without so much as a good-bye, see you later, or any other signal that the conversation is over.

And I'm not done.

I follow him and stand at the bottom of the stairs, calling up in an angry whisper, "How in the world have I 'messed up your life'? By being kind to you?"

He slams the door to his room.

I'm left pink cheeked and open mouthed.

I storm back to the kitchen and put the milk and chocolate syrup away, shutting the fridge door with more force than is really necessary but less force than would be satisfying.

I lean against the fridge and reassure myself he's wrong. I'm not a snob. That brown-haired, gray-eyed girl whose mortification is reflected on the smudge-free surface of the Sheas' sliding glass doors is not a snob. I turn away from myself.

I put Jonah's spoon in the dishwasher and wipe the counter with a wet paper towel.

I'm so tempted to stomp up those stairs and make him listen. He's wrong—high school isn't a pyramid with all the power clustered in a chosen few at the top—it's more of a movie theater with twenty-two screens showing simultaneously. The love story in theater three doesn't care what happens on the football field in theater twelve. Actors and audiences overlap on the screen and in the hallways, but there's a place for everyone. If Jonah hasn't found his, that's not my fault. I've been more than welcoming.

An explosion of video game noises interrupts my thoughts, making me jump and drop the glass I'm carrying to the sink. His glass. The chocolate sludge from the bottom splashes onto the kitchen floor as I bobble it. The glass lands on the tile with a sharp clink but doesn't break. A minor miracle tonight. I pick it up, double-check it for chips and cracks, then lean against the counter for a second before grabbing a sponge to wipe the floor. Just as I'm thinking, *He's going to wake the baby*, Sophia screeches through the monitor and the garage door goes up.

Mrs. Shea opens the door. "Hi, Brighton! How'd everything—Sophia! Is she okay?"

"She just started crying. I was on my way to get her." I toss the sponge in the sink and wonder if I should *still* go get the baby or let her mother do it.

Mr. Shea appears in the doorway. "Let me guess, Jonah's video games? Go check Sophia, dear. I'm going to have a talk with him." He bellows, "*Jonah!* Turn that down!"

They both rush up the stairs, leaving me purposeless. I head into the living room to retrieve my purse and put away Dad's book.

I play with my phone; texting Amelia: **I'll b home soon. Call me after u leave Peters.** I can't wait to tell her the whole story and have her get all worked up—not that I want her to hate Jonah.

I just want to listen to her rant for a while and tell me that I'm right.

Instead I'm stuck staring at my father's photo on the back cover of his book and trying to shrug off words that shouldn't have stuck. *Teflon.*

Mrs. Shea coos at Sophia, her soothing noises broadcast over the baby monitor. I can hear Mr. Shea's and Jonah's angry voices too. It all makes me cringe. Family drama should be kept private; I feel like an unwilling voyeur.

"Sophia was sleeping. Did you even consider that before

you decided to turn your TV to hearing-damage levels?" Mr. Shea's voice is hardly quiet. He's speaking loud enough for the baby monitor to pick up his words.

It doesn't catch Jonah's reply.

"You never do think of others, do you? Go. Drive the babysitter home. I can't even look at you right now."

15

JONAH

☀ *8:28 P.M.* ☽

ROAD RAGE

Brighton's in the living room, looking at me with pity while pretending not to. I guess she heard Paul's lecture in all its condescending glory.

"Doing some reading?" I ask, gesturing to the book in her hand.

"What?"

"So tell me, what's your favorite part?" I'd paged through Mom's margin notes once. It had been crap like: *Was Jonah overly attached to his imaginary friends?* And *So true! Jonah did wet the bed.* I can only imagine what ammunition Brighton's collected to go tell her minions.

She's blinking a ton and tracing the cover. "Um, I've always liked his whole idea of '*doing one thing every day to make the world better.*'" She swallows and gives me a look that I'm supposed to believe is sincere.

I'm biting my tongue so hard, I'm shocked I don't taste blood. Mom probably wrote a whole list of bathroom-mirror sticky-note quotes. Probably added things like, how when I was seven, I used to answer, "What do you want to be when you grow up?" with "I want to help the Easter Bunny." Or how when I was twelve, I'd written a letter to every player on the Red Sox and asked them to help out a family in our neighborhood whose house had burned down. How, up until January, I'd tutored at the after-school program at one of Hamilton's elementary schools. How I used to be a kid she was proud of.

"You tell anyone *anything* that you learned about me from my mom's highlighting and stuff, and I will tell them their perfect girl is a psycho stalker I caught going through my underwear drawer."

"No! What? It's not like that." She shuts the book and stands, touching the cover almost reverently and taking far too long to slide it back on the shelf. "It's just that . . . You see . . . My dad . . ."

"Look, we're not doing that thing where we trade stories about our families." I'm sure hers is perfect. The last thing I want is for her to think snooping through Mom's books or hearing Paul's scorn gives her permission to ask about mine. "Let's go."

She follows me into the kitchen. She's picked up the glass and spoon I purposely left out because my stepdad has fanatic rules about cleanliness.

"Paul said to give you this." I hold out the check and grab my keys from the hook beside the door to the garage.

Through the baby monitor, his voice mingles with Mom's. "Your son has got to learn some responsibility. He doesn't think of anyone—"

Brighton reaches over and flicks the volume off. "Okay. Well, thanks for the ride."

"Not my choice," I call from halfway down the stairs to the garage.

By the time she catches up, I've already started the car. I back out while she's still fumbling with her seat belt.

Can this night get worse? Brighton Waterford. In. My. Room. In. My. Car.

The first time I saw her was in the hall on my first morning at CP High. She'd been hanging posters for a food drive. Not just a food drive, a *pet* food drive for the local animal shelter.

"Who's that?" I'd asked the student assigned to be my guide and "orient" me to the school, Preston something. It's not like I was interested or anything, it's just she's the type of girl you notice.

"Don't even dream it," scoffed Preston. "A little piece of advice to save you some time: Brighton Waterford is *not* interested in you."

When I responded to her name with "Waterford? Like the crystal?" he'd given me a look and a "Dude," both dripping with scorn and showing how damn masculine he thought he was. I had to fight so hard to stop myself from reminding him his name is *Preston*.

Whatever. I only know it's crystal because Mom and Paul got some for their wedding and threw a fit when I broke a wineglass while packing. But I didn't get a chance to explain, because Brighton had come over with a hair toss and a smile.

"Hey! Are you new? Welcome to Cross Pointe. Where are you from?"

I said, "Hamilton" and caught the look she and Preston

exchanged in the beat before her "Oh. Well, welcome. I bet you're going to love it here."

I'd snorted and she'd looked offended—a look that was glossed over with a quick reply—"Sorry I can't chat. I need to hang these up. If you need anything, let me know"—and a rapid exit. Perfect manners. Perfect girl.

The name fits her—shiny and pretentious. And there's no escaping her within the high school; she's like the town's poster girl for model teenage citizen. Besides her save-the-world-from-everything campaigns, her face smiles down from the video announcements broadcast every morning. *Video.* Because what's the point in having networked hi-def projectors and a state-of-the-art video-editing lab if you can't use them in flashy ways? And even among all the too-peppy students speaking way too cheerfully, way too early in the morning, she stands out: all smiles and school spirit while urging people to buy prom tickets, vote in student elections, support the Cross Pointe Cougars in playoff games, come to Gay-Straight Alliance meetings, see the spring musical . . .

In fact, I bet if I bothered to check the Facebook pages of any Cross Pointe students, the one thing they'd all have in common is her on their friends' list.

And now she's in my car too.

The car where—*dammit!* Like she didn't do enough damage tonight.

I can't think about Carly right now.

Brighton interrupts my brooding to say, "I'm sorry you got stuck driving me. I know it's not how you wanted to spend your night."

"It's fine." I do not want the drive to turn into a round of socially acceptable small talk. I gesture to the stereo. "Put on whatever."

"Whatever you were listening to is fine." She presses the power button and flinches back from the loud barrage of screaming and thudding.

I doubt she can hear my laughter till I turn it off and spin the dial on my iPod to illuminate a list of bands. "Probably not your taste. What do you want to hear?"

"Anything's fine."

There is nothing more annoying than people with no opinion. "Rap?"

"Sure."

"Country?"

"I guess."

"Classical?" No one can like rap, country, *and* classical.

"If you want."

"God, how can you stand to be around yourself?"

"Excuse me?" But her voice doesn't go up in a question, it goes down in annoyance. "I don't understand why you're so determined to dislike me."

Does she really want to go there? Because I will. "How do you think people describe you? They say, 'Brighton Waterford, she's so . . .'"

"I don't know." She stares at her nails. "I hope they'd say *nice.*"

"Nice?" I scoff. "Nice is the word you use when you can't think of a real adjective. It's what you say when something doesn't make an impression. Socks are a 'nice' gift. That's the word you want people to use about you?"

"What would people say about you?" she challenges.

It's a fair question, but it doesn't have just one answer. My old baseball team would go with *quitter*; apparently Carly would choose *cheater*; anyone at CP High would say *loser*; while my mother would say *maladjusted*. My dad wouldn't sugarcoat it; he'd called me a *traitor*, a *disappointment*, and worse before he left.

I offer the words that seem truest: "Cynical? Jaded?"

"And *those* are better than nice?"

"Yes, because nice is for people we forget." This answer finally silences her.

I've reached the edge of my neighborhood and have to turn onto Main Street. Each of the neighborhoods in Cross Pointe connects to Main Street, and each has its own pretentious name: an Estate, a Hunt, a Grove, or a Glen. "So, where do you live, Bright?"

She drops the iPod and her cell phone into the cup holder. "Don't call me that!"

I shrug like it's no big deal, but I know she'll be Bright in my head from now on. This is what it takes to get an opinion out of her, a stupid shortening of her name? Nicknames probably aren't snobby and proper enough for her. She'd probably prefer I call her by her full name, while genuflecting.

"Turn left on Main. I live in Ashby Estates." She picks up my iPod again and scrolls. "Wait! You have 'You're a Mean One, Mr. Grinch'? Really?"

The smile she sends my way is the first nonplastic one of the night; it's a little lopsided and a hell of a lot sexier than when she poses. I turn away.

The song's from a playlist I made for Marcos when Carly

and I took him to see Santa at the mall last Christmas. I reach over and place my hand on top of hers, ready to press the skip button.

Her skin is so soft.

Soft skin? Carly and I just—I jerk my hand back to the wheel before my thoughts veer down the revenge-screw path.

"I don't get why you'd *choose* to be grinch-y," she persists, a cheerleader tone creeping into her voice. "People would like you if you'd let them. You're a great guy, I can tell."

"You're right! If I just listen to Brighton Waterford's guide to popularity, my life will be perfect."

She stares at me, shoulders pulled in and forehead creased. "So, you don't want anyone to like you?"

"No, unlike you, I don't want *everyone* to like me. There's a difference."

She abandons the iPod again, turning in her seat to face me. "Since you're so brilliant, tell me, who should I want to like me?"

"People you respect. People *you* like. As long as you're passing a class, why do you care if your teacher likes you? And why does it matter if the stoner kid whose locker is next to yours—"

"Phillip Walters is not a stoner!"

"It was an example. My point is, why waste energy sucking up to people who don't matter? Why are you sucking up to me? I don't matter in your life."

I turn into Ashby Estates; more straight rows of matching houses in varying shades of dull. I wonder how often people try their keys at the wrong front door.

These McMansions alternate between models with a

cross gable and those with a wraparound porch—I'm disgusted I still remember those terms from Paul and Mom dragging me along on real estate trips, so they could pretend my opinion counted.

"Everyone matters." She sounds like she's quoting Scripture or a manual on how to be a good person. Perhaps it's another quote from that book. Maybe that's next week's sticky-note mirror message.

"Yet everyone doesn't matter to *you*," I retort.

"But it's important to be liked."

"Why? Because it got you a 'Works Well with Others' in kindergarten and prom queen now?"

She squeezes her hands into fists, and I wonder if I can make her mad enough to hit me.

"No!" I hear her swallowing breaths as she fights to calm down. Her voice is still shaky when she says, "That's my driveway, the third one on the left."

"Then why?" I demand as I turn the wheel.

"Because . . . because it's nice!"

"Ah, and we're back to *nice*," I answer triumphantly as I put the car in park. Her house is beige. It has a cross gable.

Brighton sputters, practically trembling with repressed rage and frustration. I want her to yell. I want someone to yell at me so I have an excuse to yell back. "C'mon, Bright, use your words."

Her mouth drops open. She clenches her fists so tightly her hands shake and she blurts out, "But you *have* to like me," before bolting from the car.

16

Brighton

☼ 8:41 P.M. ☽

16 HOURS, 19 MINUTES LEFT

Stupid! Of all the idiotic things I could've said, *why* had I said that? What happened to "Thanks for the ride," "See you at school," or simply "Bye"?

I refuse to let myself run up the walk to my front door. "You have to like me"? No, he doesn't—have to or like me.

I shouldn't care. I shouldn't.

Teflon.

I don't care.

I'm shrugging it off as I fit my key in the door. Every light in the house is on, a clear sign that Evy's home and wandering around like a lost soul. I need to pull it together.

"Brighton!" Evy pounces, ripping the door handle from my hand.

"Hey! Welcome home." I offer a hug, and she flits in and out of my grasp. She's effortlessly stylish in black linen shorts and a printed red shirt. It's the type of shirt I wouldn't look at twice—too busy and bright—but it hugs her skin, drawing attention to her waist and making the most of her chest. Her dark curls are twisted into a careless knot and anchored with a swizzle stick. The outfit probably took her ten seconds to throw together and makes me self-conscious about the hour and a half it took me to get ready for school—and the fact that I don't, and never have, measured up to Evy in interest factor.

"Yeah, thanks and all that. Want to help me unpack?" she asks.

This will translate into me unpacking and organizing while she sits on her bed and tells me stories about all her college friends and college adventures. It's our typical routine, and I'm about to agree when her eyes light up. "Or maybe you have other plans. Who's the guy? Hey, handsome."

I look to see what she's grinning at: Jonah's standing in the still-open doorway.

"Hi," I say. It takes all of my effort to keep my feet planted on the foyer's Oriental carpet instead of fleeing up the stairs. Looking directly at him is out of the question; I aim my gaze over his left shoulder at his car parked halfway down the driveway.

"You forgot your cell."

Jonah hands it over and is gone before I even manage, "Oh, thanks."

I stare at the back of our front door until Evy puts a hand on my shoulder and spins me around to face her amused grin. "Wait. Wait. *Wait!* I thought you were babysitting—who was the guy? Did my little sister finally learn to lie to Mom? I'm so proud. And, nice choice: he sizzles!"

"What? No. That's the couple's son."

"And did you tuck him into bed and read him a story?"

She raises her eyebrows and pulls her lips into a scandalized smirk.

"The *older* brother of the baby I was watching." Why did I inherit all of the insta-blush genes in our family? "It's nothing like that. He doesn't like me at all. Wasn't that obvious?"

She winks and nudges me with an elbow. "Sounds like grade-school flirting. Next he'll be pulling your hair and calling you dorkhead and cootie-face."

"Ha. Not likely." I grab one of her suitcases from the foyer floor and trudge toward the stairs. "What do you have in here? It weighs a ton."

"Shoes." There's another knock on the door. "See, this is when the hair pulling begins," Evy says as she reaches around me for the knob. "I knew he couldn't resist my little sister."

She pulls the door open with a flourish so I'm face-to-face with a scowl. I drop the suitcase, flinching at its thud. "Did I forget something else?"

"I locked my keys in the car." His scowl deepens.

"Accidentally?" Evy asks, laughing.

His eyes drift past me and land on my sister. She's assumed an audience position, leaning against the green wall of the hallway. I'm sure all he sees are her chest and long, tanned legs crossed at the ankles.

"I wouldn't have spent the past two minutes cursing at the car door if it was on purpose." But he says this with a smile. *She* gets a smile. "I'm Jonah."

"Evy. Smart idea not to curse in front of The Innocent. It makes her so damn huffy."

"It does not!"

They share a look like they're on some exclusive team. I hate feeling like an outsider.

"I'll drive you home to get a spare key," I offer.

"I'm blocking you in. My phone's in the car; can I use yours? I'll call AAA and be out of here."

"Sure," I answer.

Evy points to the cell in my hand. "Genius, if you'd figured it out sooner, you could've saved yourself a trip to return hers."

I hand it over with an apologetic look. "Don't be mean. He was probably busy worr—"

"Busy being a moron and locking my keys in the car." He fishes a AAA card out of his wallet and turns to face the door while he dials.

I stand watching until Evy hooks her fingers in the back of my collar and drags me backward into the kitchen.

"Let go of me!" She does, and I stumble until my hip hits the counter. "What's wrong with you?"

"Wrong with *me*? What's up with the Miss America act, B?" She assumes a pose that's straight up and down, feet at a forty-five-degree angle, fluttering lashes, and head tilt.

"I did not stand like that!"

"You did! And you're broadcasting puppy-dog affection on every channel. Back off a bit, B, make him work for it."

"I do *not* like Jonah Prentiss," I hiss in a whisper. "And I do not need guy advice."

"Just listen," she orders, and as usual I shut up. "Whether or not you like this guy—someday there's going to be a guy or girl you do. The smile-and-nod routine you were doing back there? That's not going to get you anywhere with anyone who's worth your time. And for the record, I approve of *this* guy—he doesn't treat you like you're made of porcelain like your usual fan club. So drop the act, okay?"

She stands there, hands on hips, eyebrows arched, waiting for my nod of agreement. I'm not going to give her the satisfaction. She doesn't get to waltz home and tell me what a failure I am at dating and life in general.

She tilts her head toward me and clears her throat. Over her shoulder, I can see Jonah approaching from the foyer. If I don't concede now, she'll make me regret it.

"Fine," I say, and she smiles triumphantly.

Jonah hands me my cell. "It's going to be at least an hour. They gave me some crappy excuse about how since I'm not in any immediate danger or stranded, I'm not considered a priority."

"I'm sorry. That stinks." An hour? I want him to go sit on his car, or pace the driveway, or do anything but be in my sight. I want away from how anxious he makes me and how much he makes me second-guess myself.

Evy sits down at the kitchen table and uses her toe to push the chair next to hers toward him.

"Of course you're welcome to stay," I add, but my own invitation is a weak, awkward echo of hers.

"Thanks." Jonah sits and scans the kitchen. Ours isn't as immaculate as his. There are fingerprints on the stainless-steel surface of the fridge. Evy's left a plate by the sink and a soda can on the counter next to a stack of mail she's gone through and an open catalog she's doodled on. All of this will have to be cleaned up before the memorial tomorrow.

I look stupid and out of place standing, but don't feel

invited to join them. Which is ridiculous. Evy is *my* sister, Jonah is *my* babysitting charge's older brother.

Who hates me.

But I can fix this—I'll use this hour to *make* him like me. Once he does, I'll get him to come volunteer on Sunday. Then I'll never have to think about him again.

Decision made. So, by Dad's logic, I'm 80 percent closer to him liking me than I was a second ago. Funny how I still feel totally unwelcome in my own kitchen.

I keep standing, trying to make it look like I want to by leaning against the marble countertop. *Everything looks better when you're wearing a smile.* I flash some teeth, trying to find a balance between the Miss America of Evy's accusation and the grimace I'd like to wear. "Can I get you anything, Jonah? A drink?"

"No," he says, then adds, "Sorry if I ruined your plans." This is addressed to Evy. Apparently my plans don't matter.

"No worries. I'm in for the night. I was going to make tea and wait for my boyfriend to call. Brighton's about to walk the dog. You can go with her."

"Never? No." If I had been sitting, I'd have bolted to my feet in protest.

"Um, I'll wait by my car if walking the dog is a private task for you." Jonah gives me a look of curious disdain.

"No, that's not what I meant."

But my words are overpowered by Evy's opening the French doors to our back porch. She whistles and shouts, "C'mere, boy! Where's my baby?"

Nearly two hundred pounds of drool lumbers into the kitchen. Jonah's chair is forced back when Evy's "baby"

pushes his way over to inspect him. Jonah tolerates the sniff-
ing and even scratches behind the demon dog's ears. *Saint
Bernard? I don't think so.*

"Who loves me? Never loves me. Good boy, Never. Such
a good boy," Evy coos, and the dog turns his attention to her.
Jonah stands up to avoid being beaten by the dog's tail, which
immediately overturns his chair.

"Never?" Jonah asks. "That's some dog."

"See, I wasn't saying you couldn't come—"

"Never: Not Eve's Replacement. My mom got this big,
beautiful boy right before I left for college. Didn't she, buddy?"
Evy scratches his chin, and he rewards her with a lick that
leaves visible slobber across her cheek. Gross.

"And he never listens to anyone but her, so it's appropri-
ate." I scowl—not that either of them notices. They're too
busy lavishing affection on the beast, who has a habit of
chewing up my shoes and jumping on me when I sit on the
couch so I can't get up until he decides to move or someone bribes him with a cookie. "I'm not walking him. I can't.
He was just in the backyard, I'm sure he's fine."

As soon as the word "walk" leaves my lips, Never bounds
over, jumps up, and knocks me down. Then he proceeds to
lick my face.

"Get him off me," I beg, but Jonah and Evy are too busy
laughing.

When I'm near tears, Jonah does, by holding up a leash
Evy must've given him. He manages to get Never to sit while
he fastens it. I hate the dog and she knows it. The thing
weighs nearly as much as the two of us combined, but he listens to *her.*

"I can't walk him," I repeat. I put my headband on the counter and pull my hair into a ponytail so I can splash my face with water from the kitchen sink and remove the drool. All my makeup comes off along with it. My first instinct is to run upstairs and fix it, but Jonah will hate me with or without mascara and sandstone eye shadow.

"Don't be a baby. He needs a walk—" Her cell rings. "And look, there's Topher, so I can't do it. Have fun. I'll listen for the AAA guys." Evy zips out of the room, cell phone to her ear, cooing to her boyfriend in a tone similar to the one she used with the dog.

"I can't," I say to Jonah.

"He's just a dog. You're the owner. Tell him what to do and he'll do it."

Like it's that easy.

Never hasn't listened to a command from me since he was actually lap sized. The woman at obedience school kept correcting Mom and Evy, telling *them* to speak softer—that *my* normal-volume instructions wouldn't be effective if Never got used to obeying commands at a yell. But they didn't listen and she was right. By the time he was knee height, all the cookies, cheese, and peanut butter in the world couldn't convince him to sit or stay for me.

Jonah holds the leash out, but I just shake my head.

"Fine. I'll walk him then. What's a good loop so I don't get lost? Everything in this town looks the same."

He's wrong—of course—not only do things *not* look the same, but all the streets in Cross Pointe are laid out in a grid. I don't understand how it would be possible to get lost. I open my mouth to give him a route, then change my mind.

"You know what, I'll come with you."

If he were any of my guy friends, I'd link my arm through his, but Jonah would flinch or say something scathing. For now anyway.

Seeing him with Evy has given me hope; he's *not* a 100 percent miserable all the time. He *will* like me. I just need to figure out how to get him to take the chip off his shoulder and give me a chance.

"You're great with Never. Maybe you can teach me how to walk this beast without getting trampled." I offer the flattery in a "my hero" voice and pair it with a smile. He stares for a second, then turns and walks out the front door, dog by his side.

We head down the driveway, the automatic lights flickering on one by one as we trigger their motion sensors. He casts a forlorn look at his car as we pass.

I can't think of anything to say except things that would sound lame or like I'm sucking up: *You're so good at walking the dog. Don't feel bad about the car; anyone could make that mistake. Did you know your shoulders are really broad?*

My cheeks blaze, but at least it's dark and he can't see them or read my thoughts. He's staring again though.

"You don't look anything like your sister."

"Really? You think?" I smile. He's initiating conversation; we're already doing better than earlier. "Evy and I used to be mistaken for twins when we were younger. My mother took total advantage of this by dressing and styling us alike for holiday photos until Evy rebelled."

"Twins? She's all curls and curves and flash. You're . . ."

The smile freezes on my lips. "I straighten my hair." Also, she wears push-up bras and too much makeup.

"Your hair's curly like that?" Jonah sounds astounded. "God, you won't even allow your hair to have personality. I've never met anyone as repressed as you." His expression of disapproval is illuminated by a streetlight as he stops to let Never sniff.

My hair? He's even critical of my hair? "You know, most people like me. Or, if they don't, they're not rude enough to tell me."

"Rude, or honest?" Jonah asks.

"Rude," I insist.

Jonah snorts. It's the most infuriating sound I've ever heard.

"What's that supposed to mean? You think people *lie* about liking me?"

"You said it, not me."

"No, *you* said it first. You said *rude, or honest.* So tell me your version of the truth—I dare you."

"You *dare* me?" He laughs and shifts the leash to his other hand while considering this. "All right. If you really want to know, people like you because there's nothing there to dislike—that's not a compliment. You're vanilla ice cream. People like to build their sundaes on top of you because you go with everything. But vanilla on its own is boring."

"I'm boring?" Now isn't a good time for my Teflon coating to fail, but I can't make this insult not hurt.

"Look at you."

I do. Khaki capris, a navy pin-tuck tank. I'd worn light gold sandals to school, but traded them for white flip-flops for the walk. It's an outfit I bought straight off a mannequin in Cross Pointe's most popular boutique—I'm sure their stylists know fashion a little bit better than Jonah.

Never's pulling at the leash, so he and the dog continue down the sidewalk.

"I am *not* boring!" I call after their shadowy shapes. I make my hands into fists. One of my nails hits a tender spot from earlier, but I keep forcing them tighter. "And I like vanilla!"

Jonah's laughter drifts back. "Are you coming?"

"I'll prove I'm not boring!" I stomp to catch up. "Turn left here, there's somewhere I want to go."

We turn out of Ashby and we're back on Main Street. How could Jonah possibly think this town is confusing?

"Wait here, I'll be right back," I say once we pass the awnings for the art gallery, stationery store, and a clothing boutique to reach Yates Pharmacy. "Please," I add.

The bells hanging above the door chime as I open it, and Mrs. Yates looks up from her place behind the counter. "Honey, we close in five minutes," she calls at me.

"I only need one," I answer and storm the aisles, searching for what I want. While it isn't exactly the same, it will do. I hurry back to the register, and Mrs. Yates is waiting with a smile.

"You came out at nine p.m. just for this?" she asks.

"It was an emergency." I smile at the bottle I'm rolling between both hands; it stings each time it coasts over the marks left by my nails. "But how about I add this too?" I hand her a Snickers bar.

"I remember being a teen—fashion and chocolate are always emergencies. Have fun."

17

JONAH

☀ 9:01 P.M. ☽

LONGEST HOUR OF MY LIFE

A Brighton rebellion. I'm curious what she'll buy in the pharmacy. Or maybe she won't *buy* anything—maybe she's proving she's not boring by shoplifting. Jeff once stole a Matchbox car after his older brother called him a chicken. But Jeff was eight, and I really can't see Brighton pocketing anything without paying.

Bells signal her reappearance. Never barks once and strains to go sniff her. I tug on his leash and he sits, but his tail beats impatiently against the ground. I know how he feels. Is she walking slowly on purpose? If she's waiting for me to ask, I won't.

"This is for you." She tosses me a candy bar—a very bad throw, but I stretch up and catch it automatically. "And *this* is for me." She holds up a glittery-green bottle like it's a trophy.

"That's it?" My voice sounds harsh, even to me, but seriously, nail polish?

She frowns at me and continues to turn the bottle so the

glitter reflects in the streetlight. "What were you expecting? It's a pharmacy, not a tattoo parlor."

"I don't know, something more impressive like hair dye or condoms or something."

"This *is* impressive! I've been wearing Pointe-Shoe Pink since I was twelve." She curls the bottle into her palm and tightens her other hand into a fist. "Wait! Condoms? Why would I need—"

"Let's head back; they might be there." I turn Never and head toward the crosswalk. I can think of a reason for condoms . . . if she were Carly.

Carly. She'd dyed her hair a few weeks ago. Had there been some bigger significance to that? Some late-night dare, or had she done it to prove a point? I hadn't asked. I'd been too shocked to do anything but stare.

I kick a piece of mulch that's dared to stray from a perfect flower bed. Is it too early to call her and try and explain? Once my car's unlocked and my phone's accessible, do I want to? If she knew who I was with right now, she'd never believe me.

I want my old life back, but do I want to grovel? She wouldn't even listen to me. Didn't trust me. My stomach prickles, and I have to stop myself from grinding my teeth.

Brighton continues to talk about her nail polish—are there really people in the world who care this much about colored fingertips? I roll my eyes at Never, wishing Paul would even consider getting a dog this awesome. He gave away his cat as soon as they found out Mom was pregnant, so I'm sure anything that sheds, slobbers, or is remotely interesting will be categorized as *"absolutely not."*

I'd love to see how Never handles a game of fetch. Maybe if AAA's not there yet.

"I almost got this color today, and I let my mom talk me out of it. No, I didn't even let her talk me out of it, because that implies I did some talking. I just let her bulldoze me. 'You don't want that color, baby; you always get the same color. Go, sit.' And I did, just like a dog. Not like *that* dog, but like one that's obedient." She throws these words at the sidewalk without looking at me.

"Here. I'll show you how to walk him. I had a boxer when I was little. A Saint Bernard's not that different." I loop the leash over the hand she extends. God, her wrists are tiny. She's not rail thin or sickly like a lot of Cross Pointe girls, but her wrists are tiny. I bet my fingers could wrap around and overlap two knuckles. I shake off the urge to try, jerking my hand off hers.

"Now, you *walk*." I start down the sidewalk, and Never stands up and follows, panting, tongue dripping.

She manages a few almost-controlled steps before Never begins galloping.

"Give him a command!" I yell as she struggles to sprint behind him, then digs in her flip-flops to try and stop him; they're useless on the sidewalk. The little bottle falls from her hand in a metallic blur. I ignore it and run to catch up. Time seems to freeze in the moment when the edge of one foam flip-flop catches in a sidewalk seam and folds beneath her foot. Her exposed toes scrape along the concrete, and she pitches forward. My mouth opens in warning but is too dry to speak—I'd be too late anyway. On pure instinct, I grab her arm with one hand and the leash with the other.

"Never, sit!" I command. The dog obeys and I turn to her. "Dammit, Brighton. You've got to be in charge! He's the animal; you're the master."

She starts crying. Crying. I used the same furious tone with her as I had with the dog. She's got a torn shoe, a bloody foot, she's shaking, and she'd told me she couldn't control a dog that outweighs her. And I yelled at her.

I'll show you how to walk him.

All I did was watch her get dragged. Dammit. I exhale through my teeth.

"Hey, it's all right. Let's see how bad this is." I kneel and lift her foot, carefully remove the destroyed flip-flop. The white foam is covered with gravel and spattered crimson. I wiggle each of her toes. Thank God I can handle gore, and it's too dark for her to see what I imagine is as painful as it is ugly. "I don't think they're broken, but they're pretty shredded. You okay to walk? I'll take the dog."

"No," she says, and I debate whether I can carry her and manage the dog. Take the dog and come back for her? Knock at a house and ask for a ride?

She lifts her chin. The tears on her cheeks and lashes reflect in the streetlight, but she isn't crying anymore. "If you can walk him, so can I."

"What?" My fingers tighten on her ankle, leaving a smear of her blood across bones that feel thin and breakable. I watch her hands clench in quick fists.

Without answering me, she tugs her foot from one of my hands and the leash from the other.

"Never, heel." Reminding the dog to "heel" and "leave it" every few inches, she limps back to where the nail polish lies on the sidewalk. I look between the drops of blood on the pavement, the dark smears on my hand, and this girl. Her ponytail is knocked crooked, and she blows a lock of hair out of her face as she walks toward me. It slides right back across her cheek, clinging to the tear tracks.

She stops in front of me. Crying has made her eyes shinier and a darker gray. Or maybe they look darker because they're full of determination instead of passive smiles. Or maybe I'm being a moron and it's just the streetlights.

"Can you hold this? I want two hands on the leash."

I accept the polish, holding it in the hand that doesn't have the remnant of her flip-flop. But before I do, I brush that piece of hair off her cheek and tuck it behind her ear.

I have to look away before I ask, "You're sure you're okay?"

"I said I was." She chokes up even more on the leash; Never's flank is practically pressed against her leg. "But thanks for asking."

While I stare at her legs, she starts walking careful steps that keep the injured toes on her bare foot from touching the ground. I wipe the feel of her skin and hair off my hand, shove the nail polish in a pocket, and catch up.

18

Brighton

☼ 9:26 P.M. ☽

15 HOURS, 34 MINUTES LEFT

I let go of the leash as Jonah pushes open the door. Gripping it so tightly has done nothing to help my sore hands. Never bounds over to his water bowl and then to Evy. He lowers his mouth—still streaming water—into her lap. She smiles at him like he's performed a miracle but doesn't put down the phone until she sees me.

"Hang on a sec, Topher. Oh my God, Brighton! What'd you do?"

The words "He made me walk your dog" sound whiny, even in my head, so I leave them there. "I tripped."

"You okay?" When I nod, she's satisfied. "Well, don't get blood on the rug. The AAA guys haven't come yet, by the way."

I turn to Jonah. "I'm going to get Band-Aids." Then I start up the stairs, walking on my heel to keep bloody tracks off Mom's ivory carpet.

He follows, answering before I can ask: "Let me help you clean that." He passes me at the landing but waits outside the bathroom door. "Please? I feel bad."

Feeling bad is a step closer to liking me. It's almost an apology. He's offering to help and waiting for my permission. "Thanks."

"Where are the Band-Aids? And peroxide? And cotton balls?" he asks. "Oh, and here." He hands me the nail polish.

The counters, which had been immaculate and organized this morning, are now covered in Evy's shower caddy and cosmetic bags. I dig through her clutter and pull out the supplies he requests.

"Should we move down to the kitchen table?" Having him in my bathroom seems way too intimate. I get *naked* in that shower every morning. The way-too-flimsy-but-never-seen-in-public bathrobe Evy gave me for Christmas is hanging on a hook behind his head. "You really don't have to do this."

"It's not a big deal. Sit." He points to the lidded toilet and takes a seat opposite on the edge of the bathtub. "Do your nails and try not to flinch. This is gonna hurt."

I pull nail polish remover from a cabinet and sit, reaching over to snag some cotton balls from the bag. Jonah props my foot on his knee, soaks a cotton ball in peroxide, and presses it to my toes.

My determination to be brave shatters with the first contact of cotton. Pain flames through my toe, and I have to grasp the side of the counter to keep myself from wrenching my foot away from his hand. I gasp and exhale a whimper.

"Your small toe's the worst—even part of the toenail's torn off. The rest shouldn't be so bad."

"It's okay. I'm okay," I repeat softly, wincing as he dabs my next toe and a new sting fires through my foot. I set my ring on the counter and concentrate on wiping off Mina's handiwork. My fingers shake slightly as the blush of color smears and dissolves.

Jonah leans in and blows on the bubbles forming from the peroxide—like Dad used to when I skinned a knee.

"I bet you're a great big brother."

"What?" He looks up at me, puzzled.

"Sophia looks like you," I add.

"You think? I'm not sure that's a good thing." He smiles a little. Almost. "She's a chill baby, I'm going to miss her when I leave for State in the fall."

His hand rubs my insole as he talks, the light touch masking some of the pain throbbing from my toes. I look from his face to my foot, curious if he even realizes he's doing it.

"Oh, no. Sorry, I'm getting blood on your shorts." I try to pull my foot back, but his fingers hold firm.

"It'll wash out. Don't worry about it."

"I've got stain stuff under the cabinet."

"It's fine." His clipped words kill my efforts to free my foot and get the Spray 'n Wash. My cheeks burn with color—like they always do when I feel chastised—and the nails on my left hand end up a little smeared.

He crumples the Band-Aid wrappers into a ball and lowers my foot to the floor. I wipe at a stray speck of glitter on my thumb and desperately seek something to say. He softened when talking about Sophia; another question about her, maybe?

My gaze rises slowly from my nails, drifting up his shirt to his face, and locks on the brown eyes that are studying me. "Thank you—" The other words of my gushy *like-me* speech die in my throat.

He nods and stands. I do too, and the space between toilet and bathtub is far too small for both of us. I can feel the heat radiating off his body, hear his breathing. I wait for him to step away.

He doesn't.

"What do you think of the color?" I ask, lifting a hand and holding it out to him.

He cups it and leans back to create enough room between us to examine my fingers. "It's very *green.*"

But I'm looking at his hand cradling mine, not my nails. He has kind hands. Can hands be kind? His are.

I want to find a flippant reply, something that will keep him smiling with amusement not condescension, yet all my mind will repeat is: *he's being nice.*

If only I could freeze time and figure him out. Make a list and uncover the secret to receiving a smile like this. Instead, I suppress the shy grin that wants to spread with my blush, and force a practiced smile. "You like it? Maybe it'll start a trend. All the girls in Cross Pointe will be wearing green nails."

His fingers drop mine, his mouth drops into a scowl, and he crosses the bathroom. "It's nail polish, who cares?"

My words dry up. I shrug and lean back against the countertop.

"You're about to knock your ring down the drain." He points.

"Oh. Thanks." I don't bother to explain it wouldn't fit down the drain. Instead I guide it back onto my finger, careful not to hit a nail. The green of the gem and the polish are a perfect match.

"Is that real?" he asks.

"My dad gave it to me for my twelfth birthday." It was my last birthday with a father.

"Because you're really careless with it," Jonah adds.

Careless? I've been hyperaware of its weight on my finger all day. It's an anchor, keeping me grounded and prepared for whatever Mom might need. A reminder that when I get past the stress and emotions of tomorrow, it's all for *him*.

I wish I could communicate this to Jonah with a look, because I can't find the right words. Normally if I'm in a situation where I have to utter the phrase "my dad" to anyone but Amelia, I'm suffocated by pity and the subject is changed.

"Don't worry, I won't lose it," I finally say.

"AAA's in the driveway," Evy calls from the kitchen.

"I wasn't worried." He shakes his head like he's disappointed in me. "If you lose it, he'll just buy you another one, right?"

My mouth drops open, but he's already disappeared into the hall and heading down the stairs.

His retreat slaps like rejection. We'd almost been getting along while he played medic. Had he thought my hand squeeze was romantic instead of friendly? Standing practically pressed together, holding hands with me might've seemed like something it wasn't. Because it wasn't anything.

He definitely wouldn't want it to be anything.

He didn't even seem to notice that he was sitting on the edge of my *shower*. He had no reaction to touching my bare legs. Even the skimpy robe hanging behind his head didn't make him pause. Plus, he has a girlfriend.

The girl in the mirror agrees with me, nodding as she continues to pose with her hand in a ridiculous posture— like it's being held by a ghost. I shake my head at her and watch as she spins the emerald inward, makes fists, then reacts to tacky nails hitting tender palms. I examine my hands as I leave the bathroom. There are flecks of glitter in the welts—decorations on my marks of stress and shame.

19

JONAH

☼ 9:41 P.M. ☽

I'M LATE FOR AN APPOINTMENT WITH NYQUIL SHOOTERS & MY PILLOW

Evy follows me to my car. She's detached from her cell, and her grin is all sexy mischief. I don't care what Brighton says, they don't look alike.

"So, do I want to know what you and my baby sister were doing upstairs?"

"Depends. Does blood make you queasy? I was fixing the damage Never did to her foot. She can't walk that dog and you know it."

Evy shrugs an acknowledgment. "I didn't think you'd let her get *hurt*."

"She's not my responsibility." I'm annoyed. Evy pushed her into a task she knew Brighton couldn't handle, and yet it's *my* fault she's bleeding? It's one thing for me to blame myself—another to hear Evy say it. "Who owns a dog they can't even walk?"

"Hey." She grabs my arm and pulls me to a stop. "B's . . . Don't be too hard on her. Just give her a chance."

A chance to do what? God forbid anyone's hard on Brighton—the girl lives a charmed life and now I'm supposed to feel bad for not joining her fan club.

I shake my head and call a greeting to the woman in a AAA polo shirt. "Thanks for coming."

"I need your card." I hand it over.

"And your registration," she adds.

I point at my glove compartment and bite my tongue to keep from saying: *If I could open my door to get my registration, I wouldn't need you.* I lean against the trunk, trying to give the woman room to work but impatient to get the hell out of here.

"Voilà. Door open." The woman steps away and I practically dive for my registration and owners' manual, handing her the thick file then digging my cell out of the door pocket while she writes stuff down.

I need to get away from here. Fast. Get anywhere. But is there anywhere left for me to go?

New text messages.

They've got to be from Carly. She's realized she's being insane. I can be there in twenty-five minutes if I push it . . .

But do I want to? I'm half-crazy with the desire to call her, but if I do, I can't think of anything I actually want to say. My stomach twists.

You cheated on C? No way you got someone hotter.

Not. Carly.

The next text's not either—it's from Carly's friend, Sasha: **U dirtbag, loser, jerkwad. You didn't deserve her.**

What the hell has Carly been telling people?

The AAA woman's holding a clipboard out to me, the

front door's opening and shutting, Evy's calling something up the walk, and Brighton's limping down it. I scrawl my name and thank the woman. The sooner she leaves, the sooner I can get in my car and go—but she climbs in the truck, turns on the cab light, and starts on more paperwork.

Three more messages:

Where U at? Get. Here. Now. Beer.

A CP chick? Heard she's butt ugly.

Where RU?

The last one's from Jeff—and he's left a voice mail too. Can I go to his party? It's easy to picture how it's going down: Carly sitting on a countertop entertaining a group with stories about what a crappy, cheating boyfriend I turned out to be. Her audience soaking up the lies. The stories mutating and spreading as people wander in and out of earshot to refill their cups. By the end of the night I'll be seen as a total tool—a Cross Pointe sellout. It'll look like I'm too embarrassed to show my face. Like she's telling the truth and I slunk off to lick my wounds. She's taking Hamilton away from me, poisoning my reputation, claiming *my* friends—

Evy leans over my shoulder. "What's so exciting?" I find myself aping her sister's fist clenching and jerk away.

Headlights from the truck illuminate the three of us as the woman backs out of the driveway. I raise my hand in salute and to shield my eyes. Brighton's at the end of the walk, making careful progress down the stone steps that lead to the driveway.

The light catches her hair, her eyes, her legs. Doing things to her silhouette that I could watch all night. **No way you got someone hotter.** Hotter? Carly and Bright are attractive in totally different ways, but Brighton can more than hold her own.

She pauses on the second step and asks, "Everything all set with your car?"

My reputation is already screwed—apparently eighteen years of knowing me is worth less than a piece of paper with a phone number. And if everyone's going to believe I'm cheating scum, I at least want them to believe I'm cheating scum who nailed a hot girl.

"Brighton, want to go a party?"

"What?" she asks, while Evy claps her hands together and says, "Yes, yes, she does."

We both ignore her.

"A party. You know, people, music . . ."

"Beer, hookups, gossip, and scandals," adds Evy.

"Jeremy's party? I didn't even know you knew him. If you want to go, I'll bring you."

I'm not even sure who Jeremy is, but of course she'd assume I'm begging for an invitation to his party. "No, my friend's party. You should come with me."

"Why?"

"Look, come to the party and I'll come to your book thing on Sunday."

Her eyes go wide and she starts to nod, then pauses. "You'll really come to the library? I thought you had plans."

I'm sick of trying to coax her, impatient to get this over with. If compromise won't work, maybe a reminder will. "I said I'd go. Come to the party. You'll learn a hell of a lot more about me there than you did in my bedroom."

"What?" Evy demands, grabbing her sister's arm and dragging her down a step.

Brighton looks over her shoulder at the house and tests her sister's grip on her arm. "Okay. I'll go to the party."

"His *bedroom*?"

"He's kidding." Brighton's fake laugh is far from believable. She looks at me pleadingly.

I hold her gaze for a long moment before turning to Evy. "Hello, have you met your sister? I'm kidding." I can afford to be generous now that I've gotten my way.

Evy looks disappointed, but only for a moment. "This is perfect! You need to get out of the house and get rumpled a bit. Live a little, baby sis." She flounces over to me. "And, you? You would be an excellent person to rumple her."

"Evy, enough!" There's zero authority in her voice, more plea than order. She looks like she might curl into her embarrassment and disappear.

And Evy doesn't even pause. "Is that blood on your pants? Ew. Well, you'd need to change anyway. I wonder if there's anything in your closet that's even a little sexy—you should probably just borrow something from me."

I allow myself to imagine that for a minute: Bright in short black shorts and a red top that shows off her chest. Or maybe something low cut. Her legs in heels . . .

Except. Her foot. The one that caused the blood spatter on her pants. No heels tonight. And the way Evy's dragging her up those stone steps has to hurt. Does she not notice her sister's limping?

"Evy. Evy. *Evy*!" Brighton's repeating it with each painful footstep, but her sister's too busy blathering.

"Stop!" I call.

What am I going to do with her at the party? After the three seconds where I get *nailed-that* credit, what am I going to do when she opens her mouth? Or when they open theirs? Brighton shouldn't go near a Hamilton party, where they'd gladly devour a Cross Pointer—especially a girl they think has shamed one of their own. No, this idea is stupid. I can't do that to her.

"I changed my mind."

"What?" Evy and Brighton's voices blend into a chorus of confusion and indignation.

"Forget the party. You don't want to go."

"Didn't I just say I would?' She honestly sounds con-fused. "Why wouldn't I?"

I scramble for an angle, a way to convince her it's a bad idea. "It's in Hamilton—you don't want to go there."

She's standing halfway up the walk, one arm tight in Evy's grasp, the other hugging her torso. Her bandaged, bare foot is picked up and resting against her other calf. It's a pose that makes her look vulnerable and graceful, but her voice is anger and iron: "I already told you, I'm not a snob, so stop treating me like one. Who cares if it's in Hamilton?"

"What if we go to . . ." even as I try to remember his name, I can't believe I'm saying this, "that other guy's party? The one that's here."

"No. We see those people every day—you don't even like them." She pauses to flash me an amused smile. "Besides, I want to meet Carly."

She's walking up the path, going through the front door, and I'm still standing there wondering how I let this get so out of control. How my *screw you* to Cross Pointe, Hamilton, and Carly has turned into a giant *I'm screwed*.

20

Brighton

☼ 9:54 P.M. ☽

15 HOURS, 6 MINUTES LEFT

My foot hurts and I'm tired. I glare at the cute shoes lining the bottom of my closet; there's no way I'll be able to wear anything but flip-flops. I direct the same frown at my bed— like my comforter and pillow are somehow betraying me by being simultaneously inviting and not an option.

Maybe this is a good thing, Jonah did invite me after all—even if he tried to weasel out of it immediately after. He even agreed to come to the library on Sunday. If he meant it, if he shows—then I've done it. A 100 percent.

Somehow securing the plaque is no longer enough; I need him to like me too. Or, at least, not hate me.

Evy shows up in my bedroom as I'm yanking my shirt over my head.

"What are you doing?" I squeak and cross my arms over my bra. "Ever hear of knocking?"

"I'm helping you. Don't you dare put on something like Gramma Anna would wear."

I grab a sweatshirt and zip it up over my bare stomach.

"I don't need help getting dressed." I'm curious what she'd choose—curious but also terrified. I'd probably end up looking ridiculous in an outfit that's fabulous on her but I can't pull off at all.

"Yeah, well, I also want some details. His bedroom? And don't tell me he was kidding. You know you can't lie to me."

"It's not what you think. It wasn't anything romantic." Evy's eyebrows shoot up and I hurry to recover. "Not that it was *unromantic*, it just wasn't, you know . . . It was nothing bedroom related."

"Fine," Evy huffs. "Don't tell me. But I knew the second you walked in the door something was up and I knew the second *he* walked in our door what it was. I don't get what the problem is. Is he not preppy-boy-boring enough for you?"

"No! That's not it at all. It's not like that with us. There's not an *us*. I barely even know him. He hates everything about me." I pause to take a breath and remember the only argument I actually need: "And, he has a girlfriend."

"Then why is he taking *you* to this party?"

"It isn't a date." I want her to shut up, to stop asking questions that make me say these things out loud. "She'll be there. Quit trying to create a scandal where there isn't one."

"There's *always* a scandal if you know where to look." She pauses by my closet door and fingers the black dress hanging on the back. "Is this what you're wearing tomorrow?" Her face has softened, teasing dropping to tenderness.

Tomorrow. I forgot. How could I forget? I sink onto my bed, sitting on my hands so I won't make fists. "I should cancel. I shouldn't go out tonight."

Evy sits next to me. "Yes, you should."

"But what if Mom needs me?"

"She's fine. She called while you were out—she and Aunt Joan are at some wine bar in East Lake."

"But—"

Evy reaches over and takes one of my hands, smoothing out the fingers. "That's the ring Dad gave you. I don't think I've ever seen you wear it."

"I don't usually. It just seemed *right* today." I slip it off and put it in my jewelry box. "I'm staying home."

"No." Evy yanks on my sweatshirt zipper. "Go. Have fun. And pick out something else for tomorrow. This is a memorial, not a funeral. It's a celebration of Dad's life. He'd want you in rainbow colors."

She grabs my black dress and pauses before leaving: "You're going to this party—so get dressed."

I scowl at the back of my bedroom door—and then at my closet. Push hangers around and reject all my clothing. Figuring out what to wear to the memorial will have to wait for the morning. I can't think about Dad right now.

I need to keep moving or I won't be able to move at all. That paralyzing grief is right there, lurking in the corner, waiting for me to stand still long enough for it to pounce. But if Mom and Evy are still pulled together, then I can be fine too.

I have to make it through tonight before I can worry about tomorrow. Through this party. I don't understand the rules of Jonah's game or his expectations. Does he really want me to get to know him better? If I annoy him as much as it seems, then inviting me to the party makes no sense. If Evy's right . . .

He said I was boring—like vanilla ice cream. I glance at the white eyelet top under my hand and shove it aside. I've got short things, sparkly things, but I don't want to look like I'm trying too hard. Effort that appears effortless is always twice as much work.

I tug a hand-me-down navy blue polo dress from a hanger. Amelia's mom accidentally put it in the dryer and it's too short and tight for her Kardashian curves. When Amelia made me try it on, she clapped and said, "You actually look more Victoria's Secret Angel and less feathers-and-halo angel." It walks the line between too-sexy-for-school and oh-I-just-threw-this-on. Perfect.

Jonah's comment about Evy's curves echoes loud enough for me to put on a better bra—but I refuse to reach for anything push-up or padded.

I limp down the hallway. Now that I have time to examine it, the bathroom is chaos. Evy has piled bags and bottles all over the counter. My brush is buried beneath a shower caddy and a tube of toothpaste. I wipe off a smear of something sticky and smooth my hair out of its ponytail.

My makeup case is not in its regular spot: the left side of the second drawer. I check the third drawer. Check the cabinet.

"Brighton!" Evy calls up the stairs.

"Two minutes," I call back.

Since I can't locate my makeup, I rummage through hers. Rejecting hot pink, then glitter gold, I settle on plain gray eyeliner. It has a wide, smudgy tip that leaves my eyes thickly outlined. Attempting to rub it off results in further smudging. I resign myself to looking raccoon-like and impatiently swipe on mascara—again, too heavy and gloppy for my taste. Her shadows, blushes, and glosses are all too bright for my I'm-not-trying look, so I guess I'm finished. I fix a stray speck of mascara and frown. I shouldn't care this much. It's just a party, not prom, not anything that matters. And I look fine.

Except the two people standing downstairs are waiting to judge me. No matter what I wear, all they'll see is how desperately I want their approval.

21

JONAH

☀ 10:10 P.M. ☽

CAN I GO BACK IN TIME & TELL MYSELF THIS IS A BAD IDEA?

"Is this okay?"

I don't answer. She knows she looks good. The dress probably costs more than I made in a month when Carly and I worked at Dairy Queen. And the girl all but treats the stairs as a runway, pausing at the top so we can admire her. I keep expecting someone to cue the soundtrack of one of Carly's cheesy romantic comedies—except that would make me the date waiting in awestruck wonder, and I'm not impressed. If this were really a teen movie, it'd be Carly floating down the steps. She'd be wearing something a lot sexier.

Bright looks up at me from the bottom step and her dark brown hair slides back from her face. I suck in a breath—she wasn't lying; there is some resemblance between her and Evy. I didn't see it earlier when she'd looked about eight with the headband or when she had her hair in a ponytail, but now, with it hanging down around her face, there's something older and arresting about her.

Her eyes are still too big, still remind me of a doll's, but

they look pointed instead of round; sexy in a subtle way—
though the look she projects is much too innocent.

But Brighton isn't someone you easily look away from
either. If I'm honest with myself, she's beautiful. Beautiful.
Not that Carly isn't. Carly and Brighton side by side would be
something to see. Carly's head would barely reach Bright's
shoulder, yet Carly projects so much larger a presence, while
Brighton blends in. Or tries to.

Right now, she doesn't look vanilla at all. The guys will
drool for her; the girls will hate on her. Carly will have a fit
of jealousy.

God, what am I doing?

She carefully slides a flip-flop over her bandaged foot,
wincing a little as she lets go of the strap. She's left the ring
off. Good. I want her to stand out, but not because she's
flaunting a daddy's-girl status symbol.

"I just need to grab my purse and we can go."

Evy holds it out with a smug smile. "I'll fill Mom in when
she gets home, but we won't wait up. You two have fun . . .
but not too much. And don't get into trouble. Mom keeps a
bail fund for me—for you, she only has college money."

When *Mom* gets home. I don't think *Dad* has been mentioned all night. Who would've thought Brighton's parents
would be divorced? I bet they have one of those still-best-
friends divorces and Bright's got a second car, a second fan
club at her dad's house. Perfection times two.

"Let's go," I say. Let's get this over with.

She stays silent as we back out of her driveway, not even
picking up the iPod. Her answer to "Which way back to
Main Street?" is so quiet she has to repeat it. So quiet that I
can hear her stomach when it growls.

"Hungry?"

"A little," she admits.

"We can stop and get something on the way." Of course, now that we're on the highway, there's nowhere to stop till we get to Hamilton. I have no clue why she's gone incommunicado. Or what she likes to eat. She's staring out the window and absently rolling the hem of her dress with green fingernails. My eyes keep shifting from the road to her legs to the back of her neck.

"Are you going to tell everyone in Cross Pointe I was in your room?" she asks quietly. She's still facing away from me, but instead of fidgeting with her dress, her nails are hidden against the palms of her hands.

"I hadn't planned on it. Why? Are you embarrassed to have people know you know me?"

"Hardly. If you remember, I've been trying to get to know you at school for months." She takes a deep breath, then continues, "It's just that you said that in front of Evy, just to embarrass me and make me come."

"How else was I going to get you in this car?"

"You didn't need to." She turns away from the window and shoots a quick glance at me. "I was already going to say yes."

"Oh." I know I should apologize, but I can't make myself do it.

"Just so you know, I'm holding you to showing up at the book event on Sunday." That smile again. The slightly lopsided real one. It makes this whole idiotic idea seem more idiotic. Me, bringing Brighton *Cross Pointe* Waterford to a party. Her *wanting* to come with me.

Yeah, right.

"What's Carly like?" she asks.

I don't want to talk about Carly.

But she's staring at me, rolling that hemline, exposing and re-covering the same inch of thigh.

"Carly—" I clear my throat, "she's . . ."

Manipulative.

"Charismatic. And she's . . ."

Reckless.

"Fearless, like this one time she talked a cop out of a ticket after she got caught waving to me from Maya's sunroof. And she's the one to watch out for every year during the neighborhood Thanksgiving football game—she's short, but she'll throw mud or trip anyone that gets between her and the end zone. She's also . . ."

Judgmental, always right, an emotional seesaw.

"Compassionate. She loves animals. Never would be crazy about her, all dogs are. She's a vegetarian too. Throws a fit if I eat meat in front of her and won't let me kiss her until I've brushed my teeth."

I swallow twice, but I still can't continue. My mind is stuck in a loop of *not anymore; never again.*

"And she's *real.* Carly is who she is—she doesn't care what other people think about her. She's not defined by the clubs she belongs to. She says what she means and doesn't hide behind what she thinks other people want to hear."

Bright's gaze is heavy on my face, like it's weighted with her comprehension of my less-than-subtle insults. I need a break from that level of scrutiny. I know she can't read my thoughts, but I can't meet her eyes without feeling guilty.

"Pizza?" I ask. I'm already parking in front of the doesn't-look-like-much, but-just-taste-their-sauce place the team used to stop at every Friday after practice. It's open late and not much else is besides fast food. I bet Brighton doesn't eat things that start with Mc.

"You didn't say a single thing about what she looked like. Most guys would start with 'she's hot' and then go on to list the ways."

"I guess I'm not most guys." I yank the keys out of the ignition. "Of course she's hot."

I'm out of the car and halfway to the restaurant before I wonder if Bright meant it as a compliment not a criticism.

"I figure we'll get a pie. What do you want on it?" I ask when it's our turn at the counter after a silent wait in line.

"Whatever you want is fine."

"Seriously?" It's the iPod all over again.

She nods. I roll my eyes and lean across the counter. "I'd like a medium pie with jalapeños, olives, pineapple, and mushrooms."

Her eyebrows shoot up, but she presses her lips together and doesn't say a word. I grin and snag a table in the back. She joins me, carrying a pitcher of water and two cups of ice. I'm so busy gloating, I forgot drinks. And napkins, which she has pinned under her arm.

"They don't have chocolate milk. I checked." Her mischievous grin is a hell of a lot more appealing than Evy's, and probably much rarer. As she pours water into the scratched red plastic cups, her smile fades to seriousness. "I don't really drink. Alcohol, that is. I mean, I do sometimes, but only if I'm with Amelia or people I know really well."

"That's fine. No one's going to force you to do keg stands or anything." Because I'm clearly the type of guy who'd bring her to a party where she'd be roofied. Is that what she thinks? Or is she worried I'll get tanked and she'll need to babysit me and drive me home? Maybe I'll let her. It might be nice to lose some of tonight in the bottom of a Solo cup.

"What do I need to know about this party?" she asks.

"What do you mean? It's a party." She's winding a straw wrapper over her fingers, and I can't look away from the contrast of white paper, green glitter, and tan skin.

"Who will be there? Is it, like, for a club or something?" Her words are slow, like she's choosing them individually. It takes me a minute to figure out what she's trying *not* to imply.

"A lot of people will be there. It's a regular party—not some antisocial group like you're imagining."

"I wasn't—"

"Yeah, you were. You don't know everything, Bright, and Cross Pointe isn't the whole world. Maybe I haven't been Mr. Social there because I don't need more friends than I already have." She flinches at my angry words, and I'm glad. Happy to see her hands curl in her lap and her eyes hidden by her hair when she lowers her head.

A guy brings us pizza and paper plates. Normally they just call your name from the counter when it's done and ring you up when you go get it.

"What about the check?" I ask.

From halfway across the restaurant the guy calls, "She already paid. Enjoy."

I pull out my wallet without looking at her. I won't be her charity case.

Soft fingers on mine, freezing my hand. God, what does she do to have skin like that? It's probably from never having worked a day in her life.

"Jonah, it's fine," she says. "Your stepdad way overpaid me and—"

"I'm paying next time," I say. Then realize there won't be a next time. After this party, Bright's never going to talk to me again. My throat is suddenly tight—I pull my hand away from hers and take a sip of water. This was my goal—to get her to leave me alone. If she'd listened when I told her that at school, it would've saved us both a lot of time.

"Sure." She smiles at me, all toothpaste-ad perfection. "So, let's try this creative combination of yours. Is it a favorite?"

Of course she'd rub that in. Of course she'd make a point of paying for pizza I ordered to piss her off. She's probably trying to make me feel like a jerk. Or like *more* of a jerk. Well, mission accomplished, Bright. The piece I sling on a plate and thrust toward her is the one with the most toppings. Not that I'm petty or anything.

I help myself to a slice and watch with satisfaction as she nibbles around the pineapple, takes a cautious bite of jalapeño, then spits it out in a napkin. I swallow a mouthful and my laughter.

She tosses the napkin—and her plate—in the trash can as she walks back up to the counter. "You said whatever toppings I wanted," I call after her, smugly taking a large bite of mushroom and pineapple.

She doesn't turn around, but I do, because someone's calling my name.

"Prentiss! See, told you it's Jonah."

It's Mike Balaski and Zeke Manzano, two guys I know from Hamilton. They're standing in the doorway, letting in bugs and letting out the AC.

"Hey, man, what's up?"

"How've you been?"

They ask about Carly—so clearly the news hasn't spread that far. I dodge the question and ask if they're going to Jeff's party.

"Maybe later. We're picking up the girls from work and hitting the last show of *Shriek 3*." Mike's grinning like a fool, but I can't remember whom Carly said he was dating.

"Tell them I say hi," I bluff.

I don't hear Brighton approach but notice when their eyes drift past me and widen in approval. She announces her arrival with: "You'll want to bring a drink—it's long."

"They're talking about *Shriek 3*." At the last second I manage to strip the scoff and sarcasm from my statement.

"Yeah, I know. I heard you at the counter." She smiles and gives her head a silly-boy shake that Mike and Zeke eat up. "It's more than two hours, and it's set in the desert—you'll need drinks, trust me."

Their thanks and intros take precedence over my "*You've* seen it?"

But after introducing herself with, "I go to school with Jonah," she answers me, "I saw it last Friday."

Carly won't even watch previews for movies like that. I'm annoyed Mike and Zeke are looking at Bright with respect and interest. Why does she fall into conversation with them so easily when she and I are magnetic opposites?

"So, who'd you send to fetch your drink?" I want to

expose her for the princess she is, but preferably without looking like a complete jerkwad.

"Jeremy North," she answers nonchalantly, and both Mike and Zeke sigh—like they've forgotten all about the "girls." I'm not much better, going through my mental Cross Pointe roster and identifying the center of the basketball team. *That's* whose party she was talking about? "But only because Amelia wouldn't let go of my or Peter's hands. I don't know why she goes to scary movies; she never sleeps afterward."

"And you do?" I challenge, as Mike says, "Not so easy to scare, Brighton?"

"It's just a movie—they don't bother me."

"So, what'd you think?" Zeke asks.

Ha! This is where she'll expose herself: Bright doesn't have opinions and they haven't seen it, so she can't just agree. I lean back and wet my lips.

"It's hard to go wrong with a Lewis Marsh movie," she says. A nice, vague, Brighton-type response. "But I hope he wraps up the Shriek films sooner than later. He dragged out the Gore series far too long. There's only so many times a character can not be dead."

She's really seen them. And knows her stuff.

"I know, right? Six movies, and the plot ran out after four." Mike nods and leans in toward her. "You know, you're not half-bad for a Cross Pointer."

"Gee, thanks?" Bright laughs and they join her. I'm analyzing her posture, her voice, her body language. She's not flirting. She's just . . . charming. And they're thoroughly charmed.

"You want to come with us?" Zeke asks. At least he has the decency to aim the question at both of us.

I don't realize how I'm standing until Bright puts a hand on my arm while answering. My muscles are tense, my posture's rigid. "Thanks for asking, but we've got plans and Jonah's pizza's getting cold."

My muscles unlock under her brief touch, melting whatever the hell's wrong with me so I can say, "If you make it to Jeff's, catch up with us, 'kay?" and wait for her to murmur, "Nice to meet you," before returning to the table where my pizza is indeed cold and unappetizing.

She clears her throat and I brace myself for I-don't-even-know-what she's going to say about Mike and Zeke. Or the fact that I stopped being a functional person after she joined our group.

"It's too bad you don't have OnStar," she mutters.

Only a spoiled brat would think OnStar is standard. Paul and Mom got me a car to erase their guilt about the move—or rather, they gave me her old car after spending days pouring over *Consumer Reports* and buying Mom the one with the highest crash-test ratings so Sophia would be safe. I only have AAA because of the time my battery died. Paul hadn't appreciated driving out to the State Park in Hamilton at one a.m. to give me a jump. After that night Mom got me AAA, and I insisted Carly and I leave the dome light and music off when the car is parked.

I glare at the table. "Yeah. Too bad."

"Because then you could've had it unlocked with a phone call and you wouldn't be stuck here. With me."

I choke on an ice cube and she hands me a napkin.

"This was a mistake, Jonah. I'm not sure why you invited me, but you don't want me here—and I'm not saying that so you'll disagree. Not that I think *you* will. Just take me home. You don't even have to show up at the library on Sunday."

"What makes you think I don't want you to come to the party with me?" I'm asking purely to be difficult and because I'm pissed that she has the guts to admit it's a mistake when I don't.

She stares at me. Raises her eyebrows in a look that dares me to contradict her.

"We're already here. Just come." We're so close. Even if we just stay for five minutes, it'll be enough to replace whatever Carly's saying with my own story.

"Two slices of cheese?" The guy who brings the plate winks at Brighton. He's totally checking her out. I recognize him from Hamilton High—I want to say he's on the wrestling team, but who knows—Hamilton's three times the size of Cross Pointe. Ironically, it would be easier to be anonymous at the school where I was anything but.

The possible-wrestler is still hovering. "Let me know if you need anything else. *Anything.*"

He drops a napkin beside her plate, his name and number bleeding in black ink. I'm bothered and that bothers me. Why do I care? She's not my girlfriend—we're not on a date. Except—*we could be*—this punk doesn't know we're not. Neither did Zeke and Mike. No one has questioned my place across the table from her. What, they don't think I'm competition? And this loser thinks Brighton's in *his* league?

She smiles politely but turns away in dismissal. Turns

to me. I take the napkin and use it to wipe the condensation off my cup. The digits blur to black-green starbursts. I'm an idiot. Next I'll be tearing my shirt and beating my chest.

"Did you want this?" I ask, holding out the sodden, ink-stained mess.

She waves it away and gives me her perfectly imperfect grin. "Not even a little. You can keep it."

22

Brighton

14 HOURS, 9 MINUTES LEFT

Jonah does a decent job on the toxic pizza, stopping when only one slice remains on the tray. Does he actually like that flavor combination, or did he chose it to prove a point? I decide not to ask since we're finally having a normal conversation. It's like seeing his friends reminded him that kindness isn't fatal.

Granted we're only talking about college, how we both have no clue what we'll pick as majors.

"One time, this guy my mom was seeing asked what I wanted to be after high school," I say as we get back in his car. "I answered, 'A college student,' and he thought I was being rude or making fun of him because my answer was so vague. It was a mess; he was insulted and I felt awful."

Jonah laughs and turns down another side street—a baseball rolls around in his backseat, pinging off something metal each time he turns. This street curves too, more roads and driveways branching off in all directions like a spider's legs. There's no logic to these streets, or to the houses either.

Duplexes, capes, saltboxes, and a condo complex all share the same street. One house has a sign advertising a beauty salon out front. Two streets later there's a house with a yard crammed full of bright plastic slides and toys. Maybe it's actually a day care center? Some yards are landscaped and tidy, others have peeling paint and out-of-control weeds. We pass a building with plywood on the front windows. The houses are placed at random—some close to the street, others down long driveways. It's like a giant opened his fist and sprinkled buildings—new, old, large, small—all over the landscape. It makes me uncomfortable—and the fact that I'm uncomfortable makes me *more* uncomfortable.

Jonah makes a sharp left turn.

"I don't know how you can think Cross Pointe is hard to navigate. This is like a maze."

He shrugs. "But in Cross Pointe everything looks the same. Here, we've got landmarks. There's the park where I had Little League. Back there was the house we all thought was haunted. That stop sign is bent from when I hit it while Carly was trying to teach me to drive stick shift. And that's the Digginses' house."

He pulls over, parking along the grass between two other cars. A long driveway leads back to a small, white two-story house. "We're here."

His words trigger my anxiety. I don't want to unbuckle my seat belt or leave the car, or for him to remove the key from the ignition. "You could go to Cross Pointe parties instead. It'd be a whole lot closer and good for you."

Jonah's smile looks suspiciously sneerish, but he's facing the windshield so I can only see half his face. "Good for me? How do you figure?"

Darn. Now I need an explanation. "Well, it'd be good for you because . . ." What would my father say? I search for a line from his book. "'Adapting to change is an important life skill.' You should embrace the fact that you live in Cross Pointe now and get involved."

That sounds sufficiently sane and is actually pretty true. Jonah apparently isn't a loner in Hamilton: the boys at the pizza place were cute and friendly; he has friends who throw parties and a girlfriend. For him to choose isolation now isn't normal or healthy.

His jaw shifts like he's grinding his teeth. "I leave for college in a few months, and I'm not coming back. Why bother?"

"Because you're missing out on things. Aren't you lonely? Everyone's really nice."

He continues staring out the window, the portion of his face I can see folded into disapproval. "They're nice to *you* because you're Brighton Waterford."

He gets out of the car and I scramble to follow, protesting as I shut my door. "No. They're just nice people! Do you know that *everyone* else in the school volunteered at least once this year? Wait, what does that mean? Because I'm *me*?" This has the flavor of an insult, but I'm not sure why.

He leans back against his car—the blue of his shirt blending with the blue frame in the semidarkness of the road. "Kindness is your social weapon of choice, but it only works because you've grown up within the system and it's what people *expect* of you. You get to be the 'nice one' only because you've got everyone trained to think you're so sweet and innocent."

"Trained?" I sputter. I can't even train Never. "That's not true."

"Oh yeah? I'll prove it. Give me your cell phone."

I hand it to him immediately . . . then realize I should ask: "Why do you want it?"

"Who's your best friend?"

"Amelia."

"Okay, I'm calling her." He presses the speakerphone button, and the rings echo off the empty street.

"Hey, B! Finally! Where've you been? I called you hours ago! Are we still going to Jeremy's, or do you want to rest up for tomorrow? I thought you'd be home early? How late does this couple stay out? I can't remember the last time my parents were awake past nine thirty. Not that I'm complaining."

"True or false," says Jonah when Amelia's excessive cheer dies off. "Being mean to Brighton's like kicking a puppy."

"Who is this? Jeremy? Did she go to the party without us? True. Though, not *her* puppy; Never'd slobber you to death. Who *is* this? Is she okay?"

"I'm fine, Amelia," I call.

"There you are! What's going on? Is someone being mean to you? Hold on—speakerphone—Peter, someone's being mean to Brighton."

"What? Our Brighton? Who?" He sounds baffled and angry. "You okay?"

"I'm fine. No one's being mean."

"Where are you?" Peter asks while Amelia adds, "Are you sure?"

"Hamilton," answers Jonah.

"Need us to come get you?" I can already hear Peter's keys jingling in the background.

"Why *Hamilton*?" I wince at the insult in Amelia's tone.

"I'm going to a party here."

"Party? Whose?"

"A friend of a friend's. It's fine. Promise."

"Which friend? We have the same friends! Who are you with? I feel like I should ask in case the cops are looking for you in the morning." Amelia's voice is one part concern and one part melodrama.

"Jonah Prentiss," he answers.

"Jonah? The new guy, Jonah?" In the pause before she continues I count in my head: *1-2-3-4.* "Brighton . . ."

"I'm fine."

"I know who that is. He used to be a hell of a baseball player," adds Peter.

"We don't know him. We don't know you, Jonah," states Amelia. "So you're definitely a no-go on Jeremy? I really thought you'd like him. Wait, I thought you were babysitting. How'd you end up in Hamilton?"

"I was babysitting Jonah's sister. It's fine and I'm fine. I'll call you tomorrow." I ignore her Jeremy remarks. I'd told her I wasn't interested *before* she set us up on the surprise movie date, after the movie date, and at least five times a day all week. Jeremy's a great guy, just not right for me.

"No. Wait. Speakerphone *off,* B."

I roll my eyes, but take the phone from Jonah, hit the button, and hold it to my ear. "Yes?"

"Do we like him?" she asks in her most serious voice.

"We don't know him, remember?"

"But *could* we like him? Please tell me this is not just about the volunteer thing. It's totally unfair for Mr. Donnelly to put so much pressure on you because he wants his name hanging in the hall. *Please* don't do anything stupid over that. Jonah's cute. Tell me this is because he's cute."

"It's not like that." Or it isn't *just* about the volunteer thing. I wish I could explain what it is like—but then I'd have to understand it myself.

"I don't believe you. But you're okay? Safe and stuff? Promise?"

"Yes. I'll call you tomorrow. 'Night, Ames." I hang up and start handing Jonah the phone before remembering it's mine and tucking it into my purse.

"I proved my point. Both of them jumped to your defense." He's a few steps farther away than I remember, kicking the curb.

"Of course they did, and not because they think I'm helpless—they're my friends." I hope crossing the distance between us emphasizes my next point. "I can't wait to meet yours."

We both turn to look at the house. The front door, which had been sealing in the music and conversations, opens to reveal a couple attached at the lips. Their bodies are entangled, and they stumble down the steps without breaking off their kiss.

I look away from them to Jonah. Does he kiss like that, like the only thing preventing him from suffocating is someone else's lips? Carly's lips, I mean.

I'm blushing and staring and he notices.

"What exactly were you answering with 'We don't know him'? How much of a loser Amelia thinks I am?"

"No! Not at all." We're standing far too close, but I'm not

backing off now. If he wants space, *he* can step back. But I can't answer either. My cheeks are already flaming; if I admit she was asking if I *like* him, I might combust. "Cross Pointe isn't evil, it's not unfriendly. You just need to give people a chance to get to know you. Tonight, I'll come to this party with you, and maybe next week you and Carly can come to one with Amelia and me. At least think about it."

He snorts. "Oh yes, we'd love that."

"Come on," I say taking a step toward the driveway. "Let's go inside and I'll invite her myself."

23

JONAH

☼ 11:03 P.M. ☽

O'CRAP O'CLOCK

The closer we get to Jeff's door, the more conflicted I feel about Carly. It's like all my anger has iced over. I don't know what I want to do anymore. Flaunt Brighton to make her jealous. Apologize. Yell. Pretend I don't care. Actually stop caring.

It's just that walking down this driveway, I can practically see the ghost of past parties. We'd be the couple kissing on the front steps. Or fighting on the driveway. Or dominating at Ping-Pong on the old, lopsided table in the basement. Or, most often, I'd be the guy stuck holding her beer so she could use both hands to reenact some gossip for her overeager and easily amused audiences.

I miss the days when we were new. When it was the two of us working the same shifts at Dairy Queen and she'd dare me to eat whatever ice cream–candy combinations she mixed up. Those nights I'd go home and stare at the ceiling of my old house too buzzed on kisses and candy to sleep.

I haven't felt like that in a while. And I think there's a lot more missing than a massive quantity of sugar.

We're at the front steps—I know I should tell Bright about the breakup, that she, named after crystal and just as delicate, could be shattered by the reception waiting on the other side of this door. I almost turn around and head back to my car. Almost.

But Brighton is old enough to take care of herself; confident that the world is full of good intentions and sweetness. It isn't my job to protect her. She's the one who insisted. She led the charge down the driveway.

Sink or swim time, Bright. Let's hope the world really is as nice as you claim. I hold the door and follow her into the Digginses' house.

The front hall's empty, but the lights and noise from the kitchen spill our way. Heads turn toward the open door, and people tumble out to meet me.

"Prentiss! How are you, man?" booms Sean. I still think of my former teammates by position; he'd been my second baseman. He's a good guy. Dependable. Laid-back.

Eliza hugs me tightly. "I heard from Sasha. How are you doing? I mean, with the whole thing?" The hug's a little too tight—her eyes and body giving not-so-subtle hints that she wouldn't mind being the one to cheer me up.

I say thanks and pry her off me, slapping palms with Felix and nodding to the crew behind him. Maybe this won't be so bad.

And then they notice I'm not alone.

"You're not Carly!" is Felix's brilliant reaction. Followed by a smirk and an equally brilliant, "But I'd like to get to know you."

She holds out a soft-skinned, green-nailed hand to my former first baseman. "Hi. I'm Brighton." And smiles at the group, utterly unaware that all hell's about to break loose.

"Bright-ton?" repeats someone, while Eliza crosses her arms and scoffs, "What kind of name is that?"

"A rich snob name, of course," answers a female voice. The speaker is out of sight but earns plenty of chuckles.

Bright lowers her unshaken hand. Felix isn't being rude—yet—he's just too busy gawking to notice.

"You're from Cross Pointe?" asks Sean.

She nods. "It's nice to meet you all. Jonah speaks highly of you and Hamilton."

Her speech is so formal and her posture's tin-soldier straight. Her hands are clasped in front of her around the handle of her bag—making her look like a kid playing tea party and reinforcing Cross Pointe's snotty reputation.

There are scoffs and laughter. More people join the crowd. It's about to be a massacre—she hasn't even taken ten steps and they're practically pushing one another out of the way so they can see her social takedown. Ready to hate her because of her zip code when all she's done is smile. I need to say something, anything, to defuse this, but before I can, she turns to Eliza and delivers the fatal words.

"Are you Carly? I'm dying to meet her!"

The room breaks into fifteen competing conversations. *"Cross Pointe snob!"* and *"Look at her!"* are distinct above the roar.

Brighton turns to me in confusion.

Eliza grabs her arm. "Are you kidding me? Jonah, is she kidding?"

Bright steps closer to me, not even realizing that she's

reinforcing the conclusions they're all jumping to. I'm tempted to step away, to physically demonstrate I'm not paired with her. Instead, I stay frozen and watch it unfold. This isn't what I planned.

"Priceless! Totally what Carly deserves." A catty voice slices through the room, but I'm too distracted to figure out who spoke.

"What's going on? What'd I say?" Brighton's eyes swim in hurt and reproach as she whispers her questions to me.

"Jonah, we should talk," says Jeff. He'd been my catcher and best friend. Yeah, we should talk, except there's too much to say. Months of stuff to say. Nothing will make any sense—but despite this, we should talk.

I follow Jeff through the kitchen, and Brighton follows me. Eliza shoots her predatory glances, someone whistles, and someone else offers a shout of encouragement. Really? There are people who are glad Carly and I broke up?

"Where is she?" I ask. Carly should be front and center, leading the attack or at least reaping a victim's share of sympathy.

"She's upset. She stayed home." Jeff's answer is sharp, an accusation.

The party crowd thins on the other side of the kitchen— away from the food and the game of flip cup taking place on the table. We hover by the door to his mom's home office, where Jeff used to be stuck reading for thirty minutes before he was allowed to join the rest of us playing catch in the park. He looks from Brighton to the room. I open the door.

"Bright. Sit here a minute, okay? I need to talk to Jeff. I'll go get you a drink. Water?"

"No. I want to know what's going on. Now." She plants a fist on each hip and stares up at me expectantly.

"I just need a minute. Then I'll introduce you to everyone." I try again to herd her into the office.

She resists. "I'm not going anywhere until you tell me what's going on."

"Suit yourself."

Before she follows up with another question, Jeff says, "Please tell me you work fast. Tell me there was no overlap. Carly's been obsessed with you cheating since your move. Now you show up with a new girl hours after you broke up?"

"Wait. What?" Her hands slip from her hips and she leans back, clutching the counter behind her.

I ask Jeff, "Have you talked to Carly? Has Maya?"

"Maya's spent half the night on the phone with her. Sasha's with Carly at her house." The crowd has moved, followed us. They're hoping for a scene and waiting for a chance to spit their questions and judgments. "God, Jonah, did you have do this tonight? My parents are only out of town for one night, and Maya's going to spend the whole time dealing with Carly's drama."

"*She* broke up with *me*." My answer's defensive, but does he really think this is what I wanted or how I expected to be spending Friday night? "Did you know she was going to? Thanks for giving me a heads-up."

"Time-out. My turn." Bright pushes her way between the two of us. "You and Carly broke up? Today? *What?*"

I don't get to answer because Eliza invites herself into the conversation, "Can you blame her?"

"Yes!" Brighton turns toward her. "He's crazy about her!"

I groan. She may be well intentioned, but she's not helpful.

Eliza chokes on her indignation, and more people press around us. "You're going to stand here—the one he cheated with—and defend that? Bingley, it's too bad you've got all that money and no way to buy yourself some *class*."

I'm trapped in the corner between the door and a wall of gossip-hungry ex-classmates. And Brighton.

"What?" She sputters the word, her face as red as the rooster painting hanging on the wall behind her.

"Let's not be too hasty," Felix adds. "She's pretty smoking. I never would've thought Prentiss had it in him—juggling two of them? You're a god."

"So it's true?" Maya joins the group, her cell clutched in one hand, her cheek still imprinted with its outline.

"Wait! Just wait a second," I say. Everything's going to hell. This is the lie I wanted to sell, yet now that people are saying it, now that Brighton's face is crumpling under their accusations, it's all so screwed up.

"We aren't dating," she protests.

Felix whistles. "A god. A god I tell you, if he can get that girl without having to date her."

Maya's pushing through the crowd to Jeff's side. "Oh, Carly . . . ," she simpers into the phone, "No, she's really not *that* pretty. Honest."

"Is she looking at the same girl as me?" Felix asks the room.

Eliza snorts. "I bet she sleeps with anyone."

"Shut the hell up!" I bellow. The group stands with their mouths open, fingers frozen above cell phones. "You don't know what the hell you're talking about. I never cheated on Carly."

There are tears in the corners of Brighton's eyes, but she's blinking them away. Her voice is soft. "Jonah? I don't understand."

"There isn't sex ed in Cross Pointe? What's to understand?" Eliza's scorn makes me want to muzzle her.

"You've got it all wrong," Brighton protests.

When the murmurs and doubts continue, her voice goes higher. "The idea is ridiculous. I've barely even spoken to him before tonight. I was babysitting his little sister."

I turn to face her, blocking her view of the crowd and its of her. She looks like a caged animal, her eyes flickering around the room. Her posture screams panic. I keep my voice quiet and try to calm her: "Don't worry about it. I'll explain later."

"No. Why would they even think that? What have you been telling people? Is this why you were so desperate to get me to come to the party?" She pushes past me. "Jonah's not dating me. Or anyone in Cross Pointe. No one in CPHS even knows who he is."

24

Brighton

☼ 11:11 P.M. ☽

13 HOURS, 49 MINUTES LEFT

Jonah gapes. Someone in the crowd makes a taunting *ohhhh* sound. And I can't stand to be in this crush of judgmental strangers for even another second.

"Excuse me. Excuse me. Excuse me." I have to ask every person individually before they move aside and let me pass. Someone steps on my bandaged toes, and I mash my hands into fists to keep from crying out.

"Bright. Wait!"

I'm done listening to Jonah. I say, "Excuse me," to the last girl standing between me and the front door. I know I'm demonstrating just how very "flight" I am, but I also know it's justified.

Jonah catches up with me about seven steps into the lawn. He puts a hand on my wrist and pulls me to a stop. "Will you just wait five seconds so I can explain?"

My eyes go from his frustrated face to the open front door where a crowd waits for more drama. They're pushing one another to have front-row viewing and actually manage to knock a kid off the steps and into the bushes.

Jonah turns and yells "Back off!" and flips his middle finger before pulling me a few steps farther across the lawn and out of sight.

He looks at me and sighs. I refuse to let myself feel sympathy. Feel anything but anger.

"Why didn't you tell me about the breakup?" I demand. "Why exactly did you bring me to this party? To embarrass me?"

"Yeah, because you didn't embarrass *me*? Thanks for calling me a loser in front of all of my friends."

"At least I told the truth! You don't get to play story time with my reputation."

"It was a misunderstanding. I'll explain."

"Like they'll listen! They've already decided I'm a horrible person! Is everyone in Hamilton so rude? Do they always assume the worst and attack before they know the facts? How can you possibly be friends with people like that?"

"Spoken like a true, judgmental Cross Pointe snob," he retorts.

I flinch, taking a step backward and holding up a hand so he doesn't come any closer. "*I'm* judgmental? They even attacked my name!"

"Um, guys? Sorry to interrupt."

I hadn't heard them approaching, but there's a guy and a girl standing a step behind Jonah. It was the girl who'd spoken, and she doesn't sound sorry at all. "Hi, I'm Maya. This is Jeff. I need to borrow Jonah for a minute."

"Take him for as long as you'd like. I'm done with him."

"Brighton, just—" He holds his hands up in a helpless shrug.

"Go. Your friends want to talk to you—I don't. I'll call Amelia for a ride."

"Bright, please . . ."

I huff as he gets my name wrong—again.

"Good-bye, Jonah." I turn my back to him and don't exhale until their voices are shut behind the slamming of the front door. Then I bend over, hands braced against my knees, and try to breathe. I can't. I can't believe. He just—

I won't let myself cry. He's not worth crying over. I thought I was making progress. I thought we were almost friends. I thought he was cute.

But then again, I also thought he needed me. Needed a friend in Cross Pointe and someone to be nice to him. After seeing how he swaggered through that door and the way everyone here flocked to see him, it's clear the last thing he needs is another friend. He's got a houseful of people who care about him, and *they* don't want me anywhere near him.

I fish my cell out of my bag. There's a text from Silvia on the screen: **OMG! You'll NEVER guess—**

I close it without reading the rest. I don't want to guess right now. Or gush. Or smile. Or stress about whether every word I say is what someone wants to hear.

I just want to go home.

I can't be crying when I call Amelia. She'd call the police and have them come wait with me. Or yell at Peter to break every traffic law and get here faster.

I gulp a deep breath. Hold it a beat. Take myself to the same mental place as before a complicated dive. Exhale.

Dial.

Voice mail.

"Dammit!" I stamp my foot. Gasp. The pain rocketing from my toes is excruciating. I can't breathe or swear or cry.

"Hey, it's Amelia—but you already know that since *you* called *me*—" begins to play in my ear, but I hang up before the beep. I don't even have the address for her to plug into her GPS.

I head down the driveway to get the street name and number off the mailbox and then call Peter. If he doesn't answer, I guess it's Evy, though the thought makes me cringe. She won't let me live this down, even though it's her fault I'm here to begin with. If she hadn't been home, I would never have said yes. I wouldn't be stuck in some sketchy town at a party full of people who think I'm one step up from an expensive pole dancer.

Black plastic numbers on the wooden pole read "3845."

But 3845 what? I don't even know the street name. I lean against the mailbox and look down the cracked stretch of asphalt, trying to figure out which way to walk to find a street sign.

There's a group of fireflies in the bushes at the far edge of the yard. They show up as little more than pinpricks of light in the darkness. Blinking yellow, then disappearing, and one strange one that glows the color of solid flame. A mystery that's solved when a shadow detaches from a tree trunk and taints the muggy air with the smell of cigarette smoke. He steps closer, passing through the flickering light of a streetlamp and revealing a guy who is taller and bigger than Jonah. He crosses to me with a confident swagger, then leans across the mailbox.

"No, you don't. I caught you."

"What?"

"Every time Jeff throws a party, the mailbox gets destroyed. Smashed with a baseball bat. Or egged. Last time someone used a cherry bomb, and we had to pick up mailbox shards from all over the yard. It was not fun to do while hungover. Please don't make me do that again."

He's smiling.

"I'm not going to. I just needed the address. Is this your house? Are you related to Jeff?"

"Jeff's my little bro." The guy grins wider. "I'm Digg."

"*Digg*?" I ask, then realize how rude I sound. "I'm Brighton."

"*Brighton*?" he repeats in parody of my question, but he smiles again. "Digg's short for Diggins, my last name. And, you know, I think I'm going to believe your address story. You look too sweet to be involved with mailbox sabotage. I'm glad I found you. It's like you were an angel just waiting to be discovered."

I blush and laugh. "Well, I don't know about that."

Digg laughs too. "That was even cheesier out loud than it was in my head, but you can't blame a guy for trying. Can we make a pact to forget I ever said that?"

He's got these amazing blue eyes, so bright I can see them in the streetlight, and the type of eye contact that makes it possible to admire them without staring. "I'll think about it," I tease.

He stubs out a cigarette butt on the post. "C'mon, now that you've seen the driveway, I'll give you a tour of the rest of the house."

"Actually, I was leaving. I just need to call a friend with the address. Speaking of which, 3845 *what?*"

"Oakmont. But at least let me wait with you until your ride comes."

Digg is handsome and seems harmless; best of all, he wasn't there to see everything that went down. I nod.

"Good, but let's wait inside. Away from rogue eggs or mailbox debris when the inevitable happens." He slings a hand around my shoulder and leads me back down the driveway.

His hand is *huge*; it engulfs my whole shoulder and part of my arm. He seems taller now that I'm standing next to him; my head barely matches the height of his bulky shoulders. Yet his hand and eyes aren't anywhere near my chest and he's left a friend-sized space between us. I don't even feel a twinge of what Amelia calls "perv alert."

"Why do people destroy your mailbox?"

Digg chuckles. "Damned if I know. Probably because my dad works for the post office. Guess it's supposed to be funny?"

"Oh." Definitely doesn't sound funny to me. I move to turn back across the lawn, already nervous about the reception waiting on the other side of the front door, but Digg doesn't follow.

"C'mon." He gestures toward a door off the garage. "Let's go to the basement."

Since the party was in the kitchen, I agree.

Except the basement is more crowded than the kitchen—the sounds of electronic explosions, shouts, music, and chatter all compete within the large rectangular room. The white tile floor does nothing to absorb any of the noise, and every sound echoes: the splash of a cup that's knocked off the Ping-Pong table by an accidental elbow, the soundtrack of a video game, the yells of the players seated in rocker chairs on the floor, the squeal of a girl who slides in the spilled beer, and a chorus of "chug, chug" from a trio of guys.

I almost accuse Digg of lying to me—I wanted to find a quiet place to make a phone call, not to join the center of the party—but then I realize that the assumption was mine, not anything he said.

We're separated from most of the chaos by a beat-up gray sectional couch. It's facing away from the action, toward the stairs, a small bar area, and the door that opens to the driveway. Digg flops down on it—momentarily distracting its only other occupants: a couple tangled at lips and legs. They look over, smile, and reengage.

I sit next to him. Feeling awkward and then uncomfortable when he spreads his legs to cover the space between us and my thigh ends up touching his. Trying to make it look like a casual shift, I lean away from him. Digg doesn't move any closer. I'm being an idiot. That's how guys sit—I'm overreacting. One night with Jonah and I'm seeing danger everywhere. This guy looks like he stepped out of an advertisement for Abercrombie: clean-cut, welcoming smile, and a T-shirt and shorts broken in to fit him perfectly. I need to stop ogling him and think of a conversation topic, but he beats me to it.

"So how come I don't know you already, Brighton?"

"I don't live in Hamilton. I came with Jonah Prentiss— we're just friends."

"Ah, Prentiss. I haven't seen him in ages. I'll have to catch up with him later."

"He moved—to Cross Pointe, that's where I'm from."

Digg nods. "Now it makes sense. I've been going through the yearbook in my head, trying to figure out how I could forget someone like you. Cross Pointe, huh? So Prentiss brought you slumming?"

I sit straight up on the couch. "What? No! I would never say that, or even think it!"

"Relax, I'm just teasing you." He puts a hand on my arm and gives me a gentle shake. "Loosen up a little. After being at college for a year, I could care less where people come from. And I'm hardly going to complain about a new, gorgeous face at a party where I've known most everyone since they were grade school booger-eaters."

He's right, I'm totally on edge and acting like a priss, but even talking to someone welcoming, it's hard to shake the feeling that I'm on hostile turf. I exhale, then make the conscious decision to lean back and smile. "Where do you go to school?"

"I'm a freshman at State. Got home on Tuesday."

"My sister's a sophomore at Glenn Mary; she flew in today. She said her first week home last year was like readjusting to life on another planet."

"It's not so bad. I mean, it's weird reconnecting with everyone from high school. And it sucks having rules and curfews again, but it's good to have my mom do my laundry and get food from a cabinet, not a cafeteria."

"It's got to be nice being done with finals for the year. I still have two weeks and all that stress standing between me and summer."

"Ah." He nods. "Is that why you're so tense? Damn finals."

He moves like he might give me a back rub, so I sit up

and lean away, pointing to the various baseball pennants and paraphernalia tacked to the walls around the room. "Are you a Phillies fan?"

"Hells, yeah! Aren't you?" He leans in to finger the edge of a poster tacked to the wall behind my head.

"Sure." I try to think of a follow-up question.

"Good, because I'd hate to have to despise you. You're too damn pretty to despise."

I blush and roll my eyes. He's flirting, yes, but it's casual. Familiar. In fact, his praise makes me *more* comfortable. In control. I know how to respond to guys in these situations. It's Jonah's personalized barbs I can't handle.

"Let's grab drinks and I'll give you a tour of the rest of the house."

"The rest?" I instinctively lean even farther away. "That's okay, I don't need to see the bedrooms."

Digg laughs far too loud—people turn to see what's so funny, and while I couldn't answer if they asked, I find myself laughing along. He stops only when he starts coughing. Then he puts a hand on my shoulder like he's so winded he can't hold himself up.

"You kill me. I didn't mean the upstairs. I mean the kitchen and stuff."

"Oh. I've already seen them." And have no desire to revisit the site of the earlier drama or run into any of those people. "Let's stay here."

"How about Ping-Pong? One of the perks of it being my table is I can call next game anytime." Digg's stretching his legs out in front of him and drumming his thumbs on the couch. I can tell he's getting bored, that he doesn't want to just sit any longer, but when I look behind me at the party crowd, I see all the faces that attacked me in the kitchen.

"I'm hopeless at Ping-Pong."

He's on his feet and holding out a hand. "Then you've come to the right place. I've got skillz with a z, and I might be willing to teach you."

"I'm fine right here." I sound painfully lame and rude. Any second he's going to bail and I'll be left alone again. "Maybe in a little bit. Tell me more about school."

Digg's still standing in the middle of the tile floor. He shrugs and points to a mini-fridge. "Drink?"

"Diet Coke?"

He crouches and opens the fridge. "Okay. What do you want in it?"

"Just Diet Coke. I'm not drinking tonight." I watch his back, which is wider than the little fridge.

He turns around with a snort. "Why the hell not? This is a party, you know."

"I know, but I have plans in the morning." Speaking of which, it's getting late and I have to try Amelia again. I pull my phone from my purse—11:30.

"One drink won't kill you."

"No, thank you. I'll stick to soda tonight." I text her. **Call me.**

He smiles at me over his shoulder. "Compromise: a shot, then a Coke chaser."

My phone is still silent. Where is she? I can taste frustration on the back of my teeth as I answer: "Just the soda. Thanks."

"Suit yourself. Diet Pepsi okay, or are you a Coke purist?

There's probably one here somewhere . . . ," he says over the metallic fumblings of cans being jostled.

I exhale, relieved he finally let it go. "Either is fine."

There's the hiss of two cans popping open, and he takes a swig from one and fumbles some more. I send Amelia another message: **You there?** I consider texting Peter too—most likely Amelia's lost her phone or let the battery run out.

"Trying to find you a straw. I know there are some down here."

"That's okay, I don't need one."

I start to stand. I could get twenty sodas in the time it's taken him to find one. Digg slams the fridge, passes me the can, and sits back on the couch. He's opened a beer for himself and raises an eyebrow as he sips it. "You're sure you're good with a soda? I'd be a bad host if I didn't ask one last time."

"I'm sure." I'm sick of this conversation and the insinuation that I'll be more fun if I'm drinking. I don't feel like "being fun" tonight. I feel like getting home. Why hasn't Amelia gotten back to me yet? I could excuse myself to go find the bathroom, but then what? My alternative to sitting here and making awkward conversation is to go outside and hope I don't get hit by mailbox debris while waiting for my phone to beep or ring. At least down here with Digg I blend in. And it shouldn't be much longer. I hope.

25

JONAH

☼ 11:13 P.M. ☽

EPIC FAIL

"Do you think she's okay?" We're standing in the foyer, and I'm waiting for Jeff or Maya to get around to telling me whatever the hell they thought was so important. Trying to pay attention to them when all I want to do is go find Brighton and make her listen to whatever version of the truth it takes for her to forgive me.

"I think," says Maya, "that you're a tool for coming here with *that* girl."

"Why did you, man?" asks Jeff. "I mean, assuming you're *not* sleeping with her, and from her reaction, I'd say that's pretty clear."

I look out the window. She's gone. She really left.

"I don't know."

"Well, as much as I hated to interrupt your screaming match—and she deserved a chance to rip you a new one—you should know we have an incoming: Carly's on her way," says Jeff.

I groan. "I can't do this tonight."

"And she's out for blood," adds Maya, shifting her hands to her hips. "Can you blame her?"

"Hey." Jeff slides an arm around her waist. "Calm down."

"But—"

"Carly's more than capable of serving Jonah his balls on a plate—sorry, man, you know it's true—don't let it ruin our night. Please?" He kisses the tip of her nose, and Maya fights to stay frowning.

"Fine. I'm going to go call and see when she'll get here. And let her know that girl left." Maya flounces out of the room, but not without giving me one last angry look.

"Her cell phone battery can't last much longer, right?" Jeff jokes. "Come on, let's get you a drink."

He gets one for each of us, and we sit on barstools in his kitchen. He's telling a story about Maya or baseball. Or maybe about Maya at one of his games. He punches my arm lightly to get my attention. "You know, watching the door isn't going to make her appear any faster—or slower."

"Yeah." I pry my eyes off it and face him. "Do you think she'll be okay? She won't go wandering off and end up on Brunswick Street or anything, right?"

"Brighton?" He blinks and looks confused. "From the way she handled *you*, my guess is she'll be just fine. I'd start worrying about Carly."

But he doesn't know Brighton. And she doesn't know Hamilton. I should never have let her leave by herself.

"And here she is," says Jeff, and I whip around, ready to talk about green nail polish or the library thing or whatever— as long as she's in one piece and willing to forgive me. But it's Carly whose voice carries into the room.

Maya's back is the first thing to emerge from the front hall—she's walking backward and gushing sympathy at Carly. Next is Sasha's white-blond hair hanging straight down around her angry face.

Carly's last to enter, stepping from behind the other two. I can see the evidence of how her night's gone. Though her makeup's been fixed and her hair's styled into some complicated braid thing, her eyes are puffy and there are telltale she's-been-sobbing blotches outside the lines of her cherry lip gloss.

She's pissed: her posture, the straight line of her eyebrows, and her smashed-together lips make this clear. But she's shaken too. Her hands are more hugging herself than crossed.

Carly steps forward. "How could you?"

She doesn't wait for an answer, marches past me and grabs either side of Felix's face. Kisses him. An exaggerated kiss where she rakes her hands through his hair and breaks apart with a sucking sound.

"How did that make you feel?" she demands and I wonder if I look half as shocked as Felix does. To him she says, "Thanks."

He manages a dizzy-looking leer and says, "Anytime."

"Well?" she asks, shaking her hands in my direction. She makes a sound of disgust and storms out of the kitchen. Maya stays to glare at me, but Sasha follows her and then a door slams upstairs.

I look at my full cup, tempted to gulp it down. Instead I slide it toward Jeff and Maya. I stand. He gives me a punch in the shoulder. "Good luck."

26

Brighton

☼ 11:32 P.M. ☽

13 HOURS, 28 MINUTES LEFT

"Hey, Brighton. Jonah thought you left." The couple from earlier comes down the stairs and heads straight for Digg and me. It was Jeff who spoke—he's actually smiling, but his girlfriend isn't.

Digg clearly doesn't appreciate his brother butting in, because before I can answer, he's already asking, "What do you want?"

They both ignore him, so I do too, playing with the tab on my untouched soda as I answer, "I'm waiting to hear back from a ride. Tell him not to worry, I'll be gone soon."

"You can't leave already. It's early," says Digg. He puts a hand on my arm, like he expects me to bolt out the door this very moment. His touch makes me want to. I pull away.

"Stay," agrees Jeff. "Jonah will be glad you did."

"Where is he, anyway?" I ask, ignoring the blatant lie.

"He's with Carly," says Maya. "Knowing those two, it's probably going to be a while. I'm sure they're getting back together. He looked *so sad*."

I keep my face perfectly still, frozen in a socially acceptable bland expression.

Jeff shrugs. "I think they're done. So tell me about Cross Pointe. What's our boy doing if he's not playing baseball?"

"Was he any good?" I ask.

Digg chokes on his beer, and Maya almost drops her cup. Even Jeff is looking at me like I'm crazy. "Yeah. He was an All-State pitcher sophomore and junior year."

"Oh." My cheeks go hot, but really, why should I be embarrassed? It's not like Jonah voluntarily shares information about himself with me, or anyone at Cross Pointe. I do know the CP team roster, though, so I can say with a 100 percent certainty: "He doesn't play anymore."

"We know. So what's he up to? What'd you mean by 'no one knows him'?" Jeff asks, sitting on the arm of the couch next to me. Maya fits herself against him, and the two of them look at me expectantly.

"Um . . ." The blush has spread from my cheeks to my neck. I can't think of a single thing to tell them, and they're starting to exchange looks as my silence drags on. Do they think I'm hiding something or that I'm the type of girl who apparently goes to a party with complete strangers? I wish I could spin the question around: ask *them* about *him*. Or the version of Jonah that lived in Hamilton, because *he* seems completely different from the guy I pass in Cross Pointe's halls.

"He . . ." I pause again. "He just does the typical stuff, I guess."

"Yeah. I guess." Jeff looks disappointed. Maya squints suspiciously.

They watch me through another few seconds of video-game gun noises, then she takes Jeff's hand and tugs him away. "I'm bored. Let's check what's going on upstairs."

Digg gives them a curt wave, then turns back to me. "Little brothers suck, huh?"

I smile noncommittally and check my phone.

27

JONAH

☼ 11:34 P.M. ☽

MY LIFE IN PAST TENSE

I trudge up the stairs and rap my knuckles on Jeff's bedroom door. "Carly."

"Go away, Jonah."

The thing is, I didn't feel anything when she kissed Felix. Maybe because I knew it was her being petty. Maybe because I was too surprised to be jealous. Or maybe . . .

I take a deep breath and knock again.

"She doesn't want to talk to you," says Sasha.

Walking away now is tempting. I can say I tried and go back downstairs and get blitzed, or just go out to my car and leave. Maybe I can drive around until I find Brighton. If she called someone from Cross Pointe for a ride, they can't be here yet. And maybe she'll listen to me.

Not likely.

I look at the door again. I've seen Carly and Ana in these situations so many times. But this fight isn't about a shirt that was borrowed and stained or snooping through someone else's text messages. I don't feel like participating in all the screaming and name calling that the Santos girls go through before they get to their "I'm sorrys" and hugs.

But ours isn't the sort of history I can shrug off. Or want to shrug off. Years and years of friendship before it changed to girlfriend and boyfriend. I've texted her first thing in the morning every day since I've had a cell phone, and except for the rare fights we've had over the past two years, I've ended every night with her voice breathing, "sweet dreams" in the phone at my ear. My stomach twists when I think of a lifetime of mornings and bedtimes without her. And without her, the only action my phone will see will be Mom calling to ask me to pick up diapers or tell me when to be home for hellish family dinners.

I knock harder.

"Carly, I know you didn't come all the way over here just to kiss Felix. Come out so we can talk."

The door opens a crack, and one of Carly's red-rimmed eyes peers out. "What do you have to say?"

"I'm not doing this through a door and with an audience." Sasha's standing on Jeff's bed to see over Carly's head. "Let's go outside."

"Don't listen to him. He's only going to tell you more lies," says Sasha.

"Carly. Please." The door opens some more, and I put a hand on her shoulder. "Come on."

"Fine. But don't expect me to believe a word you say." She shakes off my fingers, then turns and leads the way down the stairs and through the front door like it was her idea.

I follow her outside, but I'm moving slower.

"What are you doing?" She's backtracked from the driveway to where I've paused on the lawn. Unless Brighton's ducked behind a hedge in some twisted version of hide-and-seek, she's really not here.

I can't win. Whether I lie or I tell the truth, whether Carly believes me or doesn't. So the question that remains is simple: How much of my pride do I want to maintain?

"I'm looking for Brighton."

She pulls her shoulders back and meets my eyes with a gaze that's all cool anger. "Want to know how I knew you were cheating? You could never handle being alone for most of the week. You hate being alone."

This stuns me because it's not true anymore. I did. I hated being alone—and it used to be I never was. Days started with texting Carly, eating breakfast in her kitchen or in her car on the way to school. Classes/hallway/lunch were one nonstop group conversation, and afternoons meant playing baseball with Marcos on the days I didn't have practice with the team. Then homework, dinner with my parents, followed by video games with the guys or a shift at work with Carly, a movie or some TV with making out or more if her siblings weren't around, and a phone call before I went to bed.

Maybe loneliness is an acquired taste, or maybe it's like plunging your hand in ice water—it hurts like hell in the beginning, and then you go numb. Either way, I'm good at being alone now. An expert.

"For the last time, I'm not cheating. I'm looking for her—so she can tell you we're not sleeping together and you can tell her that *I'm* not the one who's gone around telling people we are."

I brace myself for an argument. Another twelve rounds of *"you're* lying/am not."

But when Carly opens her mouth and asks, "Why are you here?" the sentiment isn't anger, it's disappointment.

"I don't know." It's one of the most honest things I've said all night.

"You need to do better than 'I don't know,' because I can't think of a single reason that doesn't make you a complete jerk. Either you wanted to rub my face in it or if you're telling the truth and nothing has happened between you two, then you wanted to call me a liar and humiliate her." Carly's words make my stomach sink. Both reasons are too close to true. I *am* a complete jerk—I'm worse than a jerk. "You weren't always like this. I felt guilty when you left—but Sasha said not to and she was right, because a couple hours later you're showing up here with the very girl you swore you've never touched. It doesn't matter if that's true anymore. I don't know you."

"Carly. Carly! Stop!" My voice echoes off parked cars and tree limbs. It's loud enough for them to potentially hear in the basement. Even over the music. "I don't know what you want from me."

"She's exactly what I was afraid of." This is Carly's vulnerable voice. The one that cries during ASPCA commercials or calls me at two a.m. to tell me she misses me.

"What do you mean?" Without thinking, I lean forward and cup her elbows. It's natural to touch her. Unnatural to stand apart.

"Jonah, you had no choice about the move—I get that— but you never let me into your new life. We used to share everything, and now I only get a part of you. I don't understand. What's so good about Cross Pointe that you couldn't share with me?"

"So *good*?" I step back and take a deep breath. Then take another one. My hands are shaking. My voice is too. "You want to hear the truth about my new life, Carly?"

The words are a boulder, sitting on my chest, crushing the air from my lungs and making it impossible to lift my head and look at her when I continue. "It sucks. I hate Cross Pointe. I'm a loser there. Both at school—where I'm invisible and ignorable—and at home, where I'm a disappointment and a screwup. I spend my whole week wishing I were *here* and avoiding talking to anyone *there*."

My confessions poured out in rushes. Now I'm breathless and panting as I wait for her reaction. Wait for her to laugh or scoff.

Or . . . shrug. "Jonah, it's a *town*. You moved, okay? It's not the end of the world. People move all the time—you need to start dealing with it. People *change* all the time. You can't go flipping out because I dye my hair or get a new job or apply to a college you didn't know about. Life didn't just freeze because you live in Cross Pointe now."

"Whatever. I didn't say it did." I'm leaning away, shoving my hands in my pockets.

"Come on! Quitting baseball. Asking a zillion questions about everyone *here* but not offering a single detail about your life there—it makes so much more sense now."

"Don't act like you've got me all figured out."

"But I *do*." She reaches out and touches my shoulder. "Jonah, I know you. I guess I just didn't realize how hard this move was for you."

She approaches me and holds out her arms. I lean into the hug, and she rests her head in the space between my shoulder and chin, a space that's always seemed designed for her. I inhale the scent of her hair spray and cherry lip gloss while I rub her shoulder. Too relieved, exhausted, and surprised to say anything.

"You should've told me," she coos. "I would've understood."

"I *tried* to tell you. You were too busy giving me shopping lists."

"What?"

"All you ever want to hear are stories about their money."

"What!" she repeats. It's not a question this time, and she's leaning back to look up at me. "When have I *ever* cared about money or designers? I think you might be confusing me with Brighton."

"How about when you asked to see the label on my new jeans?"

"Um, to get you *out* of them?"

"And the limo, and the earrings, and cupcakes from that ridiculous CP bakery. Do you know how expensive all that is? I don't have a job anymore, Carly. I'm scraping the bottom of my bank account to get you all these things you 'need' to be happy."

"*I need?* Jonah, you used to talk nonstop about how ridiculous everyone was with their money. It was the one thing you *would* talk about." She's blinking back tears. "The limo was fun, the earring are pretty—but what I really wanted was for you to say, 'I still love you.' I wanted you not to be too embarrassed to bring me to Cross Pointe. I wanted to walk down their Main Street holding hands, without you worrying that everyone who saw us would think I was your maid or something."

"They wouldn't have." This was a truth I wouldn't have believed earlier in the night, but that didn't make it any less true. "Carly, they're not like that. At least, not most of them."

"I wish you'd just been honest with me. I don't want us to fight anymore."

"Me either," I say.

She reaches up and places a thumb on each of my temples, rubbing gently at tension I hadn't paid attention to until then. It makes me smile, thinking of all the other times she's massaged away stress: before my baseball games, after the SATs, all those nights when my parents yelled and yelled and I escaped to the cheerful chaos of her house.

Then she's pulling my head down. Kissing me. My mouth responds. Immediately. Instinctively. But it no longer feels right.

I turn my head to break the kiss and end up with a mouthful of braided hair. "What are you doing?"

She tries to smile; it looks forced and wobbly. Her voice when she tries to tease sounds fake. "Jo-nah! You really need a definition?"

"You broke up with me."

"Yeah, but I get it now that you explained." She tries to slide her hands up my chest. "Don't you think we could . . . I mean, shouldn't we *try*?"

"No." I take a step back and cross my arms, too surprised by her actions and my answer to elaborate.

"Is this because of Brighton?"

I swallow and look around the driveway, like her name

could make her appear. God, I hope she's okay. "It has nothing to do with Cross Pointe. It's about *me . . . us.* I don't think our breakup was a mistake."

"Since when?" She's giving me a don't-be-an-idiot look.

"Since . . ." *Since I realized that the most appealing part of dating you is your zip code.* I can't stay with her for her access to my old life or because then I can pretend my whole world hasn't changed. "We had two great years . . . but it hasn't been good lately."

"You get that I believe you now, right?" she says, but she's taking a step backward too. "I know you never cheated."

"Yeah, but it was never just about that flyer. If we were still solid you would've laughed at that. Or *asked* me. We don't work anymore—you just noticed sooner than I did."

Carly looks embarrassed, but when she stops shaking her head, her expression has hardened. "You're making a mistake."

"Well, it's not the first one I've made tonight." I reach out to touch her hair. A farewell gesture that can't be interpreted as an invitation for more. "I'm sorry."

She jerks away, hands going up to smooth her braids. It's an excuse to lower her head, not because she cares about her hairstyle. She whispers, "I guess that means good-bye, Jonah," before running across the driveway and yanking open the door to the basement and the heart of the party.

28

Brighton

13 HOURS, 18 MINUTES LEFT

The door from the driveway slams shut behind a girl.

A short girl. A pretty girl with a crown of braids and a pissed-off expression.

It's her.

The girl whose picture was in the frame I dropped and destroyed.

Carly.

She's scanning the room. I pull my shoulders in, slide down on the couch cushion. While trying to become invisible I unintentionally lean closer to Digg. He responds by putting an arm on the back of the couch, his thumb touching the bare skin inside the collar of my dress. I want to jerk away, but I want to remain unseen more.

Carly calls to someone at the Ping-Pong table. She crosses the room to join the group of players. I don't exhale until she's passed the couch. Only then do I pull away from the finger that Digg's started tracing along the back of my neck and open my mouth to tell him a hasty I've-got-to-go-*now*.

I'm not fast enough.

"Oh. My. God. You're her!" The words make my skin prickle. For a millisecond I think Digg's touching me again, but no, his hand is hovering near my shoulder. I see it when I turn to look. Carly's stopped just beyond the couch. She's shoulder to shoulder with the girl who hugged Jonah when we arrived, and the girl's expression is pure vindictive victory. Her finger is still pointed at me.

Carly back steps until she's directly in front of me. "*You're* the girl from Cross Pointe. He said you left—what the hell are you still doing here?"

I flinch from her words. Her anger. Flinch right back into Digg, whose hand clamps down on my shoulder and pulls me toward him. The movement throws me off-balance and I almost fall into his lap. The hand I throw out to stop myself braces against the bare skin of his knee.

Carly's eyes narrow. She smirks and shakes her head. "And now you're hanging out with *him*?"

Digg laughs. "Nice to see you too. Want to catch up on *our* old times later?" He ends his statement with a wink.

She curls her lip in disgust. "Go to hell, Daniel. And take her with you."

"Cute, as always," Digg—Daniel?—answers. "I forgot how feisty you are."

I'm so aware of the fact that I haven't said anything yet. But this makes it even harder to form words. I don't know what to deny first or how to stand up to her accusations.

"Actually, this is perfect." She laughs, but it's not friendly. "No. Seriously, you two are just perfect together. Don't let me interrupt."

She reaches out, and I think she's going to hit me. I

squeeze my eyes shut and tense for the blow. I'm caught off guard when she shoves my shoulder instead, sending me careening back into Digg's lap. His arms tighten around me, and when I open my eyes, his are looming close. His whole face is too close, his beer breath sticky on my cheeks.

"Careful, angel."

I yank myself out of his grip and away from him. Carly's gone to join the group. Digg's scooting closer on the couch. "What was that about?" he asks.

I pick up my soda and raise the can to my mouth, ready to avoid answering and hide my embarrassment behind a sip. Before my lips close around the rim, a coconut smell makes me freeze. I hold out the can like it's radioactive. "This isn't just Pepsi."

Digg shrugs and taps his can against mine. "I splashed a little fun in it. Drink up."

I stand. "I told you I didn't want to drink."

"Ahhh, c'mon, I even used the flavored rum—it'll taste like candy." He reaches for my wrist, but I take another step back.

"I told you I didn't want to drink." My voice is louder, but my words are the same. I don't need any additional arguments.

"Man, you're wound tight. That's 'zactly why you need to be a good girl and drink up. You'll have a much better time if you relax." He chugs.

My breath is coming in quick gasps. "Listen, asshole, what part of *no* don't you understand?"

I could just let this go. Should probably just leave.

Flight.

I'm flight, and everything in me wants to run away from this. But I can't. It's the condescension. It's the disrespect. It's the assumption that his agenda of getting me drunk is more important than my decision not to drink.

I tip the can, angling it over him. It takes Digg a second or two to react, and then another second for the reaction to move from wide eyes and a gaping mouth to grabbing the can from my hand. It isn't close to empty, but there's a satisfyingly sized wet spot on the crotch of his shorts.

"You're dead," he snarls, standing up and seizing my arm.

29

JONAH

☀ 11:47 P.M. ☽

A QUARTER TO, I'M GOING TO KILL HIM

When Felix strolls by, I'm sitting on the trunk of my car try-ing to decide if I need to say good-bye to Jeff, or if it's better for everyone if I just leave.

"That Cross Pointe girl gets around," he says with a grin. He's carrying a lighter and something in a brown bag, en route to do who-gives-a-crap to the mailbox.

"Brighton? What do you mean?" I demand, already stand-ing up. My stomach sours. Something about his smile makes me want to punch it off his face.

"She's in the basement with Digg." Felix waggles his eyebrows.

I'm tearing up the walk, cursing her for having no sense of self-preservation. Digg? Really? No girl who's interested in ending the night clothed hangs out with him. I get that she doesn't know his I-get-it-on-with-anything-with-boobs his-tory, but how could she not see that he's skeezy? How could she possibly be interested in *him*?

Jeff and Maya are kissing in the front hall. They break apart as I throw the door open.

Maya asks, "How'd it go with Carly?"

I ignore her and round on Jeff. "Your brother?" I snarl. "You left Brighton alone with *your brother*? Are you insane?"

"She's fine. They're just sitting—"

I'm already halfway down the basement stairs, my feet only touching every third, fourth step. I'm sweating.

I hear his voice first. He's yelling. "You did *not* just do that!"

Digg's standing in front of the couch, a tipped-over beer at his feet, a soda can in one hand, the other clenched around Brighton's wrist.

"Let go of her!" I can already see the scene playing out in my head, charging across the room, shoving him back onto the couch. Punching him until that smirk becomes a smear of red.

He releases her wrist so suddenly she nearly falls. She's all frightened eyes and pale skin, limping toward me on her bandaged toes. And my hands are up, out, reaching for her, though I don't have a single damn clue what I'm going to do when she's close enough to touch.

"Hey!" calls Digg. When Bright turns, he flings the soda can—the liquid spilling as it spins toward her. Instinct makes me snag it out of the air like a line drive, then throw it back at him, pegging him in the chest. The splash creates another stain to match the one on his crotch. I wipe my wet hand on my shorts.

Digg's yelling an impressive string of curses, but there's too much blood rushing in my ears. I miss the first part and hear only, "—from Cross Pointe dumped her soda on me."

Brighton's voice is quiet, but the crowd hushes to hear it. "Only because *that* Hamilton scumbag spiked my drink."

"What?" I'm coiling to lunge at him. My lips pull back in a snarl that feels feral, while my muscles tense from my fists to my shoulders.

"Don't." Her small green fingernails tug on my sleeve. "I want to go. Now."

"Good," jeers Digg. "Go. Get the hell out of my house. Prentiss, living in Cross Pointe is making you a pansy."

I don't respond to Digg. Don't acknowledge the group of spectators who have abandoned the Ping-Pong table and video games. I nod at Brighton, putting her in front of me as we retrace my steps back toward the front door. I want to smash my foot through each stair rung or put my fist through the wall. I slam open the door at the top of the stairs, nearly hitting someone on the other side, but I don't stop to apologize. If I stop, I'll go back downstairs and punch Digg.

I ask Brighton if she has everything—because Carly has me well trained and we are not coming back for forgotten purses or phones or whatever. She doesn't answer, just takes fast, careful steps down the stairs and across the grass.

I'm opening my mouth to warn her I don't want to have an "OMG! That party!" rehashing in the car, when she spins around.

"Don't talk to me. Just. *Don't.*"

That's fine with me, except—"You're going the wrong way."

She continues her march away from my car. Across Jeff's lawn and his neighbor's too. I jog to catch up and then plant myself in her path so she has to acknowledge me.

"Wrong way? Like you care where I go or where I end up or what happens to me. You are a jerk."

"So I've heard. Multiple times tonight." Yet it sounds wrong coming out of her mouth.

"Yeah, well, I don't care. It's true. Jonah, you're vile. I'm disgusted I ever wanted your approval. Don't you dare show up at the library on Sunday. I don't ever want to see your face again."

"Fine. I won't," I snap. But being *un*invited to something I never planned on going to stings worse than her name-calling.

"I deserved to know about your breakup."

"Deserved? Entitled much? It's none of your business."

"You set me up as a pawn in your twisted little jealousy game. Say whatever you want about Cross Pointe, no one I know would have brought you to a party like this and abandoned you to fend for yourself."

"I thought you *left*."

"I was going to. I *am* going to. As soon as possible."

"I'm not stopping you." I step to the side and throw out my hands. "Go. Do you have any idea *where* you're going? Not all of Hamilton is safe at night."

She pauses. Looks around like perverts and drug dealers are going to materialize on this half-dead lawn. And I feel like a jerk, again, for scaring her. Again.

"How are you even going to get home?" I ask.

"Amelia," she says. "Or Peter. I'm just waiting for someone to call back. Where's a safe place I can wait?"

"Just come with me. I'll take you home." I reach out a hand toward her, but she takes a step backward.

"I wouldn't want to *inconvenience* you. This is me leaving you alone. Just like you asked. And you know what else?

I don't care what you think of me. I've spent so much time trying to be nice to you and trying to figure out why you're so mean to me, but I'm over it."

"Dammit, Brighton! Did you not notice I had your back in there? That I left with *you*? Give me some credit."

She looks me dead in the eye. "First you have to deserve it."

30

Brighton

☼ 11:55 P.M. ☽

13 HOURS, 5 MINUTES LEFT

I'm starting to falter. I feel like a paper doll that's been crumpled up and tossed aside. All the adrenaline, or whatever it is that's kept me moving and yelling, is starting to drain out of my system.

I pause and lean against a tree. Bite the inside of my cheek to keep tears out of my eyes.

"Hey, are you okay?" Jonah's voice sounds like a whisper now that he's not yelling. "What the hell happened with Digg, anyway?"

"Nothing. Nothing happened with Digg, all right? He spent half the time trying to paw me, the other half trying to get me to drink. And then, when I said no to both, he went ahead and spiked my soda. But, no, nothing happened. So you can stop pretending to care."

Saying the words aloud makes me feel like vomiting. Nothing happened, but something could have.

"Jesus, Bright, of all the guys in the party, you end up with Digg?"

"I really don't want to hear it." My stomach is burning, less nauseous now, more like it's full of something hot and uncontainable.

I turn and continue to walk across lawn after lawn, fumbling in my purse for my cell phone. I'm not spending another second with this guy. I'll call Evy, I don't care if she makes me listen to a lifetime of teasing.

"Bright." Jonah's jogging to catch up. He puts a hand on my arm, but I shake him off.

"I asked you not to call me that. My name's only two syllables, it's not hard to remember." I keep walking—ignoring the pain in my toes as I push myself to go faster.

"Brighton, wait. I'm sorry"

I've cut diagonally across a driveway and reached the street. Now I need to decide which direction to go. With Jonah's words about unsafe sections of town in my head, both look equally menacing.

"Really sorry," he says.

"Sure." Left. I'll go left. The street lamps look a little brighter that way.

"Will you stop and listen for a minute?" Jonah demands. "I'm trying to apologize!"

"There's—what?" I bite my tongue in surprise. I'd been planning on telling him there was nothing he could say that I wanted to hear, but I hadn't expected a real apology.

"You're right."

He's looking directly into my eyes, all the walls down and nothing but sincere regret reflected there. After spending the night watching him add layers to his emotional armor, this level of vulnerability is unnerving. I drop my phone back into my purse and breathe a cautious, "I am?"

"I'm sorry. I've been a bast—an idiot all night. I shouldn't have brought you here, at least not without telling you about Carly. And Digg"—he clenches his jaw for a second and takes a deep breath before continuing—"I didn't—I'm really sorry, Brighton."

I can still hear crickets and a dog barking. A sprinkler, muffled party noise. Cars passing and a TV blaring from the closest house. But all these things, and even the grass, trees, and houses, seem removed from this moment. It's just Jonah and me, eyes locked, as things shift in ways that can't be measured.

"Thank you."

"Are you okay?"

I nod.

"I can't believe you dumped a drink on him. That's priceless. I wish I could've seen his face." He claps a hand on my shoulder as he praises me, and the touch seems to surprise us both. He grins and I find myself smiling back, my cheeks flushing.

There's a flash in the distance to our right. A sharp *bang.* My body decides to jump and gasp. It decides that it's going to breathe in quick, inefficient inhales and exhales that make me feel like oxygen is missing or that none is getting to my lungs. The air is smoky, and Jonah's hand is still on my shoulder. I'm trembling.

"Hey. Brighton." His voice is soft, like how you'd speak to a frightened animal. How he probably speaks to Sophia when she's upset. "It's all right. It's just Felix blowing up the mailbox. You're okay."

"Why?"

"Because he's an idiot and he thinks it's funny. That's a

good enough reason if you're Felix." Jonah squeezes the back of my neck. "Brighton, you're all right. Really."

I could care less about the mailbox, but suddenly I'm almost crying. My mouth tastes sour, and I can't stop shaking. It's too much. What could've happened. The stress of tonight. All of it.

"You okay?" He stoops to look into my face, and I know my quivering lip is a dead giveaway.

"I just . . . I just feel so dirty. Like I need a shower. He was such a perv. And the way everyone in there was looking at me . . ."

Jonah's face creases for a second. "You're probably going to say no to this, but . . . follow me."

The way he says "follow me" isn't an order. It's more of a question. As if he's asking, "Will you?" As if he's asking, "Do you trust me?" He's waiting for me to take the first step.

I do.

"How's your foot?" he asks.

I start to say "it's okay," then change my mind and go with the more honest, "It hurts less than it did."

"It's not far." He crosses the street and turns down a side road.

"What is *it*?" I ask. I hate surprises. And after everything that's happened tonight, I've earned the right to be wary.

"Signey Park," Jonah says, as he steps off the street and onto a sidewalk bordering a grassy field. "More specifically, this. It's nearly as good as a shower." He points toward a sprinkler that's rotating and watering large swatches of the field.

"What?" I half laugh. He can't be serious.

"C'mon. I dare you."

"You dare me? I'm hardly dressed for—" My words fade off as Jonah runs across the grass and plunges through the jets of water. Then he swoops back across the lawn to me and shakes off like a dog.

"Any girl who can take down Digg can't possibly be scared of a little water." He cups a hand and beckons me closer.

My mind is listing all the reasons this is a bad idea. The consequences if we get caught. The impracticality of what I'm wearing. My hair. My makeup. My sore toes. The general wrongness of it.

I place my purse on the ground and head toward him, gasping as the first drops of water splash against my calves. "It's cold."

"Quit being a chicken." He holds out a hand, and I accept it. My fingers are warm and secure in his—the only warm part of me—as we step through the direct spray of frigid water.

Emerging out the other side, he takes his hand back to wipe his eyes. "See? I knew you could do it. Not so bad, is it?"

For a moment I study him through the spray. He isn't the boy I saw in Cross Pointe's halls—someone I thought was lonely and isolated. He might be both of those things, but if so, it's by choice, not a lack of social skills or opportunities.

Everything about Jonah is different here: his posture, his tone of voice, the way he presents himself to the world, and the way it treats him back.

I've never really known him at all—but more than ever, I want to.

I don't answer him, just plunge back through the curtain of water. Pausing to laugh and catch a few drops in my mouth. Flutter my fingers through the spray. Spin.

31

JONAH

☼ 12:08 A.M. ☽

JUST A FEW MORE SECONDS, THEN I'LL STOP WATCHING

If she knew what she looks like dancing and turning in the water, she'd never leave. Or maybe she would. In fact, if she knew what I'm thinking as I watch her spin around in that dress stuck to her like a second skin, she'd probably step out immediately and ask for a robe to cover her head to toe. She stretches her arms up farther, oblivious to the fact that she's now revealing a sliver of white. What is it about white cotton panties that's so hot? Carly has a collection of thongs, lace, and things I accidentally tore, but it was when she had on white cotton that I—I groan involuntarily.

She's laughing. Like a kid laughs—a full-abandon belly laugh—and it's contagious. Finally she emerges from the water, breathless and dripping, wringing out and finger combing her hair. "I must look a mess."

I watch her cross the lawn. The wet dress is glued to her from collar to hem. She tugs at it self-consciously, but when her hands move, it re-sticks to her skin. Good dress. God, why would she ever straighten hair like that? It looks like sex, like she's just had it or wants to.

I almost forget to answer her . . . "No. You don't."

She flicks some water at me, pairing the action with a smile that makes looking away crucial.

This girl.

I can't pin her down. Every time I want to dismiss her: with the dog, with the pizza, with Digg, she surprises me.

Tonight's been insane. And this side of midnight doesn't seem any more logical. Any minute now things will fall back into their crap patterns. I mean, things haven't *actually* changed. Paul's still a pretentious snot, I'm still stuck in Snob Town till I leave for college, and Brighton . . . she's still *Brighton*.

So we shared a night and a sprinkler and a few conversations? It hardly qualifies me as her friend. I bet there's a sign-up sheet to be her sidekick that stretches three months into the future.

Behind her, the timer on the sprinkler moves to *off* with a click; the streams of water fade to a dribble. Somewhere else in the park, another sprinkler will be turning on. If we chase down that sprinkler, spend the whole night going from one to the next until we've exhausted all options, can I stretch out this moment?

She's still rubbing the makeup under her eyes—completely unaware that its smudges are hot. Completely unaware that she looks like a guy's dream right now. It's all I can do not to touch her—just to put a finger on her damp cheek or bury my face in those curls, slide a hand along the back of her dress, and pull her to me.

God, I'm as bad as Digg.

A cheesy pop song ringtone cuts the air and both our heads swivel toward her purse sitting on the ground at the base of a tree. "It's got to be Amelia."

She's not in a hurry to get to the phone before it goes to voice mail, so I'm not either.

"Don't answer it," I say. Then, realizing it came out as an order, elaborate: "We've had a few minutes where neither of us is annoying the other—I don't want you to answer that phone, talk to someone from Cross Pointe, and have it ruin everything."

"How would that ruin—" She's cut off when the phone starts to ring again. And I'm glad to be spared this explanation. I was already far too honest.

The pop song cuts out, and there's a brief silence where we stare at each other. Her head is tilted like she's puzzled, and I just want to know how I get to keep *this* version of her. Not the please-like-me plastic girl from earlier, but this one with mysteries and layers and—

We each take a step closer at the same time.

We're interrupted by a third repetition of the ringtone. It cracks the moment and our eye contact.

"I have to get it. She's not going to stop calling until I answer." Brighton shakes off her hands and then looks at them. "My phone's in the outer left pocket, can you grab it? You're less drippy."

Girls' purses are like holy ground. Carly freaked if I looked in hers, even to do something simple like grab her cell phone or take out her lip gloss. And I remember vividly a Mom lecture from when I was eight. " 'Go *get* my purse' does not give you permission to go *in* my purse," when all I'd wanted was a piece of gum for my baseball game.

I stick a tentative hand in the pocket, waiting for the objection. There isn't one, and I pull out her cell. It's no longer ringing. I hold the New Voice Mail screen out to her.

She tries wiping her hands on her dress, but they just come away wetter.

"I'll hold it for you," I offer.

She laughs and nods. "Seven, five, three, one."

Her password? She's sharing it without a moment's hesitation. I punch the numbers on the screen, then hit the button to retrieve the voice mail. She twists her dripping hair over her other shoulder and steps closer. As I extend the phone toward her, my hand grazes her cheek. She smiles at me.

As the message begins, she moves still closer. Another two inches and her head would be against my chest. I'm leaning in, my semi-wet shirt touching her dripping sleeve.

"Brighton? Baby?"

The voice that comes out of the phone is definitely not Amelia's and I'm standing too close to pretend not to hear it.

It's mom-aged, sentimental, and thick with alcohol. Brighton's eyes go wide and she stiffens, her arm drawing away from mine.

"Auntie Joan just left. We were talking at dinner, and remember that Thanksgiving when you and your daddy decided to get up early and surprise everyone by putting the turkey in?"

I should give her privacy. I take a step back, so I'm holding the phone as close to her and as far from me as possible, but I can still hear the message. Bright's eyes are closed now; her expression looks hurt, nervous.

"Only you put it in the pan upside down and forgot to take the giblets out before you put the stuffing in?" Her mother gives this sniffly laugh and blows her nose near the phone. "I miss him . . ."

Finally Brighton snaps out of her embarrassment trance and grabs the phone from my hand, but it slips through her wet fingers and falls to the ground. I back away to go wait by a bench. She reaches for it and fumbles, hitting speakerphone instead.

"Oh, baby girl—I wish you were home. Some of your tea and a chat would be so perfect right now . . . but Evy says you're out—"

Finally she presses the right key and shuts the damn thing off.

I'm bracing for an awkward exchange, watching her take deep breaths and smooth her dress down with whiteknuckled fists. Her face, when she finally lifts her chin, is blank. Even if she doesn't look as giddy as she did three minutes ago, she looks serene. It's got to be an act, but I'm not going to call her on it.

"Where should we go now?" she asks.

"What?" I'm still amazed she looks so calm. Maybe because she knows my parents are divorced too, it doesn't bother her that I heard her mom blubber. "Didn't you want to go home?"

"We can't get in your car like this." She wrings a handful of water out of her dress and squelches her good foot against her flip-flop. "We've got to dry off at least a little. And I doubt we're really supposed to be in the park after sunset. Is there anywhere good to go for a walk or sit and get some coffee?"

My own sneakers spray water through the toes as I shift

my weight from one foot to the other. "But what about—" I point to her phone, feeling like a jerk for bringing it up.

"Oh, good point, I should text Amelia and tell her I'm all set. You'll take me home, right? Eventually?"

"Eventually," I echo with a grin. If she can ignore the voice mail, then I'm sure as hell not going to worry about it. "Hamilton doesn't do froufrou coffee houses—and even if they did, it's after twelve. Nothing much is open. But no one is going to bother us about a park curfew. Jeff and I used to come here all the time when we were younger. That's how I knew about the sprinklers."

Her people-pleaser smile melds into her real one as she looks up from her text and asks, "Did you really just refer to Bean Haven as *froufrou*?"

"Maybe I did— Are you going to argue with me? I only went there once. It was so *pink*. I tried to order a small coffee and the worker said, 'You mean a *teensy*.'"

She's laughing as I lead her to the path toward the playground. The playground Felix and Jeff had graffitied at twelve. I'd been too scared to even be their lookout. Their favorite curse words are still painted in runny letters on the bottom of the slide for all to see. It's so rundown and beatup compared to the eco-friendly, native-plant-landscaped parks of Cross Pointe. I wonder if Brighton's noticing the cracks in the concrete, the weeds, or the broken swing.

I've never noticed them before.

Yet it was Cross Pointe that brought out my own graffiti artist—the first week after the move I'd gone so far as to buy the paint and everything. But when I'd stood outside the perfect shops on perfect Main Street with the can in my hand, I'd become as chicken as I'd been at twelve. Maybe if I could've painted something with social commentary, like Banksy does, but to just scrawl sloppy letters across the storefronts? I couldn't even think of what to write. A swear, like an eleven-year-old showing off his cool factor? "I hate this town"?

In the end I dropped the spray paint into one of the trash cans spread out in even intervals.

"What are you thinking?" she asks. "You look so serious. Does this park have bad memories? Want to go somewhere else?"

"No, the opposite. See that field over there? That's where my Little League team played. I practically lived there. I learned to ride my bike on these paths—my blood's probably still on some of these tree trunks. I wasn't very good at turning or braking."

She laughs and follows my finger as I point out the landmarks of my childhood. "I'm sure you crashed just for the Band-Aids. I bet you were a tough guy even back then."

Suddenly, it's easy talking to her. I want to tell her more, show her more of my town. Redeem Hamilton from the first impression it made. I lead the way to the swings and hold one for her as she sits before lowering myself onto the next one.

"Before the divorce I used to live less than a block from here on Arroyo Court. Jeff, Sean, and I used to meet here to play catch. I kissed my first girlfriend—way before Carly—on the slide over there."

"So you were a stud? You dated a lot?" She leans her cheek against the chain and looks over at me.

"Some. I don't know about a lot. I had a few girlfriends

before Carly." She's got this half-amused, half-preoccupied smile on her face, and it's driving me crazy. I grip the chains tightly before asking, "What about you? Not that I'm keeping up with Cross Pointe's gossip, but I haven't heard about you and any boyfriends."

The half smile locks in place, frozen in a look that's supposed to be lighthearted and natural. I can read her better now; I know it's not. She examines her hands, seems startled to find her nails green, then hides them in her palms and pushes off with her good foot. Her words get carried away with her swinging motion. "Sorry to disappoint, but there's not much to hear."

I stand up and grab the chains on both sides of her swing. Hold her hostage. "Oh, come on. Don't give me that." She has to know how guys look at her. Has to know she could have her pick of almost any guy in school. I refuse to believe she hasn't played with that power.

When she shakes the hair out of her eyes, I can see she's not flirting, she's serious. "I keep waiting for the day when I wake up and realize one of the boys I've known since kindergarten is suddenly breathtaking and makes my pulse race or something cliché like that."

"So there's no guy at Cross Pointe who's good looking enough for you?" I give her a gentle push and watch her arc away from me. Her hair trails like a live thing.

"No! That's not what I mean at all! There are plenty of guys who are hot, but I've known them so long. They're the same boys who used to show off their burping and farting skills. Thinking about dating any of them feels . . . weird and slightly incestuous."

"Incestuous would be weird."

She finally laughs. "Stop teasing me! I'm serious. Amelia tells me I should just suck it up and pick a guy—otherwise I'll go off to college 'dangerously innocent'—her words, not mine. But if I know I'm not going to feel about a guy the way he feels about me, then I'm setting him up to be hurt. How can I do that to someone I like? Even if it's not *like*-like."

I was going to make a crack about "*like*-like," but her answer doesn't seem funny anymore. "Good question. I don't disagree."

"Plus, I think they're all still secretly impressed with the noises and smells they can make."

"They are." I laugh louder than the comment really deserves and almost prove her right about my gender's immaturity by twisting her swing sideways. Instead, I put an extra step of space between us and look around for something distracting that *isn't* her. She lets herself slow to a stop. She's not looking at me either.

If "awkward" had a flavor, it would taste like this moment. Like my mouth opening and closing as I try to think of something to say. Or sprinkler water and the one sip of beer I had tonight. Or the ghost of Carly's lip gloss and the laughter that just fizzled.

I rap my knuckles against the cold metal frame of the swings. A hollow sound reverberates down the pole, and I open my mouth again. I don't know what ruined the moment, but I want it back.

Maybe the moment was damned to fail. I mean, Brighton. In Hamilton. With me. It's an equation that has no solution.

I look away from her, across to the other side of the park,

and suddenly I *need* to see it again. I'm already off the playground sand and on the sidewalk before I call, "There's somewhere I have to go. It won't take long. You can either come or stay here."

I'm not sure which I'd prefer.

32

Brighton

12 HOURS, 35 MINUTES LEFT

He's leaving without me.

It's my fault too. He'd started opening up about his life, baseball, girls. So what do I do? Ruin it all. Could I sound more ridiculous? Oh, why don't you date, Brighton? *Well, you see, guys smell.* Way to be eight. Does he think I include him in that category? Real smooth. He looked so embarrassed *for* me—though I'm more than embarrassed enough on my own.

I really mentioned burping and farting. Like that phone call from Mom wasn't bad enough. I knew she'd have a meltdown tonight. I knew it.

He paces next to a trash can with his eyes fixed on something I can't identify.

Just this once, Evy can handle Mom. They'll be fine.

"Wait up! Please."

As soon as I reach him, he's off again, like he's afraid our destination will disappear before we reach it.

"Where are we going?"

"Wait and see, Bright," he says. Then adds, "Sorry." He's staring at something across the street.

"What? Why?" I look around for whatever's inspiring his apology and come up with nothing.

"Called you Bright again. Accident, I swear."

"I didn't even notice."

For the first time since he started on this manic mission to wherever, Jonah looks at me. His brown eyes settle on mine and stay there; my cheeks react with a blush.

"My dad used to call me that: his Rainbow Brite."

"Do you miss him?"

"Every day." It's just a smidge more than twelve hours until his memorial. My stomach twists. My throat is constricting. I want to look away, but his eye contact is the only thing keeping me steady. "Tell me about *your* dad. Do you still see him a lot?"

"No, never. I wish I could hate him. Then at least it would be mutual."

"Jonah, come on. You know your father doesn't hate you."

He kicks at a rock on the sidewalk and answers in a tight voice. "Yeah. He does. He blames me."

"He couldn't. He's your dad."

"He blames *me*." He's stopped walking and is pacing the same three squares of sidewalk. The emotions spill out of his voice and into his stride: furious, fast steps that change direction without pattern.

"Paul was my physical therapist. Mom met him because of me. Because I screwed up my right ankle sliding into home plate and couldn't drive myself to appointments. Dad's convinced I *knew*. He couldn't get rid of me fast enough."

My chest feels tender from talking about Dad, and my heart aches for Jonah. Not wanted? By his own father?

"He said I chose sides by not telling him—even though I had no clue. And that Mom and Paul were still a family, and a kid belonged with a family. He, on the other hand, was now a bachelor, and a teenager didn't fit in his new lifestyle. I guess he doesn't want me in the way while he bar hops. I doubt he's out looking to find me a new mommy."

I hug myself because I know if I touch him, he'll stop.

"And then he sold the house without even telling me. Called me after he was in a hotel. I'm surprised he called at all. I guess I should be grateful. He coulda called from Florida and said, 'By the way, I've moved.'"

"Why?" I gasp the word and cringe at the unfairness of it all. No wonder Jonah's bitter.

"He and my mom agreed it'd be easier for me if I didn't have to see the house packed up. They equated it to a body in a casket—it's better I remember my home as a 'happy place,' not empty rooms full of boxes. Like I can forget their fights and only remember the good times."

He stops pacing and looks at me. His face is all naked emotion. His eyes scream of need. My instincts demand I look away. Run away. I don't want to be needed. Not like this. Not in a way that requires me to share more than space and conversation—a way that requires me to share *me*.

"Do you get this?" He swallows and drops eye contact, shoulders slumping. "Forget it. Your parents' divorce was probably all 'please' and 'thank you' and no hurt feelings."

I'm too stunned by Jonah's story to sugarcoat my own. "My parents didn't divorce. My dad died. Heart attack."

He freezes on the sidewalk and lifts a palm to cover his face. "Crap."

"Don't—" I know what I should say: "It's fine. I'm okay. You didn't know." Some variation of "Don't worry, you're off the hook" followed by a subject change.

I tug on his sleeve until he lowers his hand and opens his eyes. He continues to look . . . tortured.

I bite my lip and swallow. "I *do* know what you mean. I wasn't allowed to go to the wake—no one would let me see him . . . after. For years—years, I convinced myself it wasn't true. He was in another room. Or still at work. He'd gotten some extra-needy client who took all his time. And soon, really soon, he'd be home. Sitting next to me at family dinner—his lefty elbow bumping against my righty—or leaving sticky notes with we've-got-a-golf-date reminders or saw-your-math-test-I'm-proud-of-you messages on my bathroom mirror or in my lunch bag."

I feel naked, but there's no way to cover up the parts I've just exposed, so I clench my fists instead. "I get your need for closure."

"It's not the same, Brighton. It's not the same at all. I had no idea. I'm sorry."

I've never seen pity on his face before. I don't like it.

"I'm sure it's hard, but it'll get better. It takes time."

Even the tone of his voice has changed.

I step away from the hug he's offering, hold my hands up toward him. "Stop. Just stop. Please."

Jonah's arms drop to his sides and he's a split second away from getting pissed. "I was just—"

"Not *you* too. I've spent five years in school with people

who know and treat me like a tragic character because of it. 'That's Brighton Waterford, her dad died—handle with care.'" I take a step toward him, starting to bridge the chasm that's grown since I refused his hug. "Except you. Maybe that's part of why I wouldn't leave you alone—even when it was painfully obvious you wanted me to."

"Because I was an ass?"

"Because you treated me as badly as you treated everyone else. You haven't coddled me. I'd rather you be an ass than act like I'm breakable." I hold my breath as I watch him think this through. He's quiet for longer than I'd like. Studying me more intensely than I'd like.

"Are ass and coddler my only options?" he asks.

I laugh. "Shut up."

"When did he die?" It's a question in his regular voice, and I realize the flip side of Jonah not being here when it happened. He might not baby me, but he also doesn't *know* already.

The smile slips from my face, and I swallow a few times before answering. "Five years ago. Exactly five years. There's a memorial service tomorrow. I should be fine by now, right? I should be able to talk about him. Mom and Evy talk about him all the time."

"So, go ahead. Talk."

I *can't.* I turn away from him to catch my breath.

"So where are we headed?" I ask.

"We're here. This is my old house." Jonah pauses to study it for a moment before he leads the way up the driveway.

He sits on the steps of a back deck, and I join him. He's staring at something invisible, something that has

significance to him and not me. All I can see is this backyard bleeding into his neighbors', blending with the one
beyond that. Is he thinking about his old life or his new one?
About me?

We're sitting so close. My damp dress is cold in contrast
to the heat that radiates off him. I'd like that hug now—if
I could think of a way to ask for it without being lame. His
face is unreadable. The faraway look of an in-class daydream.
He looks unreachable, and sitting two inches away, I'm
lonely.

"How do you—" I jump when he speaks. He clears his
throat and starts again, "How do you handle something like
that? I can't even handle a divorce at eighteen."

"My mom went to pieces"—I shiver thinking about her
days and days in bed, leaving only to go to the bathroom or
refill whatever was in her travel mug and throw TV dinners
in the microwave for us. "Evy lashed out at everyone: cursing at Mr. Donnelly when he asked how she was; getting a
speeding ticket in Dad's car when she didn't even have
a permit. And that was *after* she ran over his golf bag, then
dumped the whole thing into the lake at the club. I didn't
have a choice. I had to deal with it.

"It was when Evy packed herself a can of beer for lunch
instead of a soda that Mom finally snapped out of it and
began parenting again." Spilling confessions to a recently
tarred driveway and the sandbox in the next yard is easier
than to his face, but I have to see his reaction. I've never said
any of this out loud before—not even to Amelia, though she
was there to see some of it. I look at him and hold my breath
while he shakes his head.

"Crap," Jonah says again. His hand touches my shoulder.

Just briefly, lightly, but it keeps me from flying into a million pieces and chases the goosebumps off my arms—replacing them with a flash of heat. "What about you?"

"Me?"

"Yeah. You were, what, twelve? What'd *you* do?"

I shrug. "Nothing exciting. I turned behaving into a science." I lean back, rest my head on the step behind me, and list an action on each star that's visible through the cloudy sky: "I cleaned up and tried to get Mom to eat. I made straight A's—I worked well with others. I was good enough at it that I convinced everyone I was okay."

"Brighton . . ." Jonah shifts to mirror my position. When I turn, his face is only inches from mine.

"I acted nice and lied and said I was fine. I chose kindness as—how'd you put it? Because you were so right—'my social weapon of choice.' And I did what I thought he'd want me to do. Signed up for all the clubs he did. Not the sports, though. I'm horrible at golf and basketball. And, for a while, I slept with a copy of his book under my pillow—tried to convince myself that those words on those pages were *him* speaking to *me*.

"*That* was the book I was looking at in your living room, Jonah. It's one he wrote. I wasn't snooping, I promise. I just didn't expect to see it there and was feeling a little lost. I wanted him to give me some answers. But—" I choke on the words "but he can't" and spit out an automatic—"but I'm fine."

His forehead is wrinkled. I'm hit by an urge to reach out and trace the creases, so I fold my fingers more tightly into my palm. The pain is a welcome distraction, brings some clarity.

This is insane. I barely know him. My family doesn't

discuss these things. We don't talk about my dad in public. And if we do, it's with big smiles, a polite "I miss him very much," and a quick change of topic. The tears and mourning—Evy and Mom save those for dramatic scenes within the privacy of our house. Usually taking a positive event—Christmas, graduation, prom—and tainting it with tears and "I wish Dad were here. Don't you wish Dad were here?"

"You're not fine," he says, giving me a long, searching look. He turns his face to the stars. "But you will be."

His fingers flex on the step beside mine. They're so close I feel their heat in the air around my fist. Lying there, beneath the weight of the whole sky, I feel lighter.

"So will you," I answer.

33

JONAH

☼ 12:43 A.M. ☽

TOO LATE TO GO BACK

She's trembling slightly, causing her curls to quiver against my shoulder and making me feel even more useless. God, I want to touch her—bury my fingers in her hair, feel the skin of her neck, learn how her hand fits in mine. But I won't. She clearly didn't want to be held on the driveway, and instead of accepting the hand I'm holding open, she balls up her fist and moves it farther away.

If I sit next to her any longer thinking of all the ways I *can't* touch her, I'll go insane.

"You're cold."

"No, I'm okay—" she protests.

"And we're pretty much dry. We might as well go."

It was the wrong thing to say. I can tell as soon as I pull away and push myself off the low step. Her face goes straight to a neutral smile, and she resorts to her old standby of agreement.

"Sure."

It's not until we're back on the sidewalk that I actually

pause to look at the house. It's so small compared to Paul and Mom's McMansion. It doesn't have vaulted ceilings or chandeliers. There isn't even a second floor. It's a simple two-bedroom ranch, but until Mom and Dad started fighting every night, it had always seemed big enough.

"It's a nice house," she says.

I study her face—she means it.

"The shutters used to be green. And Mom had tons of flowerpots everywhere. I was constantly tripping over them when I walked home after Jeff's parties. I swear she used to place them across the path as a sobriety test." I turn my back on the house. "It's hard to imagine someone else living there. It still feels like mine."

"But you have a new house now. In Cross Pointe."

I snort. "That is not *my* house. Cross Pointe will never be my home."

I freeze for a second as a new thought shivers down my spine: it *will* be Sophia's. She'll feel about that house the way I feel about this one. But with a couple of important differences—and I'm not thinking about her allowance this time. No matter what I hate about Paul, I can't accuse the guy of not being borderline-obsessively crazy about his daughter. He'd never curse her out and pull a Houdini like my dad.

"You know, Jonah." Brighton's voice cracks the fuzz that's forming around my thoughts. "If you focused even half the energy you spend hating Cross Pointe on *not* hating it, you might wake up one day and realize what a great town it is."

I don't bother pointing out how lame she sounds. She knows—there's embarrassment in the way she's suddenly fascinated with her curls and won't look at me.

I'm better at awkward silence; I've had more practice. She doesn't last thirty seconds before continuing, "I get that you're doing a whole angry-loner thing, but why didn't you join the baseball team? Jeff said you were really good."

I can't answer this question while standing still. Talking about baseball makes my stomach twist. It makes my palm itch for the feel of dust and leather and stitches. I start across the park to my car. "I could've. I could've walked on to the team and made the current pitcher look like a water boy."

"You're too good for them?"

"I am." I grab a handful of leaves off a tree and shred them as we continue across the park. Each rip makes me want to destroy more. "But it was more about my damn ankle."

"It didn't heal right?"

"It's fine. But if I hadn't gotten hurt playing baseball, Mom would never have met Paul and I'd still be living back here. And my teammates—my *friends*—were already upset I was leaving and ruining what should have been our best season yet. How could I make that worse by playing *against* them?"

She reaches out like she might touch me. Her hand trembles in the air around my arm, but then she pulls it away and tucks it behind her back.

"Imagine how well the Cross Pointe team reacted when they found out my stats. Or when the coach tried to recruit me and I said no."

"What'd they do to you?" Brighton's voice is protective. Of *me*. My lips twist into a smile at the idea of her facing off with the players.

"It's fine. They got over it. Their season went well. They

didn't need me. But I miss playing every damn day. I miss everything about my old life."

"I get that you're angry, but you never gave us a chance."

"Did the town give me a chance? From the second I walked into school people were eyeing me like I was a science experiment . . . or dinner." We're out of the park, back on Jeff's street. I open my hand, and the contents spill and dot the sidewalk with leaf carnage.

"We're not used to new students! The last one before you was Maggie back in freshman year, and you—" She's tilting her head, peering up at me from the corner of her eyes. "You're different."

"Yeah, I know. Hamilton kid." I gesture toward the cracked sidewalks, the patched and potholed pavement, the crooked post that's missing its street sign, a streetlight with a flickering bulb, a beer can and Doritos bag lying against a blocked sewer drain. Things I never would've noticed before Cross Pointe.

"Give it up, Jonah. It's not about where you're from. Nobody cares where you're from." She crosses her arms and picks up the pace, marching past me.

We're walking by shrapnel that used to be Jeff's mailbox. I kick a piece out of the way and look at his house. Most of the lights are off. It's almost one, so some kids probably had to leave to make curfew. Or, more likely, people cleared out when they saw Digg being a tool.

We reach the car while I'm trying to piece together an explanation. I lean against the bumper and try to come up with something that will make Brighton see why I couldn't link arms and sing "Kumbaya" with her and the rest of CPHS.

Her voice is quiet when she says, "You didn't even try to fit in. You alienate anyone who talks to you." She puts a hand on my arm—her fingers are so cold. I want to cup them in mine and warm them up. I want to cling to them.

"My whole life was here."

And now it's gone. My family. My dad. My house. Carly. My team. It's gone. And most of my friends will scatter to colleges soon. There isn't anything tying me to this town anymore. I lace my fingers behind my neck and drop my chin.

When I look up, she's still standing next to me. Touching my skin with impossibly soft fingers.

"You don't have to love Cross Pointe, but can't you think of anything good about it?"

She's staring at me with a look so earnest it aches to maintain eye contact. My chest is heaving like I've just finished sprinting, and my insides feel like they've been scoured with sand. Honesty shouldn't be this painful. I swallow.

I watch her blink and suck on her bottom lip—*I* want to suck on her bottom lip. I wish she was closer. Against me. Or farther away. Home in her room. No longer a temptation.

"Never mind," she mutters, retracting her hand and retracing her steps. Climbing inside my car and yanking the door shut behind her.

It's not until she's out of earshot that I have the courage to be truthful. I mouth my answer to the space she'd just occupied: *You.*

I spend another thirty seconds standing there—rolling my neck in a circle like I used to do before winding up, trying to push the tension out of my muscles and find that calm and centered mental place I lived in on the pitching mound.

We're both tired. It's been a long night. The last thing either of us needs is a confession or more talk about emotions. I'll just—

Her car door opens.

"Jonah?" Her voice is so small, so soft. It sounds almost frightened; the thought that she still might be scared of me makes me sick.

Screw it.

"*You*, Brighton. That's what—" I say, turning around. She looks terrified. Or hurt. "Are you okay?"

She presses a fist to her mouth and says, "I'm sorry," around her fingers. With her other hand she points to the front of the car.

"Did some idiot hit me?" I exhale my disgust and palm my phone, ready to start texting to ask who saw what. Except, no. The front of my car is intact. No more beat-up than it had been before.

It's the windshield she was pointing to. It's not busted or cracked. Instead there's a message scrawled on it in letters that shine in the streetlight: PENCIL DICK LOSER.

I punch the doorframe without thinking and then have two reasons to be swearing.

"I'm so sorry," she says again.

"It's not your fault," I spit out between swears.

"You don't have any Windex in your car, do you?" she asks, coming to stand next to me.

"Sure. It's right between my vacuum cleaner and my toilet brush. Why the hell would I keep Windex in my car?" As soon as the words are out, I curse myself.

Pencil dick. Does she think it's true? I just finished telling her what a loser I am, but does she think the rest of it's true too?

She's leaning over the windshield, wiping at the letters with a napkin she must have gotten from my glove compartment.

"I'm pretty sure it's lip gloss," she says over her shoulder, leaning further in a way that pulls her dress up. I want to slide her off the hood and prove it isn't true. She stretches, going up on the toes of her noninjured foot and revealing just a hint of white. I groan.

"Are you okay?" Brighton straightens, and her dress falls back to midthigh. I look away from her legs before I develop any more antigraffiti proof. But she's not helping the situation when she reaches out and takes my hand in hers, studying my knuckles. They're red but not split. "You're going to have a bruise. I'm sorry."

She covers the injury with the cool palm of her other hand. The gesture is so comforting, I want to close my eyes and forget everything but her touch. But her voice contains all the pity I don't want to see on her face. Pity for the loser with undersized man-parts.

So, instead, I yank my hand back and say, "Oh, I forgot *you* were the one who slammed my hand into the door and wrote on my windshield. Wait. You weren't? Then why the hell do you keep apologizing for things that aren't your fault?"

She flinches.

I glare at the car, where Carly's handiwork has been turned into a smudge that covers half the windshield. "You made it worse." I know I'm being an ass, but I can't take

back the words or look at her hurt eyes. Or calm down. I.
Can't. Calm. Down.

"I'm sorry," I manage, but it sounds like a growl.

"Saying 'I'm sorry' afterward doesn't give you permission
to act like a jerk." There's pain in her voice and also anger.

"I know."

"You're not mad at me."

"I know."

"Good. Now give me your keys and let's see if the windshield wipers are more effective than I was."

She trades a stack of napkins for my keys, and I feel like
a scolded child as she starts my car. Blue fluid squirts onto
the glass, dissolving and wiping away the pieces of napkin
but only beading on and further smearing the glossy graffiti.

"Let me try again with the napkins," I say as she says,
"Maybe more fluid?" I'm leaning over the windshield when
she hits the wiper stick. The spray catches me full in the face
and I jump back to prevent my hands from getting caught in
the blades. I use one of the napkins to blot windshield fluid
from my cheeks.

I glare at her around the napkin, and she's covering
her mouth with both hands. Laughing. Or trying not to.
But her eyes are shining with amusement and her cheeks
are pink with the effort.

It cracks something in me. I want to pull her hands away
from her face and see that smile. I grin at her. "You did that
on purpose—but I guess I deserved it."

She's openly giggling now, adding spaces between words
to catch her breath. "I swear. I didn't. Promise."

"I'm keeping my eye on you," I say. "Napkins aren't going

to cut it. Check the backseat. Is there anything back there?"
I look away as she scampers over the console and probably
flashes some serious thigh. The idea makes my blood pound.
I shift and try to think of *anything* but the fact that she's in
my backseat.

She picks up my glove and a Frisbee. "Looks like you're
out of luck."

"Figures." Marcos had begged to help me wash my car
last weekend. He'd manned the hose, Carly had been in
charge of music and snacks, and Ana had shoved all the junk
and clothing in the backseat into plastic grocery bags. Those
bags are still sitting in the garage in Cross Pointe, pissing
Paul off.

I swallow down the memory. The fact that I won't have
to worry about Marcos dropping his sponge in the dirt, then
using it—gravel and all—to wash my car doors. And that I
won't get to play "expert" for Ana's boy questions: *So, if a guy
gets this funny look on his face every time you catch him looking at you, what does that mean?* There's got to be a way I can
keep them in my life, even if Carly and I are broken up.

"Um, you could take off your shirt?"

Her voice cuts right through the knot in my stomach.
"What?"

I love that she's blushing and studying her absurd green
nails when she clarifies. "You've got a shirt on under your
polo. What if you used that?"

"Brighton I-don't-know-your-middle-name Waterford,
are you asking me to *strip*?" It's so good to laugh that I do for
longer than I should. And when she stops blushing and joins
in, I have to plant my feet to keep myself from going to her.

And I fail at it. I'm opening the back door before my brain's caught on to what my fingers are doing. "I'm scandalized," I tease, offering her a hand and helping her out. Then, while she's still standing that close, I pull off both shirts. When I feel her eyes on me, I'm grateful I haven't stopped working out just because I quit baseball.

"Here, hold this," I say, handing her my polo. Then, with a little bit of swagger, I take the two steps to reach the windshield and attack the lip gloss. I hope she's admiring me the way I admired her. I flex a bit as I lean farther.

"Jonah?"

It might be wishful thinking, but I think she sounds a little breathless. I grin. "Yes?"

"Your phone's about to fall out of your pocket."

"Oh. Right. Here, keep it safe for me." I toss it to her, and she *barely* catches it. I resume my show. The shirt is working. This should only be another minute and then—

"Um, you have a missed call. And a voice mail . . ." She sighs. "From Carly."

I freeze, and something in my face or posture, or something in her, deflates so that the moment is flattened, all humor gone.

"I think that's almost good enough to get us home, don't you?" She hands me my shirt and the phone. "I'm just going to wait in the car."

I pull on my clean shirt and curse. I attack the windshield with one hand while thumbing my phone to voice mail with the other. I don't want to listen to Carly yell right now. Or whine. Or whatever she's going to say in the voice mail— though judging by the nice message she left on my car, it's not going to be fun.

I don't want to play it. But I don't want Brighton to think I'm scared of listening. And I don't want either of us to be thinking about it the rest of the night. I press the button, grit my teeth, and hold the phone to my ear.

"Hi . . . So, if you haven't seen your car yet, I'm sorry. And if you have, I'm still sorry. I didn't do it, Sasha and Maya did. But I didn't stop them either. I probably should have."

She's using her *I'm-cute* voice, but I'm not amused. Then she sighs, low and long.

"Also, can you tell Brighton I'm sorry? I didn't know that Digg was spiking her drink, but I should've known he was doing something. *I should've warned her. Not that she needed me to—she handled Daniel just fine on her own."*

Her voice trembles a bit and I can picture her shutting her eyes, trying to pull herself together.

"That didn't stop you from flying to her rescue . . . But whatever. I'm sorry about the car. I know we should probably talk at some point, but can you wait till I'm ready to call you? This is . . . it's just hard, *Jonah."*

34

Brighton

11 HOURS, 52 MINUTES LEFT

Jonah gets in the car wearing a face I've become quite familiar with. It means this-subject-is-closed and includes him pressing his lips together, swallowing, and looking away. I let it go. It's none of my business whether he and Carly are together or broken up, or what she said in her message.

I'm glad I had a minute in the car by myself. I need to be less pathetic. He's rejected me tonight—more than once—but the second he pulled off his shirt, I was all but drooling and tilting my head to get a better angle.

I just wish I knew what he was thinking. I know him so much better than I did a few hours ago—he knows me better than people who've been in my life for years—but I don't *know* him yet. I don't know if he's angry or hurting or what is going on behind those brown eyes that haven't looked at me once since he sat down and buckled up.

I hope I get the chance to, if not tonight then tomorrow or—

No.

Not tomorrow. I lean against the window, dizzy with the knowledge that I forgot what tomorrow was. What today is, since it's now after one.

I've spent a whole day—from the moment my alarm clock buzzed at 5:25 a.m.—wishing I could go back to bed. I wanted to sleep straight through Saturday and emerge unbroken on Sunday. But now, with less than an hour between me and my covers, it seems hard to let this night go. There's not enough time. Things have shifted—Jonah's ideas of me, mine of him, mine of me—and I'm not ready for tonight to end.

There was *almost* a moment out there where—I swallow and clench my fists—where I let my imagination get away from me.

He turns the key in the ignition and eases the car away from the curb. This time as we wind through the streets of Hamilton, I don't look for the mismatch between buildings; instead, I wonder if they have any connection to him. Was that his orthodontist? Does he have friends who live in those condos? Did he date anyone who grew up on this street? Or wipe out on his bike on these sidewalks?

"Did you have braces?" I ask.

"Where'd that come from?" He turns and flashes his teeth at me—perfect, straight. "Three years. I hated them."

"Me too." Though, really, I didn't. I felt so grown-up when I got them on. Evy had braces already, like most of her friends and a lot of mine too. It was like joining a club. I loved color coordinating the bands to the holidays. I loved the routine of it, the lists of rules about what to eat, what not to eat. I basked in the monthly praise from my orthodontist about how I was his favorite patient because I kept my braces so clean.

I'd lied to Jonah. And it had come out as easy as breathing. Why? Was he going to think less of me if he knew I proudly brushed my teeth every day after lunch in middle school? He might tease me, but he wouldn't care. And it's not like he's now feeling all chummy because of our shared loathing for orthodontics.

"That's not true."

"What isn't?" He gives me a confused look as he puts on his blinker to turn on to the highway.

"About hating my braces. And you know what else? I'm not nice."

"Oh-kay?"

I'm already blushing, and I want to let this go. Or say "just kidding" and push things back toward normal, but I can't. "I just realized—I'm not nice. I may act nice, but that doesn't make *me* nice. I only behave like that because I want the reaction—I want people to like me." I press both fists to my forehead, shut my eyes, and try to explain. "I'm so messed up—I don't know how to begin thinking about who I *am* versus how I *act*."

Jonah takes a hand off the wheel and rubs at his temples. "Brighton, I don't want to sound like a jerk, but honestly, I'm too tired to talk about this. I don't have any answers. Remember, *my* mom was the one with the library of my-teen's-a-screwup books—including the one your dad wrote. I can't fix you. But I don't really think you're messed up."

I'd leaned forward on my seat, expecting another dose of his harsh honesty, but now I slump back, defeated. "You're right—if I don't understand me, why would you?"

"I will say this—I do think you're nice."

"Just not always sincere."

"You said it, not me."

I fold my arms across my chest and nod. That's another truth to add to tonight's unmasking. But there's a bigger question that I'm wrestling with now. The why of it all. Why do I care so much what Jonah thinks? Why do I want to hear his opinion? Why do I *need* his approval?

I settle back against the seat, pulling my curls out of the way and resting my cheek on the faux leather so I can watch his profile. It's a comfortable silence in the car, not one to be filled with babble or pointless questions. Jonah has some sort of instrumental electronic music playing at a low volume. I try to find patterns in the musical loops, and my eyelids start to grow heavy. Sleep wouldn't be the worst thing ever. It's calm here, safe, and comfortable. I yawn and let my eyes close. Jonah will wake me. I want Jonah to wake me, want his face to hover over mine as he gives my shoulder a soft shake. Says my name.

I sit up so suddenly that he startles and the car gives a small jerk to the right before he corrects it. "What? You okay?"

But I can't tell him what. So I nod and stare out the window at blurring highway signs with eyes that are now wide-awake. The "what," the latest and hopefully last revelation I'll have tonight is simple: I like him.

Like him, like him. And not only do I not know how he feels, I don't even know if he's available.

"Jonah? Can I ask you a question?"

He rolls his shoulders back. It seems an incredibly long time before he answers. "That never comes before a question

I want to answer. And we've been doing this all night—this twisted version of Truth or Dare. Can we stop now?"

I watch the highway markers count down the distance. Cross Pointe is the next exit. Less than four miles. It's probably for the best. I should get home and check on Mom and Evy. I shouldn't keep pushing this issue or asking for answers that Jonah clearly doesn't want to give. I mean, even if he's single, what am I going to do, throw myself at him?

"Fine. What's your question?"

"It's none of my business, but how did things go with Carly? Did she listen? Did you guys patch things up? I mean, the windshield thing doesn't really look that great . . . but she called you." I speak the words in a tumble and then hold my breath while waiting for his answer. Is it wrong to wish they're still broken up? Talk about not being nice— who wants the person they like to be in pain?

Apparently, me.

He brakes a little too suddenly for the Cross Pointe exit and waits until we reach Main Street to answer: "We're done. Carly and me."

I turn toward the window so he can't see my smile. "I'm sorry."

Another lie—but I'm not confessing it this time.

"I'm not. Can we be finished with questions now?"

I start to nod, then change my mind. "Nope."

He turns off the music. "Nope?"

He's single. He's probably not interested, but he is single. And I've put him through so much tonight—granted he's given me just as many trials, but I want to do something *for* him. And I've come up with the perfect idea.

"You owe me a dare. You dared me to go through the sprinkler. I did, so it's only fair. Now make a left here."

We're at a stop sign. It's been more than the required two seconds, but he's not moving. He turns in his seat, not just his neck, but turns his whole body and studies me. I don't know what his expression means, but it makes me blush. It makes me wish I had a flat iron and a change of clothing and whatever else I'd need to repair the damage from this night and the sprinkler and make myself presentable.

"Make a left here, *please*," I amend.

He laughs. "I wasn't waiting for the magic word."

I don't bother asking what he was waiting for because he turns left.

35

JONAH

☀ 1:41 A.M. ☽

BETWEEN HALF-PAST EXHAUSTION &
A QUARTER TO LUST

One left turn and her cheeks are pink.

She blushes more than anyone I've ever met. I like it. And even though I complained about it, and even though I'm exhausted, I kinda like Brighton's version of Truth or Dare too. It's like knowing each other, even though we don't.

It's an odd list of facts I've collected about her tonight: a taste for horror films, childhood nickname, psychosis behind her nail color, nervous habit of making fists, and fear of her own dog. I want to learn more.

I lean closer, wanting her hand on me. On my arm, around my shoulder, against my back, on my face, in my hair . . . I want physical confirmation of my decision and proof that the breakup with Carly doesn't mean I'll be alone and untouched. I want an outlet for all these feelings.

But what I'm not thinking is: I want *Brighton*. And with her the distinction's significant.

She's semibouncing in her seat. In one car ride she's

gone from pensive to half-asleep, and now she looks like she's snorted coffee beans. She's even turning on my iPod and shuffling through my music. The opening notes to the Grinch theme play before she laughs and flicks to the next song.

I need a break. Just one break in a night that won't quit screwing with my head. I need a break from her body and angelic eyes. I mean, it isn't *her* I want. It can't be. It was only seven hours ago that I was telling Carly there isn't a girl in Cross Pointe who is "less my type." And no matter how tempted I am, Bright isn't the kind of girl you can play games with.

And I'd only be playing.

Right?

"Right," she says. And I almost think she's psychic—until I realize that it's my next direction. I've driven past the intersection with Frost Street, but the roads are empty, so I can back up in my lane and make the turn. It feels like we're the last two people in Cross Pointe—maybe then I'd actually like the place.

My mind wants to guess where we're headed: a party, a friend's house, an empty lot—does Cross Pointe have its own version of a make-out spot? But I decide I'd rather be surprised, so I won't let myself project ahead and think about what these roads connect to and where we could be going. It's not like I've spent that much time exploring the town, so it really could be anywhere.

"Okay, we're almost there. Just turn left up here." She's grinning with sweet mischief, and I'm dying to know what she's planning.

Until I see what's ahead on the left. I pull my foot from the gas and let the car drift to a stop, the reflection of the marble sign in my headlights and a sinking in my stomach.

CROSS POINTE HIGH SCHOOL.

36

Brighton

☼ 1:47 A.M. ☽

11 HOURS, 13 MINUTES LEFT

We sit parked in the middle of the road for two minutes. I watch the clock and spend the entire 120 seconds trying to figure out what to say. Finally he presses the gas pedal—just a little bit, so that the car creeps toward the school's driveway like an animal cautiously approaching a known predator.

"*This* is where you wanted to bring me?" Jonah's voice is half question and half laugh. I wish my brain didn't find the sound more musical than the iPod's contribution to the silent parking lot.

"Yup. Park toward the back." I indicate the spaces at the edge of the lot, where juniors and sophomores are assigned their spots, and try to sound confident. Now that we're here, and seeing his reaction, I'm starting to doubt this was such a brilliant idea after all.

"At least once before you graduate, you've got to throw some balls on that field." I reach into the backseat and retrieve the glove I'd found earlier and a baseball too. I place them in his lap and watch his face. Watch his lips, really.

I want a smile—a genuine, comfortable smile—like the ones he gave his friends when we arrived at the party. But watching his lips is not a safe thing for me to be doing—especially when they're slightly parted in surprise. Slightly parted in the same way they'd be if he leaned over and . . .

Of all the stupid things, to be imagining a kiss from a guy who'll never imagine kissing me. I get out of the car.

When his door doesn't immediately open, I walk around and tap on the window. "Come on—I *dared* you."

The athletic fields are up on top of a hill behind the school. I bypass the paved paths, hoping the pain of climbing a grassy slope with battered toes will be enough to clear my head of the ridiculous and repair my Teflon coating.

His door opens when I'm halfway up the hill, but he's beside me before I reach the top.

"Really?" he asks in a voice as soft as when we'd discussed my father. My pulse has been steady through the climb, but it spikes at his question.

"Really. I hear you're a stud player and I want to see you in your full jock glory."

When he laughs and hands me the glove and ball I wonder—again—when in the night I switched from calculating the niceness quotient of every word to comfort to flirtation.

"Here, you wear this. You won't be throwing hard enough that I'll need it."

"Oh, you watch out, I bet I can throw pretty hard." But I accept the glove and march across the field to home plate. "I can't crouch. It makes my toes hurt."

"That's okay." Jonah steps onto the pitcher's mound and

twists himself all sorts of ways. When he straightens, he looks taller. More confident. Happier. He grins and I grin back. He's given me the smile I want; now the rest of this night is for him.

"What are you waiting for?" I ask.

"You've still got the ball."

"Oh. Yeah." I chuck it with all my strength, and it bounces somewhat near first base. "I should probably warn you, I never played baseball or softball."

"Never would have guessed. Now put the glove on."

I slide my fingers in and squeeze the sides together. The leather irritates my palm, and my hand feels awkward: unbalanced and heavy. "It's a little big."

"Imagine that." Jonah laughs; the sound floats on the night air, painting my cheeks in a flush and my lips in a smile.

"Ready?"

I nod, but I'm not. The first throw sails past me. The second, third, and fourth through tenth do too. I wait for him to become impatient with my incompetence, but Jonah's laughter grows louder with each missed catch.

"I *might* have exaggerated my skills a little," I confess while hunting down the ball—again—and wishing the parking lot lights were just a teeny bit brighter, or that the baseball glowed in the dark. "I'm a diver for good reason. I'm hopeless with any sport that involves a stick or a ball or a racquet . . . Pretty much, if it requires any equipment, I'm a lost cause. Even my dad gave up trying to teach me to golf and just let me drive the cart."

"I'm not giving up on you yet," he says. And even though

I can't see his face that well in the dark, I can hear the smile in his voice and it warms me.

But maybe he should, because his belief in me doesn't prevent me from missing the next dozen throws. Yet he only offers encouragement or jokes as I search for the ball, throw it towardish him so he can make impossible catches or hunt it down himself.

"Try keeping your eyes open. Watch the ball all the way into the glove."

I do. And it *does* go all the way into my hand.

"You caught it! You did!" Jonah's laughing as he runs to home plate and scoops me into a hug. "Good job!"

"Ow! Ow!" I say in response to each of his whoops, but my nongloved hand clutches the back of his shirt and my cheek is nestling into his collarbone—a safe place to view the smear of school and fields and sky as he spins me around.

"Wimp. I guess I should've warned you it stings a bit," he says, setting me back on my feet. "Your hand might be a little red. It's an occupational hazard for pro catchers like yourself. Let's check it out."

He grips the tip of the glove, and I pull my hand out. It's *a lot* red. Bloody red. The impact of the ball stressed my tortured palm beyond its endurance; two crescent-shaped cuts bleed down toward my wrist.

The celebration fades from his eyes, causing my smile to dim to artificial. "I'm fine."

"Fine? You're like a walking Band-Aid commercial, Bright . . . ton. A night with you should earn me a merit badge or something."

"It's not so bad." This isn't the first time I've created cuts on my palm, but it's the first time I've done it in years.

"My mom makes me keep a first-aid kit in the car. Let's clean you up."

I pause to find the ball—it had flown from the glove mid-Jonah spin—then follow him down the hill. It's hard to read the emotions in his posture. Is he hunched forward from the pitch of the hill, or because I ruined another part of his night? I want to see his face, and see it filled with the pride and triumph of a few minutes ago. More than that, I want to be in his arms again for another moment.

I arrive at the car blushing and wishing I could bury my tangle of embarrassment and infatuation within clenched fists.

"Hop up here."

I clumsily climb on the hood; it's not really possible to "hop up" without two hands.

Jonah holds a white plastic first-aid kit and pulls out an alcohol swab and some Band-Aids.

"You're like my own personal medic. If I needed stitches or CPR, you could probably do that too." I use flattery to deflect my own embarrassment. But also because I want to see that smile again.

I hold out my palm and study the contrast between the nails, skin, and blood. Nothing is its natural color in the thin glow provided by the parking lot lights. My nails look a reflective, rotten gray green, my skin seems translucent, inked with hieroglyphics by my blood. One puncture has stopped bleeding, the other still trickles. A single drop slips off the trail down to my wrist and falls in slow motion. I lose track of it midair when Jonah steps close—really close—and cups my hand in his.

"Admitting I know CPR seems like tempting the fates. Don't get any ideas—I've no desire to prove it. And no to stitches; I nearly failed home econ, I wouldn't trust me anywhere near a needle." He erases the coded words on my palm, gently turning my hand to wipe the alcohol pad down along my wrist. My pulse drums beneath his fingers, tempo increasing as he slides his thumb across the fragile skin. He must feel it.

"How'd you get so good at this?" My voice is breathless, and I hope he knows I mean first aid, not making me flush, pant, and way too aware that his thighs are pressed against my knees as he plays doctor.

"I took a first-aid course. My dad had—well, *has*—a boat. Not that there was anywhere special to use it around here, but I bet he lives on it in Florida. He insisted I take first-aid training when I was younger. Bet he's more worried about his new first mate's ability to fill a bikini than handle a boat wreck."

He settles my hand on my thigh and tears open a Band-Aid, ripping the actual bandage in half, scowling, and shoving it in his pocket.

A topic change is in order and a change in mental picture—I'm visualizing Jonah on a boat, shirt off . . . "Um, have you ever used the training? I mean, besides patching me up."

"Yeah." His voice quiets and his fingers still on the box of bandages. "Paul was holding Sophia a few weeks ago—and somehow she got a button off his shirt. I looked over and she was turning blue. He hadn't noticed. I had to grab her and . . . Those seconds when I was holding her facedown and thumping her back . . . I think *I* stopped breathing till she started to cough."

"You saved her life." My whisper matches his and is twisted with awe for this boy I can't begin to understand.

He makes a noise that's reluctant agreement. "And I've been a dick to Paul—even though he's practically destroying himself with guilt about it. Tonight was the first time Mom talked him into going out since it happened. Sophia's fine, but he . . . he's even been sleeping in her room." His eyes twitch from the bandage box to my face, then back to my hand. He sighs so heavily that I feel it on my palm. "Sometimes I'm such an idiot."

"Oh, Jonah." If my hand weren't otherwise occupied, I'd curl my fingers around his. I don't have any wisdom to give him either, so after he applies the second bandage and closes the box I offer a distraction. "Now we'll play some more?"

"You're done playing tonight. These are barely sticking." He presses again on the adhesive striping the length of my palm. I fight the urge to close my fingers around his thumb.

"And I was just starting to get the hang of it. There go my dreams of turning pro."

He laughs.

I love his laugh.

"Thank you for this. Being up there, it was . . ." He looks at me, raises my bandaged hand, and presses it to his mouth.

My eyes grow wide and my lips part to ask a question— any question. I almost do. But then that's how this night will end: with conversation. The choice is mine; the move is mine.

I make it. One deep breath and all questions are erased by the touch of my lips as I lean forward to press them against his.

37

JONAH

☼ 2:26 A.M. ☽

HALF PAST—HOLY CRAP!

I'd be lying if I said I had no expectations. I've imagined kissing her a hundred times tonight. In a hundred different places and positions. But in the instant she kisses me, I'm not thinking about anything but *her.* The way her eyes widened with admiration and the shape of her lips when she commented about saving Sophia's life. The feel of the skin on her inner wrist and the size of her hand in mine. The thoughtfulness of bringing me here and her willingness to go back up that hill—despite her bandages and her remarkable inability to throw or catch.

And I want to teach her. Today, tomorrow, the next day. I want to teach her to catch a ball. I want to teach her how to punch guys like Digg, walk Never, and deal with stress in ways that don't end with bandages.

But right now, mostly I want to learn what she tastes like.

Press her back against the hood. Slide my hands up the backs of her legs. White cotton underwear. More!

Thoughts pulse against my brain as my mouth explores

hers. But not her, not Brighton Waterford. I won't. But, God, if she makes that little noise in the back of her throat again . . . And her legs. Does she know she's let them slide down on either side of mine?

One foot wraps around the back of my leg and draws me closer; she knows.

My body wants to rush the moment, to find out what's next, but I won't let it. With Carly, kissing was like stretching before a game. It was important, but it wasn't our final destination. With Brighton . . . well, I don't want to be thinking about Carly.

Her lips against my lips. My world shrinks to the sensation of our mouths coming together and apart. The glide of her tongue across mine, the tug and give of her mouth. I feel drugged, hypnotized. Greedy. My legs halve the inches between us, and my mouth seeks more access.

Bright shifts away and I freeze. Is this the part where she changes her mind? Realizes she could and should do much better?

She removes her arms from my neck, and I hold my breath. She slides down from the hood of my car so she's pressed between the bumper and my body. My hands are on her shoulders, shivering with the desire to be in her hair. I need to know if she wants them off her and in my pockets.

Step backward, my mind orders my reluctant legs. I do, with movements awkward and uncoordinated and eyes that won't look higher than her flip-flopped, bandaged feet.

They step forward. Her hands circle around to press against my back. She waits for me to look at her—her eyes feverish and uncertain—then her lips brush feather-light across mine. My mouth opens in a groan. She tilts her head. Her mouth and my mouth are reunited. And I'm learning her as she learns me.

Not until she pulls back and buries her face in my shirt do I remember she's fragile; I was going to treat her gently. But maybe she isn't after all. Maybe she's stronger than me.

I rub her back with one hand and lower my face to where my fingers are tangled in her hair. She smells like rain and something clean and innocent—like lemons and daisies. I know I should say something, but I'm too calm, too excited, too baffled to form any thoughts but *Hold still. Stay.*

I feel her mouth move against my shirt more than I hear her speak.

"What?" I smooth my hand through her tangles, reaching down to tip her chin up.

Her face is flushed, her lips swollen, and her eyes flicker over me, around the air. She sighs. I watch her hand curl in, nails hitting Band-Aids. She frowns and presses her palm flat against her leg. I fight the urge to crush her back against me and smother her words about *this* in my shirt; against my lips. Or buckle her in the passenger seat and drive away, leaving all consequences in the parking lot.

Her unbandaged hand reaches up to barely, barely touch my face. I lean my cheek into her palm, shutting my eyes for an instant to savor the sensation, then open them to watch her and worry about her silence.

One half of Brighton's mouth quirks with mischief. "It's only fair to warn me: Are you noisy and smelly too?"

38

Brighton

☀ 2:31 A.M. ☽

10 HOURS, 29 MINUTES LEFT

I'd really said: *That was nice.*

Those were the words trapped in the weave of his shirt. As soon as the sentence crosses my lips, which still tingle and taste of him, I realize how wrong it is. I try to breathe and erase the tangle of emotions from my face.

When he steps away and asks, "What?" my heart lurches with fear he's heard and is offended. Then comes the panic of finding something else to say. I reject all adjectives. How can I describe something that makes me feel like I floated out of myself while simultaneously making me more aware of my body than I've ever been?

His skin *feels* different than mine. I hadn't considered that skin can be masculine, but his is. I want to trace the lines of all his bones beneath the covering of stubble and calluses and textures.

No. I need to speak.

We need to talk and say what that was. The Band-Aids on my hand interfere with my attempt to make a fist.

Jonah's leaning away, shutting his eyes and shutting me out. The moment is dying.

I blurt out the first words that hit my tongue. "It's only fair to warn me: Are you noisy and smelly too?"

His laugh rebounds off the empty pavement and the walls of the school. It settles in my stomach and calms the knives of panic while curling into a different type of flame.

"Sometimes."

He slides his hand across my palm; fingertips on skin, Band-Aids, skin. Fingertips on fingertips, feeling like they might glow from the intense sensation. My laughter dies in a choked gasp.

"I really said, *that was nice.*" I won't lie to him. Not now.

My fingertips slide from his, and my other hand drifts from his shoulder to my side. I look up at him through my lashes. His eyes are dark, searching, full of something I don't understand and don't know how to react to.

"Nice?" he echoes.

I'm hollow. Cold. Like he's already interpreted this as an insult and walked away—taking with him all of the emotion of the night and all the warmth from the air.

"No." He shakes his head. "No."

I feel every slightly damp spot on my dress. I'm hyper-aware of the sweat on my lower back and palms—it's turned glacial. I'm shivering. On my way to shaking.

And then—heat!

Jonah's hands on my arms. Burning. Urgent.

"Nice isn't good enough." He leans closer, his voice dropping to a husky whisper. "I think we owe it to ourselves to do better than *nice.*"

I smile against his lips—more than willing to be convinced. When his mouth leaves mine to explore my neck, I whisper in his ear, "*Really* nice . . ."

His fingers lace through my hair.

"*Super* nice . . ."

His teeth drag lightly against the skin behind my ear.

"*Really, super* nice."

He laughs against my collarbone, and I forget what cold even feels like. Can't imagine ever being cold again. "I'm getting you a thesaurus."

I open my mouth to add another adjective to the list, but he cuts off my teasing with his lips and the only word that lingers in my head is "more."

"There it is: parking space F23. All mine."

I'm not sure which I recognize first, the guy's voice or the girlish giggle he gets in response. But the words slide over us an instant before headlights do, illuminating the moment when Jonah stiffens and I pull back in surprise.

"Brighton? *Brighton!* What are you doing here? Oh my God! Who are you *kissing*?"

Somewhere amid Silvia's questions and exclamation points, Jonah's fingers drop from mine. I miss them immediately and don't understand why he's putting so much space between us. Or why he's turning away from me. I ignore Silvia and Adrian for a moment and look where Jonah's looking: back up the hill.

The grass on the field is bled of its color in the dim light. The boundary between the concrete and slope distinguishable by a sense of lushness, not a difference in color—both look drab gray.

Jonah takes another step back and pulls his keys out of his pocket.

I feel deflated.

I want to grab his hand and run. Or yell at them to leave.

"Brighton? Adrian, that *is* Brighton, right? Maybe it's her sister? Evy?" They've parked in Adrian's space and she's leaning over the side of his convertible and peering into the darkness. "Can you see who she's with?"

"It's me, Silvia," I answer. "Hi."

"Hey! I'm here with *Adrian*." She manages to keep *some* of the excitement out of that statement, but enough leaks through to make me glad I stopped him in the hallway and sent him to find her.

"Hi, Adrian."

"Hey, Brighton . . . and hey." He gives a wave, which Jonah returns with a short jerk of two fingers.

"Brighton, is this some secret rendezvous? Scandalous! I want to know everything!"

I want to tell her to back off. To take her excitement level down from an eleven to a six and her nosiness to a three. These might be questions she wants *me* to ask *her* about how she and Adrian ended up here together, but I haven't even managed introductions yet and Jonah's posture is already coiled and defensive.

I don't want a rehashing of the computer lab scene though—where one sharp word meant a million apologies.

She leans even farther over the side of the car, to the point where Adrian's grabbing the belt loop on her jean skirt. "I thought you were single?"

"I . . ." I don't have an answer to that. It's not something

I can ask Jonah in front of an audience. It's not something I'm ready to ask him. Or think about. And he's tossing his keys impatiently between his hands. Looking everywhere but at me.

Which is probably a good thing, because I'm sure my expression is raw hope and desperate longing.

"Is that . . . the new kid?" Adrian asks. I'm not sure if it's a question for Silvia or me, but it makes me cringe. *The new kid?* They should know his name—or ask. All my earlier arguments about the merits of the town crowd back up my throat and choke me.

He tacks on a "with *her*?" in a voice that's neither quiet nor polite. The screen of a cell phone glows brightly in his fingers, illuminating his skeptical expression. He's turning this moment into a text, a status update, or a tweet.

"Jonah," I correct in a voice like flint, and I feel his eyes on me. "His name is Jonah."

"We should go," he says quietly. He gazes coolly at Adrian as he reaches around me to open the passenger door.

"Oh, you don't have to! Sorry. We didn't mean to *interrupt*! Adrian was just . . ." Silvia's apologies dissolve into giggles.

"Showing her my parking space," he finishes. "But *we* can go. You guys stay."

"No, it's fine." But my voice is hollow, and if they weren't so busy with each other, they'd hear I don't mean it. Jonah has already shut his door and is shoving his key in the ignition. "*Jonah* and I will see you guys Sunday."

I shut the door on good-byes and giggles, and he puts the car in drive.

Neither of us says a word, and this silence is thick and

ominous, like whatever is said next will have permanent consequences.

As I'm fastening my seat belt, I get it—what Amelia wants from Peter and what he gives her. I finally, *really* understand a moment from earlier in the day in this parking lot at dismissal.

Amelia with her head on Peter's shoulder.

His hand on her hair.

Peter's other hand on the key to her car.

Her car.

The car Amelia has never let me drive. The car her parents started planning a year before her sixteenth birthday so she'd have time to change her mind about make, model, and color.

And the way she'd said, "I'm tired, baby. Take me home, please." It was completely comfortable, completely confident.

And Peter's response: tracing the line of her forehead. "If you didn't keep such rock star hours, Lia . . ." And he'd smiled as she pulled his hand to her lips and murmured *shhhh.*

Eleven hours ago I'd dismissed it as cute. Now it means more. Peter isn't one of Amelia's fads or phases. They're all in. And that's what I want. That moment. That relationship. That trust. That.

The longing feels like someone has grabbed my insides and twisted. I want what Amelia and Peter have, but does Jonah fit in that picture? Do I want it with *him?*

I think the answer is *yes* and that terrifies me.

Based on how he reacted back there, his answer is *no.* His feelings were passion, not permanent. He's probably thinking I was a silly mistake, a stupid footnote on his bad night.

"Home?" There is nothing of the hoarse desire in his voice anymore; it's straight exhaustion with a sigh for punctuation.

"Yes, please."

39

JONAH

☼ 2:46 A.M. ☽

IT'S TIME TO BEGIN

I hate that kid in his shiny new Mustang. I'm less sure about the girl in the sequin tank top he had riding shotgun, but I'm willing to hate her too. I'm prepared to hate everyone at CPHS for the deer-in-headlights look on Brighton's face when she was caught kissing me.

I bet she'll micromanage the whole episode into a joke or a misunderstanding. *You thought we were* kissing? *Oh, no. Not at all. I was: insert-suitable-activity-for-an-empty-parking-lot-at-three-a.m.*

I can't think of anything that fits that category, but I'm sure she'll come up with a way to spin it. This night has been a holiday from reality, and we've reached the part where vacation ends and real life floods in.

After a drive that's too long, too short, and way too silent, we're in her driveway. The digits glowing on my dashboard are only a few hours before I usually wake up for school. She twists her hair into a knot and then lets it all drop around her shoulders, looking up and meeting my eyes for a milli-second.

I refuse to be the one who says good-bye first. I won't make this easy on her by acting like I'm okay with what just went down and offering her an awkward hug. What is she thinking, head lowered, fidgeting with the hem of her dress? That she needs to let me down gently, that I'll be heartbroken? She doesn't seem to be in any big hurry to leave the car.

I hate that I don't want her to.

"You can call me Bright," she whispers. "If you'd like."

"What?" I touch her shoulder to get her attention. The offer was spoken to her knees, and I want to see her face. Or maybe I just want an excuse to touch her.

"It sounds . . . natural coming from you. I don't mind. And we should probably exchange numbers. I can't believe I don't even have your phone number."

Her words are uncertain. It's the tone you use for a question, or when you're questioning why you're saying what you're saying.

"Brighton . . ."

"My cell's off. Here, give me yours and I'll add my number."

I dig it out of my pocket and hand it to her.

"Now you text me and I'll have your number. That's how this should work." Her voice falters and she droops. "Right?"

"There isn't any 'should.' What do you want, Brighton?" She won't look at me, and suddenly I'm angry. If she doesn't want this—me—then that's fine. I'm fine. "I'm not going to be your stray dog—you feel good because you took me in and made a project of me."

"What?"

"You didn't care if people in Hamilton saw us together, but I saw your face in the school parking lot—you didn't want people *here* to see you with me."

"That's completely ridiculous." She wears her frustration like a tight necklace. It makes her voice tense and her words clipped. "What did you want from me, Jonah? I was embarrassed."

"So, I'm an embarrassment. Just what every guy wants a beautiful girl to say about him." I reach across her to open the door. "Thank you and good night."

"Wait! Not embarrassed by *you*, by the situation. I'm not really a PDA person—and I didn't know what to say. I panicked." I catch a flicker of anger in her gray eyes before she sits up straight and asks, "What was I supposed to say to all her questions? Is there a *we*? Am I single? You really want to have this conversation now? Fine, my turn. Answer this, what am I to you: rebound or revenge?" She covers her open mouth, like she can stop the words she's already spoken.

"Neither. You're more than that. I don't know what yet . . . but it's more than that." I press my fingers to my forehead, hoping to push back the doubts and questions.

"Me either. So I froze. I'm sorry if that hurt your feelings." Small fingers pry my hands from my head and entwine them. "And just so you know, *you* were the one who stepped away from me. I may not make out for an audience, but I never would've let go of your hand."

I squeeze her fingers, back in mine. I'm not letting go first this time.

She rewards me with a smile, looks up at me through her eyelashes and asks, "We're good right now, right?"

It's the hope in her voice that almost breaks mine when I reply.

"Yes."

"That's a start. We'll get some sleep and then tomorrow—"

I stall her answer with a kiss. I'm not ready to think about tomorrow. And in case tomorrow isn't like this, I don't want to ruin right now.

The ferocity with which I want her scares the hell out of me. I want to know her favorite candies. And colors. If she's a good driver, a reality TV watcher, and as horrible with sports equipment as she says. I want to know more stories about her dad. And her favorite cereal, how she *really* likes her pizza, and the type of music she can't help but sing along with. I want to watch a scary movie with her and see proof that she's not afraid. I want to find out what she *is* scared of. If she doesn't know the answers to these questions, then I want to be there when she figures it all out.

I want.

Her.

Everything about her. I open my eyes and study Brighton, try to figure out how she's managed to get so far under my skin. And *her skin*—I want to uncover every inch of it, bury myself in it, fuse myself to her.

I jerk my mouth from hers, watching her breath slow and her eyes blink open.

"What?" she asks, a laugh teasing her lips into a smile. I suppress the urge to kiss her again and taste her laughter. "Jonah? Why are you staring at me like that? You're making me nervous."

I imagine telling her the truth: *I want you more than is*

*socially acceptable, and I don't want to want you at all. I also
don't want the night to end, because tomorrow we'll be back to
normal.*

No, not normal because Carly will still be gone and I'll
still have this impulse to touch Brighton embedded perma-
nently somewhere near my rib cage.

"Tomorrow?" I say.

She sighs and I remember.

"Your dad's memorial. I forgot."

"Me too, for a minute. And it's *today*. I don't want to go
inside and go to bed. I need to before Mom or Evy wakes
up—but I don't want to. I'm scared when I wake up, this will
all be . . ." She touches my arm to finish her statement, and
my hand is covering hers before I recognize the desire to
touch her back.

"Yeah. I know." It's far too soon for me to attend the service for her father whom I never met. If I went with her, she'd
spend the whole day answering questions about me. She
doesn't need that. Not on top of everything else. "Will you
call me tomorrow and let me know how it goes?"

She nods and traces a circle on the seat with her finger.
The same circle, over and over. "Will . . . will you . . . On Sunday, will you have lunch with me—"

"Yeah," I agree quickly, scared the question is so hard
for her to form but relieved she asked it.

"—and Amelia and Peter after the library thing?" she
continues.

"Oh." I know we'll have to see them—see other people—
but I don't want to relive the parking lot scene over and over.
We won't work in anyone else's eyes. Hell, we don't even

work in my eyes. Yet, I'm crushing her hand to my arm with my reluctance to let her go.

"They're really ni—They're good friends."

Her eyes are pleading with me to agree, but if they snub me, how will she react?

"Couldn't we—" Couldn't we what? Have a secret relationship that no one knows about? If I reject her friends so they can't reject me, where will that leave us? Am I really this lame?

Brighton leans her forehead against my shoulder. She sighs against my skin. "You don't have to come to the library. And you don't have to meet us for lunch. I'm not going to force you or be a brat about it, but I really think you could like them. If you wanted to."

"Like *them*?"

"Yeah, I know we're only juniors, and I'm not going to make you meet everyone at once . . . But I would love if you'd give Amelia and Peter a chance. I think you'll like them . . . I hope you will."

Like *them*?

"Okay." After all, stranger things have happened: like me making out with Brighton Waterford.

"Really?" She picks her head up off my shoulder and beams at me.

"Does this mean I'm no longer uninvited to box books?" I tease.

"Really?" she repeats and kisses my cheek. I want to turn for a better kiss, but she's narrating her relief: "I was scared you were going to say no. And I don't want to force you. And if you don't like them—well, then you tried and that's okay. Jonah, I—I don't want to change you. And I'd rather you never talked to me again than make yourself unhappy trying to fit into a me-shaped box."

If she knew the thoughts her last words inspired, she'd be blushing darker than she already is.

"We're going to shake up Cross Pointe," I say with a laugh.

"No, Jonah, we're not." She stretches a hand out to cup my cheek, and I wonder if she can feel me tense beneath her palm. "No one's going to care. This is the time of year where people are worried about finals and GPAs. Summer jobs and getting off wait lists and going on swimsuit diets. Maybe for a minute they'll be surprised that either of us is dating *anyone*, but that's about it. And if that's why you want me—so you can prove a point or something—then you're going to be disappointed."

I release the breath I was holding. Can she really think that? "Of course it's not."

"Jonah." She bites her lip and looks down for a few seconds before peeking up at me. "I'm not excusing anyone's behavior, and don't get mad, but maybe the reason you never became part of Cross Pointe is you never gave anyone a chance to include you."

I want to pull away, but she reaches up with her other hand, holds my face between her palms and forces me to look at her when she says, "Please don't be mad at me."

"I'm not." My voice is everything but happy. I want to lose myself in her lips, not think about this. But earlier in the night she never would have said *anything* she thought might upset me.

"Liar," she challenges.

I reach up and take her hands from my face. I'm tempted to push them back at her, but instead I flip them palm up and trace the welts on one and the Band-Aids on the other. Her scars from tonight are visible; mine are all internal. "I'm not mad at *you*, Bright. I'm mad at me, because I know you're right. It still sucks."

"Yeah, it does. Or did. But in this case, it's not a bad thing anymore. It's a reason *not* to worry about us—don't you get it? People are so self-absorbed. Except for the people who care about you and me, no one is going to give *us* a second thought. I bet Adrian and Silvia are distracted by each other and already forgot us. And my friends will love you. You make me smile; you're important to me. That will be enough."

I let myself reach for her, one hand on either side of her face, sliding up her jawline to stroke her cheeks with my thumbs. She stops talking, closes her eyes, and inhales— holds the breath for a beat—then exhales in a content sigh.

I study the curve of her eyelids, the wave of her eyebrow, the skin of her forehead as it relaxes and releases its lines. I lean in and brush my lips against the last furrow, a small indentation above her left eye, then watch the spread of pink across her cheeks and down to her collarbone.

These demand exploration, and it's against the hollow above them that I give my answer, "I know."

There are more words to say, and more questions I should be asking, but I'm transfixed by the play of pink across her skin and how it responds to my mouth, my tongue, and even my breath. Her breath's faster too, falling into a gasp, as she leans back to expose more of her neck. I slide one hand behind her head and pull on the collar of her dress with the other. Two buttons: even unfastened they barely expose any skin. Not enough. Not nearly enough.

But I can wait. There is tomorrow—today—where I'm already factored into her life.

Where I'm factoring myself back into my own life too.

40

Brighton

ONLY TIME WILL TELL

I could stay like this for hours, melting under kisses and the touch of his hands. I avoid looking at his dashboard clock or the faint, faint line of pink that may be a distant sunrise . . . or someone's outdoor lights.

"Will you be in trouble?"

He's blinking at me in confusion. I rephrase the question: "I mean, will you be in trouble for getting home so late?"

"No. They'll think I stayed over at Jeff's. I can tell them I got up early and came home for whatever reason. They won't care. Will you?"

"No. My mom waits up for Evy every time *she* goes out but hasn't waited up for me since middle school—it's a perk of being the good child." He murmurs something about *good* against my neck, and I laugh and add, "Hmm, so neither of us has a curfew. *In-ter-rest-ting.* File that fact under Things That Are Convenient and Fabulous!"

I lean toward him but then he speaks, a laughing statement tinged with some of the cynicism I doubt he'll ever lose, and I'm not sure I want him to: "Or under: Parental Oversights I Plan to Exploit."

"Maybe it's time for me to stop being the good one." The words slip past my lips in a flush of embarrassment and did-I-really-say-that?

I wonder how he'll respond—and true to his unpredictable form, he doesn't give me a visible reaction at all. At least not beyond eyes opened wider, a quick intake of breath. So I give him one. I kiss him. Once. Just once in a breath-shattering, pulse-revving touch of lips and tongue.

I stare at his smile—I caused that. It's a crazy, powerful, intoxicating thought.

Before either of us can say something to ruin the moment or uncover a new conflict—begin a new round of Truth or Dare—I scoop up my bag and slip out the car door. "Soon."

He echoes it back, his eyes earnest. "Soon."

I dance up the walkway to the door, not wanting to go to bed, but knowing Never will bark if I linger outside. Everything seems possible tonight. People can change; I can matter. I can kiss a boy. He can see me so clearly that it forces me to take a second look at myself.

Once I get through today, tomorrow and the entire summer stretch before me with so much possibility.

I shut the door and stare at myself in the foyer mirror. Never wanders over and leans his head against my stomach. I absently stroke his ears and continue to examine my reflection. My curls are wild. My eyeliner and mascara have melted and melded until I have smoky, smudgy eyes typically reserved for nightclubs or Goths. The collar of my dress has dried warped, and the left side points up while the right curls under.

I look like a disaster. No wonder Silvie wasn't sure it was me.

And yet he kissed me.

Or, *I* kissed him and he kissed me back.

I give Never one last pat and pull away. His drool marks drip from hip height down to the hem of my dress. I bend and plant an impulsive kiss on his nose before heading up to the bathroom.

While I brush my teeth, I pull out the nail polish remover. Sometime around our arrival at the party, the green glitter stopped seeming rebellious or attractive. It might be someone else's form of rebellion or someone else's preferred color, but it isn't mine. I erase the traces of sparkles from my fingers and drop them in the trashcan. I consider losing the Band-Aids too—my palm isn't bleeding anymore, but they were sealed with a kiss and I'm not ready to let that go quite yet.

I blush at the cheesy romance of the thought, but my fingers still curl protectively over the bandages.

I reach for the bottle of Pointe-Shoe Pink Mom bought for between visit touch-ups. Shake it, uncap it. Then replace the lid and put it back in the drawer. I may not want green glitter, but I don't want that either. Tomorrow I can decide on my new color, or color-for-this-week, or even if I want to be a girl who wears nail polish at all.

Though I know I'll wake with a mess of snarls, I don't braid my hair either. Or wash off my makeup.

In my room, my black dress is back on my closet door.

A note from Evy pinned to its collar with a rhinestone hairclip.

B—

    I shouldn't have taken this. Wear whatever you want tomorrow. And tell me to butt out sometimes.

    I hope you had fun tonight . . . But not too much. I want details!

Xo,

E.

But she was right the first time. The dress *is* wrong. I shove the hanger in the back of my closet.

Grabbing a pen from my desk, I circle the last line of her note and add: *Maybe . . . If you let me sleep in.* And slide it under her bedroom door. If I'm still in bed, she'll have to deal with Mom, questions from the caterers, any early-arriving guests. Evy won't be happy about it, but she's a big girl and I'm tired.

There's only one thing I have left to do before I change into pajamas and climb into bed, but I stand in front of my closet and reject my outfits one at a time: too beige, too black, too khaki, too bland. Finally I choose a navy-and-white-polka-dot blouse. Normally, I pair it with white capris, but tomorrow I'll wear it with a red skirt. And a green-and-navy-striped belt. And red shoes. And my ring. I lay it all on the back of my desk chair. Dad used to call me his Rainbow Brite—how could I celebrate him dressed in anything drab?

Even after I turn off the lights and get into bed, I'm still smiling in the direction of my chair. It feels right.

I roll onto my back and whisper up at the ceiling, "Dad, I

don't have an answer for you tonight, don't have my 'one thing I did to make the world better.' I don't even know where to begin . . . I did lots of things today—some of them good, but I made a lot of mistakes too . . . and some of my mistakes turned out to be good things . . ."

I blow him a kiss and roll onto my side. I wish he was here, I wish I could hear his voice. I think he'd say he's proud of me. I'm proud of me too. But I don't feel like *me*. Curls tickle my cheeks and my toes sting when I brush them against my blanket.

One night with Jonah and I've morphed from *Teflon* to something that reacts when scratched . . . a record or a match. No, not something that's damaged by use. Something better.

My brain's too tired to spin ideas and pick a new analogy. And why bother? Amelia will come up with something soon enough.

I shift and shake a piece of hair off my cheek—I don't feel settled in my skin. In the skin of this girl with chaos in her brain and curling around her shoulders. A girl with a rumpled dress on the floor at the foot of her bed, smeared eye makeup, flushed cheeks, and lips swollen from kisses.

Who is *this* girl?

I owe it to myself to find out.

ACKNOWLEDGMENTS

I wish I could give a cookie and a hug to each of the readers, teachers, bloggers, librarians, and booksellers who have supported me along this journey . . . Since that's creepy, I'll just offer sugar-coated gratitude instead.

Without the following people, Brighton and Jonah's story would never have made it into your hands. I am so thankful that they're in my life:

Joe Monti, Agent Extraordinaire, thank you for understanding what this book meant to me. I hope you understand what *you* mean to me too. Barry, Tricia, and the rest of the Goldblatt team—I raise a glass of jelly beans in your honor.

The talented group at Walker Books for Young Readers: Emily Easton, who pushed me with fabulous editorial notes; Laura Whitaker, who knew just when I needed to hear "I'm proud of you"; Rachel Stark, Emily Ritter, Patricia McHugh, Bridget Hartzler, Katy Hershberger, Jenna Pocius, and Erica Barmash, who did a zillion lovely, supportive, behind-the-scenes things to make my books better.

The artificially colored pieces of heaven I call Revision Skittles, whose sugar highs kept me going during many, many late-night writing sessions.

The best critique partners an author could dream of: Emily Hainsworth (Team Jonah) and Courtney Summers (Team Brighton)—whose amazing and insightful advice is ALWAYS contradictory. I would be saner without them both, but the story would be weaker. And sanity is overrated.

Team Sparkle—Scott Tracey and Victoria Schwab, without whom I'd never believe I could "write boy," and Linda Grimes and Susan Adrian, who patiently brainstormed bucketfuls of titles.

My local writing support group: Jonathan Maberry, who wins the gold in author mentorship; Nancy Keim Comley, Elisa Ludwig, Eugene Myers, Kate Walton, Gail Yates, Eve Marie Mont, Tiff Emerick, Jen Zelesko, and Heather Hebert— they will always have a place in my heart, house, and in-box.

Taylor Mysza—who wrangled my Schmidtlets so I had time to write. I'm sorry for all the times they made her sing Taylor *Swift*—someday they'll figure out the Taylors are not the same person.

The Apocalypsies—well, the world didn't end in 2012 and I'm so glad! Because we all have oodles more stories to tell, and I can't wait to read them.

And always, my family, who let me dream, explore, and get into lots of mischief; my in-laws, who are endlessly generous with their babysitting time and help; and my puggles, who are only slightly more obedient than Never, but I love them anyway.

My impish Schmidtlets, I could write a whole book about

how much I love you . . . and if I did, you'd insist the last words be: "And fireworks!" (Dear Readers, I have no idea why . . . It's just a Schmidtlet Storytime Rule.)

Lastly, St. Matt—You're pretty cute in that halo. I love you. *And fireworks!*